IN SEARCH

of the

HERO GOD

Rise of the Celtic Gods
Book 2

Kristin Gleeson

An Tig Beag Press

Published by An Tig Beag Press

Cover design by JD Smith Designs

ISBN: 978-0-9956281-7-5

OTHER WORKS BY KRISTIN GLEESON
In Praise of the Bees
CELTIC KNOT SERIES
Selkie Dreams
Along the Far Shores
Raven Brought the Light
A Treasure Beyond Worth (novella)
RENAISSANCE SOJOURNER SERIES
The Imp of Eye
The Sea of Travail
HIGHLAND BALLAD SERIES
The Hostage of Glenorchy
The Mists of Glen Strae
The Braes of Huntly
Highland Lioness
RISE OF THE CELTIC GODS SERIES
Awakening the Gods
In Search of the Hero God
NON FICTION
Anahareo, A Wilderness Spirit
LISTEN TO THE MUSIC CONNECTED TO THE BOOKS
Go to www.krisgleeson.com/music
Receive a FREE novelette prequel, *A Treasure Beyond Worth,* and
Along the Far Shores
When you sign up for my mailing list: www.krisgleeson.com

A
TREASURE
BEYOND
WORTH
KRISTIN
GLEESON

A twelfth century Irish woman
washed ashore in America
must trust a stranger to help her survive.

ALONG
the
FAR
SHORES
KRISTIN
GLEESON

To Bruce, who understood the poetry of it all

PART I

CLÍODHNA WINDS

1

LUKE

I entered my house, threw my keys and phone on the table and leaned my surfboard back against the wall. Oh so trendy, oh so cool, wasn't I just. I was the "not a bother" man. Oh so no worries. Catch a wave, follow a tune. Only the rage was there now. Tight and unrelenting. Wouldn't let me go, so it wouldn't. I'd had to force myself to unstrap it from the SUV roof and bring it in. The rage had followed me from the Connemara coast and I'd worked hard to get ahead of it, speeding when I'd dared, dodging it like some cagey hurler who really didn't want to be in this game. But the rage had caught me hard, had me up against the wall and was slapping my mind like some old fashioned mammy from the last century. Whack! *You were thinking with your other head. The one that belongs firmly in your pants.* "Yeah, I know." Whack! *You fell for the way she played the music, when you know that's a warning sign in itself.* "Yeah, I know." And all the "yeahIknows" kept coming after the old rage, whacking at me. But feck it all, that music, that woman, Saoirse. Who could resist it? Who could resist her? The other head, the one in my pants, was all about excuses. And the residual feel of her, the soft skin, the magic touches, yeah, but no. Whack.

I picked up my phone and scrolled through the photos I'd taken of her over the past few days. I sucked in the breath, the whacks coming fast and furious, until I'd deleted every one of the images. I sighed, sat down and closed my eyes. What the feck was I going to do? I couldn't stay here. I got up and went back to the car, hauling out my gear. The wetsuit, the backpack and the bits of detritus that went into making up a weekend surfing with a girlfriend.

Back in the house, I dumped the things on the floor of the sitting room and decided a can of lager would be the best thing to get that mammy to ease off on the old whacks. At the fridge I took out a lager and opened it. I pushed it against my forehead, feeling the cool ease the throbbing ache.

I kicked off my flip flops, padded over to the docking station for my phone, selected my music app and hit play on favourites. The sound took over and I felt a little rush of joy at the mad dash of bouzouki playing I heard, followed by an even madder turn on the uilleann pipes. My lads from *Moving Hearts*, though they were probably more in the way of shuffling hearts, given the age of them now, but their energy always lifted my spirits. It was Liam O'Flynn who followed on, his way with the pipes a gift that kept giving, though now only in the recordings. I laughed when his next tune was *Sí Bheag, Sí Mhór*, the irony not lost on me. Fairy mounds could feck off and those that inhabit them, I thought, and the dark anger returned.

I looked across at the image of the coastline hanging on the wall opposite me. It was a photograph that was more a work of art than anything. I'd picked it up years ago, down in West Cork. Back before surfing had become a 'thing' in Ireland and Mon and I used to sneak out in the early morning light, when the tide was right, rise up and just spin on those waves. I lifted the can of lager and took a deep drink. The pure beauty of the memory softening my emotions. I sighed. Those days and the other days and weeks and months and years were the reason to be loving the whirl of the living, the absolute joy of feeling that sea, that water carry you and breathe with you. That and the music.

But it was the music that had got me into trouble, created a call so close my teeth barely had any skin left to measure. And I wasn't even certain I'd avoided it altogether. I knew how those feckin' fairy mound dwellers played. The ones on this side, especially. The river crossers. I'd been this side so long, away from it all, I no longer felt any kith or kinship to them. That Saoirse was one, a Tuatha de Danann, really the goddess Bríd, I'd had no doubt, once Mon had shown me the light at the beach. That she didn't know what was going on, well, tell me another one. For the day that's in it. She knew who I was, no question.

I glanced at the clock. It was late and I needed to eat something, since clearly a plan wasn't making itself known at this moment. I checked the fridge and registered the condiments that I had no clue how they'd arrived and the other useless bits that always seemed to find their way in there. Nothing substantial. Pub it was. And maybe a glass or two. The choice of which pub was made difficult because all of them were shite, at least in my book. That book had high standards of music, forget about the food, or the size of the telly screen. It was early for music in any case, but not too late or early that some feckin sport somewhere in the world was playing and sure to be blaring. Ah, sure lookit, it was food I was after and a bit of drink. Earbuds in, lad, earbuds in.

I COULD HEAR the tones of the phone ringing and then the buzz vibration to signal that someone was answering on the other end. It was a relief, well, the first stage of it, in a set of several ones, but it was a beginning and a plan, or the beginning of a plan. Time would tell.

"Luke, hey," said Mon.

"Hey."

"How's things? You sorted now?"

I smiled wryly at the understatement. "Thanks a million," I said. "And a million more," I added. Because there was no underestimating the gratitude I felt for what he'd done.

"No bother, man."

Another smile tugged at my mouth at the words and tone that were all joke and surfer dude. "No, I mean it. I had no idea. What an eejit I am."

"No, no. I wouldn't have known who she was if I hadn't over-heard my father speaking about it. Well, I presumed it was her, because he was voicing his concern to my brother. She'd been spotted in Dublin, and the word was she went to The Mangle Pit. I knew you went there, so I just thought I would let you know. When there was no reaching you, I figured you were at the beach house. So I went over."

"Your father was voicing his concern?"

"Yeah, well you know him. He's got his fingers in a lot of pies. One of them probably has to do with her. Apparently she'd gone missing from Cork and they were trying to locate her."

I sighed at his words. This had come too close this time. "Did your father mention me at all?"

"No, man. He hasn't a clue what you're up to. He knows you want nothing to do with any of it any more."

"Thanks for keeping it quiet," I said.

"Ah, you're grand. You should keep a low profile for a while though. Avoid The Mangle Pit."

"No worries about that. I have no intention of returning there."

I felt a sadness at the words, but I knew it couldn't be helped.

I knew Saoirse loved that session and there was a good chance she would be there, even if she was furious with me. I felt a moment's regret at how we parted. My behaviour had been despicable, bad enough to make me shudder at the memory. Dumping her at the railway station and throwing money at her like she was some kind of whore. But still, it seemed impossible she could have been a totally innocent part in our getting together. No, she knew who I was, and more than likely had told the others my location.

I thought about the few days we'd spent together, first here and then at the beach house. We had connected, I thought. Her response was loose-limbed and unbridled, as though she was letting go of everything to do with herself and just living in her body. It had been a response that had found an equal part in me. I sighed. A pity all round. She was a great musician, and she could play tunes for me and in me any time.

"Hello?"

I brought my attention back to Mon. He was a brother in more ways than any blood tie would affirm. "Sorry, sorry," I said. "Wandering thoughts."

He snorted. "That good, huh?"

"Yeah, well."

"She would of course."

"She would of course," I said. "Given who she is."

"Given who she is," said Mon. "Put it away, Luke. Put it away."

"You're right. It's away now, locked in the press."

"Throw away the key."

"Key is gone," I said, grinning again. He was so Mon.

"Good. Now what's the plan?"

"That's the thing, now...."

"The thing is the plan?" asked Mon, humour in his voice. "Does this thing have a shape, or is it more like a direction?"

I laughed. "Well it's a direction and a shape. Southwest direction and...uh, oblong ovoid shape?"

There was a pause and then a burst of laughter on the other end. "Jaysus. Pathetic. And you say you design logos?"

"Ah, you know yourself, I don't have to name the shapes, just design them."

I could hear the smile at the other end. "You know you don't have to ask. You can come and stay with me, and I'll even let you bring your surfboard."

"My board is an excellent board."

"If you say so."

"I will let you try it out, though, in thanks."

"You don't have to thank me that much," said Mon. Raising the topic of our long running friendly dispute about our preferred surfboard told me all I needed to know about my welcome at Mon's.

"What about all the logos you have to design?" asked Mon. "You have so many high flying clients, how will they take your absence?"

"Ah, now, now, just because you haven't an artistic bone, or even a capillary, you don't have to go flinging dirt. I do have clients and they will be fine. I can still design. My office is my laptop."

I'd tossed my answer in flippantly, but I knew I would have to do some scrambling and readjusting. Refer a few of my lesser clients to colleagues. I never flaunted my huge success to Mon, it wasn't how I worked. Mon was the best surfer I knew, and anyone ever knew. But I was as good. I couldn't help my talent any more than I could help breathing. I was good, no, the best at whatever I put my hand to and it was a gift I would give back if I ever found a way to make it possible. It shaped my life and put me in the position that faced me now. And all I could do now was to use those gifts to help me avoid those who wanted to use them.

"When do you think you'll come, then?" asked Mon.

"Soon," I said. "I just need to rearrange a few things and pack up."

"Tomorrow, so?"

"Tomorrow."

Tomorrow was a new day, I thought to myself. A new person, a new me. The press was locked, the key gone. The surf was calling.

2

SMITHY

Smithy stared at the fiddle case and it stared back at him, the silence of the sitting room, bold and strong. It was a contest, this staring, the one reaching out, the other resisting. And then a swipe as his heart stretched out and the soul of the fiddle, the very centre of its hum and lilt rejected him. He could nearly hear its mocking "hey diddle diddle" now, the little taunting jig, only the cow was definitely more likely to jump over the moon than it was for him to be able to play any hey diddle diddle tune. He tried to hum it, to woo it back all sneaky like, but the nearest he got was a flat lifeless sound.

He tugged at his hair, wanting to pull each strand out one by one, because that torture was preferable to the one he was going through now. He rose from his chair by the stove. There was no fire in it, but sitting by it gave him the comfort of possibilities and he could use all the comfort he could get. He approached the fiddle case and then veered away, all sneaking gone, defeat and a creeping despair the only thing remaining. He headed out to the kitchen and was about to turn the handle on the outside door when his leg gave way and he collapsed on the floor. Feckityfeckfeck.

This time it had come without warning, taken him unaware, so he could only fall on the spot, banging his side against the countertop before he hit the floor. His ribs were healed, his stab wounds only a red line across his side with a slight pucker on the end of one. Perfect. He looked perfect. A complete deception to the man he was.

He braced himself against the back of a chair and rose slowly. Was this happening with greater frequency, or was it his imagination and growing despondency? He sighed and pulled out his phone, determined to be methodical about determining his condition. He opened an app and started to put in the data. Make it about the data, he thought. Gather data, assess. Make a plan.

He put his phone away and headed to the kettle, while avoiding the beady eye of the Powers whiskey bottle on the shelf nearby. He kept his focus on turning on the tap and putting the kettle underneath it, the water streaming in at a steady pace. Put the kettle on its electric plate, flip it on. Get the mug, get the tea bag and then retrieve the milk. Take a sniff, no, still okay. Right so. Wait and wait and wait and wait. The wait became a rhythm, but it was skittery, off kilter and not quite right. He squeezed his hand tightly. Let it be, let it be, the new mantra, the chant. Yes that was it, all right. He would be the king of the "let it be's".

Ten minutes later he was standing at the threshold of the open kitchen door, sipping his cuppa and staring out into the yard. It still looked the same, why wouldn't it? The wooden door to his forge still had the padlock fastened at the queer angle necessary to get it through the hasp and metal loop. He hadn't been inside since he'd returned. That was a step he wasn't ready for. Not yet. The commissions would have to wait longer, he told himself. What he didn't tell himself, that part that crouched like a rabid dog ready to bite him at any moment, was the knowledge that if he did try his hand at the forge again it wouldn't just be the loss of his magic he was facing, it was the loss of all of it. The not knowing. The not remembering. That knowing of not knowing would finish him. Forget despair, desolation.

A voice called out to him. He turned and looked at the gate. There she was. That woman, his woman. Saoirse. Bríd. Saoirse, Bríd. He gave her a welcome smile. Gave it to her gladly, because he knew he owed her his life. But he was coming to wonder if it was a debt, or if the debt was on her side and not his. He hoped not.

She approached and embraced him. He put his arms around her, folding her into him, seeking her heat and something more. He knew she would hold him and hold him up and any other holds that he might ask, but at this moment he could only do the simplest holds and hope that it was enough. Time, he thought. Let it be, let it be, let it be. Three was best, wasn't it? Three wishes, three leaves of a shamrock and three aspects of the goddess.

He looked down at his goddess. Her beauty was all any goddess could wish for, the auburn hair, the green eyes wide and deep as the ocean. Poet-worthy eyes and poet-worthy body that sang odes and siren calls that he still answered willingly.

"How are you?" she asked, pulling back a little.

Smithy shrugged. "Grand."

"You've been avoiding my calls and texts. Why? Is there something wrong?"

Smithy kissed her on the lips. "Of course not. What could be wrong?"

He endured her searching looks, his expression kept neutral, until she finally sighed.

"You'd let me know, wouldn't you, if something was wrong?"

"Of course I would. Aren't you my lady?" Smithy kept his tone as light as he could.

She pressed into him. "I am your lady, and don't you forget it."

He gave her a squeeze, the emotion that filled him too much for words for a few moments.

"So why haven't you phoned or called?" said Saoirse.

Her tone was lighter and he hoped he'd reassured her now but when he looked at her face he could see the concern still there.

"Nothing to worry about. I was just caught up in a few projects."

The words slid off his tongue, no consequences attached and short of slapping his mouth to stop them, there was little he could do. The words hung in the air doing the only dancing he was capable of, until he saw the light in Saoirse's eyes and he knew she would catch them up – and him in the process.

"Oh. Can I see?"

Yes, the net was truly cast and he was being reeled in, like the fool he was. "Sure," he said. "I'll just get the key."

ONCE THEY WERE inside the forge, Smithy watched as Saoirse scanned the worktops and lime washed stone walls for the new project he was meant to be working on. He could feel the cold from the slab floor seeping up through his boots, at least that's what he told himself, it explained his clammy hands and the sinking feeling.

He walked casually over to the worktop nearest the forge and did a sly trick of the hand, a shuffle of some of his projects, so that one lay bare and seemingly in progress. He studied it for a moment, struggling to recall, grasping at the wisps of memory, until they were in his hand and woven back together. If it was only that easy with other things.

The design was a kind of a twist on the old-fashioned crane for a fireplace, one a Dubliner with plenty of money, a trendy concept and no sense of taste had asked him to fashion. The idea was to look like a tree. Okay, fair enough, he'd thought that had some *blás* to it, an idea that would take you places and not to a leprechaun and a pot of gold. But instead of graceful twists and quirky turns that trees made and did, no the eejit wanted it abstract at harsh angles to give a "modern" feel to it. Save us all please. The drawing he'd been given looked like a stick figure in a game of hangman and that fella had well and truly lost the game. He had tried to put some reason into the creation and created a few semi-circular curves and angles that softened it all. He'd lost heart a bit in the middle of it, though, and had yet to finish. The hangman still unhanged, the potential for redemption still available.

"This is it," said Smithy, hefting up the piece.

Saoirse looked over at the piece he held and considered it. "Uh, right. Uh..."

"I know," said Smithy and he frowned. "It's a 'what the feck?'" He shrugged and put the piece back on the worktop. "A commission from a design novice."

"Did you say design narcissist?" Saoirse said with a small smile.

"Ah, no, now. The commission was even worse in its original concept." He showed her the drawing.

She glanced at it and frowned. "He's going to hang it on his wall?"

Smithy laughed. He was glad for that laughter and pulled her in for a quick kiss. That seemed safe enough.

"Crane," he said. "In a modern style. I was trying to put more style in, to overcome the modern part of the commission."

She stared at the drawing and then the piece, the disbelief written all over her face. "Isn't he bold."

He smiled, loving the word play he had with her. So clever, so quick. He knew she meant "bold" in the very Irish way where it meant, misbehaving, out of hand. Like a mammy reprimanding a child not to be so bold.

"Ah, very bold, all right. My efforts, though, I'm not so sure about."

She looked down at the worktop and studied it. "I don't know. I understand how you were trying to stay within the bounds of the commission."

"You know how I would have created it if it was my design?" he asked.

She looked up at him, the eyes again. Oh, those green, green eyes. Not emeralds, no, but the green of Ireland, the forty shades and all the subtleties that inferred.

He moved to her and she moved to him and they were into each other, arms around shoulders, waists and any parts that would fit pressed against each other. He kissed her and could feel the stirring and the hope that went with it, rising to the surface.

"Let's go inside," she said.

That's what he wanted, to go inside, to be inside her – not just physically but all the ways they shared in the past that meant they were wrapped and twined and whirling around one whole after two parts. But the fear threw up the barrier like some old bundle board to keep them behaving and virginal. Would it be the same? Could it be the same?

He forced a smile and nodded.

He allowed her to lead him into the house, through the kitchen, the sitting room and into the bedroom, his steps like a mournful march to the graveside, a countdown to the hangman, each joint added one by one until he was well and truly hanged.

She stopped by the bed and turned to him, put her hand on his chest. His heart beat steadily underneath it, a thud thud that told him he was alive. Sure, wasn't that enough? Alive and her, Bríd, by his side once more, his other half, the goddess to his god? But he knew that he wasn't a god, not any longer. Failing her once more, like he always had in the past, the recent past and now again, because he could never be what she needed.

She reached up and kissed him, her lips sinking into his and instinct had his arms around her, pulling her closer. The fire lit, a small flame, and he let himself fan it, take warmth from that flame, even though he knew it was best that he pull away. For oh so many, many reasons.

But she was the one who pulled away, as if she knew the thoughts that swirled around inside him, shoving, pushing, elbowing for centre position.

"Smithy?" Her eyes were inquisitive, filled with concern. "Is something wrong?" She began to examine him, her eyes running over his body, seeking weaknesses, a tell-tale sign that some physical fault had manifested itself.

Smithy shook his head and rubbed her arm. "I'm just tired, that's all. I'm not sure my body has caught up just yet."

She nodded. Hugged him. A chaste and pure hug, filled with love and caring. It made him want to lash out and cry all at once, but all he did was hug her back. A tight hug filled with all the longing that slipped out.

She pulled away and placed a hand on his cheek. "Let's just lie on the bed, together, then. We can still be together, but you can rest."

Smithy nodded, unable to utter any words and he allowed her to pull him onto the bed. She lay next to him, her head on his chest, one arm draped across. He automatically closed his arms around hers. He kissed the top of her head.

The bargaining began then. The bargaining he'd avoided and dodged. Mr Hope on the one side, so positive and certain of every dream coming true and Mr Realistic on the other side.

"More time," said the one. "Waste of time," said the other one. "Things will improve," said the one. "In your eye," said the other one. "She will love him anyway," said the one. "She'll get hurt," said the other one.

Smithy blinked, the arguments tiring him more than any physical activity. "A few more days," he told the two. He would give it a few more days. And then, if there was no improvement, he would break things off, go away for her own good. And for the good of the others as well. He would only be a liability in this terrible undertaking to get rid of Balor.

But Mr Truth was in there too, sitting in the corner and he just shook his head, because he didn't need to voice what was paramount. That they all needed Smithy to fashion the weapons to defeat Balor. How could he explain that he couldn't? That the magic was gone?

3

LUKE

I was on the move. I felt I finally could breathe. It wasn't just that the window was down, the breeze blowing my hair, it was the easing in my chest. No beady-eyed crow in the sky, watching for me, only blue horizons and a dusting of cloud. With any luck that blue sky feeling would continue until I got to Mon's place.

I had my board strapped to the roof, my instruments on the back seat and a pile of clothes in my backpack. My phone was set to a favourite tune as well. One that kept me bouncing along and just might as well have been the Beach Boys for all its lifting up and memory of surf, sea and sand. Or sand, sea and surf. Wasn't bothered, so long as they were all in there. Ah, perfect.

The perfect lasted the whole journey and was still there when I pulled into the space behind the building that held Mon's flat. The car park wasn't large, but it was meant to service the pub that sat beneath Mon's flat, and could hardly accommodate more than a few cars. The pub itself was on the fringe of town, a classic Irish rural pub that was still somehow trying to adjust to the fact that it was no longer a market desti-nation for cattle but a tourist destination. With the summer underway, these same tourists were earnest in their attentions, especially now the spa gave promises to the more well-heeled who wouldn't suffer the quaintness of town delights or the gritty reality of an Irish beach. I knew the only reason I'd managed to get a space to park was because I was still early for the Irish visitors who never really worried about catching the worm, or anything else that meant waking up before the sun had made friends with the ground, especially if they were on holidays.

I got out of my SUV and headed to the front of the building and the door that would lead up to Mon's flat. The town was waking up fast, most of the shops open now and people meandering the streets. Cars were beginning to thread their way through the main street at a slower pace, careful of the parked cars and the people randomly crossing the road. Even a one-way system couldn't hide the fact that it was a tricky thing coming into town on a fine sunny day, in the middle of summer.

Though it wasn't the season for the best waves, the ones that got the adrenalin going, the 'now' urgency that took you out there as fast as you could before it all fizzled out, I was happy to be anywhere for any wave that could give me a ride. Feel the sea spray against my face, the salt along my lips. The hum and buzz of skimming that water, that sea, that ocean filled with the power and magic that was all its own.

There were a few surfers on hand, I could see. Their salt-encrusted hair fresh from a recent spin, the wetsuits just gone off them. That faraway look still in their eyes, some with the dash of mad glint.

An arm came around my neck and pulled me back. I lost my balance momentarily, righted myself and swung around, breaking the hold. A shock of white blond hair and a large grin greeted me.

"Mon, hey," I said, unable to keep the delight from my voice.

Though I'd seen him the day before, in Connemara, it had been brief and the situation shite.

He clasped me in a half embrace, his shaggy hair flying forward. His hair had a mind of its own like his father's did, though on Mon it made me smile rather than take note. The hair wasn't the only physical characteristic he'd taken on from his father. No, there was no mistaking his parentage, but the physical resemblance was where it ended. Just one look at the mischief in Mon's eyes and the kindness that lurked quietly and you knew you had a different person altogether.

"Good journey, dude?" he asked.

"Yeah, dude," I said in a mocking tone.

I nearly choked. He was a gasman, Mon. Loved the lingo, jargon, slang and anything else he could throw in for a bit of fun. He was a great mimic, so he was, and taking the piss out of all of it, including himself, was a favourite pastime.

"Come on, so," he said. "Let me give you a hand with your gear."

I smiled and nodded, glad to be with him. Glad to be home. Because Mon was home, or the nearest thing I had. I could trust him beyond anything or anyone.

WE SAT an hour later on his sofa, drinking lager. Strong noonday sun poured into the sitting room window, highlighting the motes of dust that danced around under its scrutiny. Not quite waltz, not quite foxtrot or two-step, their rhythms were erratic and captivating. The tune was there, shadowing their movements but so quietly, it was only a faint whisper. Another time, I told them, making the promise to them and myself as a hand waved in my face.

"You were off somewhere, and it wasn't on a wave," he said and guffawed at his own silly humour.

I waved back. "No, but I am anxious to be out there. What's it been like? Empty waves?"

He laughed in earnest now. "You must be joking. No, every pretend surfer and boogie boarder has been down here this week, with the weather being so fine."

"Anything good?"

"A few good surfers, a few good waves. Best when the tide is right, in the early hours."

I eyed him. "Early hours?"

He shrugged. "Ah you know, yourself. Five am or so, when the sun is just coming up?"

I nodded. I knew. The dedication and energy for early rising just wasn't in the blood of any Gael I knew. Except perhaps a few mad surfers.

"There's some crazy Aussies and an American who aren't half bad. Just passing through, mostly. Following the Wild Atlantic Way thing, only they're calling it the Wild Atlantic Wave."

"Oh, very good," I said and grinned.

"You'll meet them, no doubt." He looked at his watch. "In about two hours we could head down. The forecast isn't bad. Maybe a few three-star waves."

"I know I can't be fussy this time of year," I said. "So, yeah, let's do it."

"Well, even if the weather turns poor and the waves are feck all, you still have the pleasure of my awesome company."

"Awesome," I said with a wry smile.

The mischief left his eyes and he became serious. "You know you're welcome anytime, for as long as you want."

I nodded. "Grateful as always."

He tapped his bottle of lager against mine.

"And your dad isn't around?"

He shook his head. "No, like I said before, he's somewhere up north, I think. Nothing to do with you. It's safe, dude, not to worry. No Tuatha de Danann around. Bar the two of us, of course."

I allowed myself a little bit of relief. Though Mon's father was my foster father and cared for me I knew, I really would rather not encounter him and see the disappointment in his eyes.

Mon shoved me in the elbow. I looked over and saw that he copped on to what I'd been thinking.

"He'd understand, you know. If you explained it to him."

I nodded, but knew he was wrong. How could I explain it to him if I couldn't even explain it to myself? Not really. I only knew what I felt and that was only in the few brief, and they were very brief, moments, I allowed those feelings to make themselves known. Even Mon didn't know the half of it, but being Mon, he trusted that my feelings were true and right and justified all the decisions I'd made. I wasn't so sure.

"Come on, bet you can't beat me on the PlayStation. I just got the latest *God of War*. It's brilliant."

I laughed. "You are joking, now. You really want to play a game based on gods?"

"Viking style, dude. Viking style. With trolls and ogres. Nothing like the real stuff." He scrunched up his face. "Be prepared to laugh. And then be prepared to lose. Lose large, lose big."

I laughed. "Hah, now who's joking? You haven't beaten me since *Lara Croft Tomb Raider* and that was only because you were better at being a girl than I was."

It was all silly trash talk as Mon liked to call it. His latest in a long line of fascinations for the fads and pastimes of each generation. But I was in the mood to humour him. I put down my lager, picked up one of the consoles on the table and prepared to put my game face on.

THE SUN HAD STARTED its descent by the time we arrived on the beach. As predicted, it was crowded enough. The signature blue flag flapped in the distance. A few shouts peppered the air. Swimmers and paddlers were scattered across the shallower parts of the water, but the majority of the people still favoured the sitting on sand part of going to the beach, the saner option in a climate whose water temperatures usually meant anything between paralysing and frigid. The small window at the height of summer could sometimes bring an exception. If the weather, the sea gods and all else cooperated.

Maybe Mananan did know I was here and had taken pity on me, because the waves were decent enough. Just the sight of them caused me to relax. More than the lager or the few hours spent playing a game of hero gods that was silly enough that I wouldn't weep at the thought or sight of it.

There was a light wind, enough to make the waves have a bit more meaning. I felt the urge stirring inside me. I looked across at Mon and he grinned back. We put our boards down and began to pull up the tops of our wetsuits that had been hanging down from our waists. We'd changed in the car park above and left the last bit until we were ready to go in, the wetsuits too hot in this weather except when in the water.

I was zipping up the wetsuit and closing the flaps when I caught sight of one of the surfers in the distance. Mesmerising, lithesome, the surfer caught the targeted wave perfectly and sailed along, bending and curving, a body alphabet of all the best ways to ride a wave. I followed the surfer with my eyes, but the rest of me was feeling the waves and the board and the curve, bend, sway just as the surfer took on those very shapes, riding, skimming sailing along in a seemingly endless perfect motion.

I stood there, watching the surfer fly away with the wave, riding it in, almost ahead of it, as if knowing where it was going and daring it to reach out and push faster. Few had that skill, even allowing for the wave's moderate size. Mon had gone ahead, his attention caught up in his board. Something stopped me from pointing out the surfer, to share the appreciation of skill and technique that seemed more inborn than anything. I kept the moment and the appreciation to myself, unwilling to take my eyes off the person for even a second, a blink, as though doing so would kill the moment, kill the wave, and the surfer would disappear under the water.

The wave died slowly, a natural death and the surfer eased out of it, a practised extrication that was a gentle appreciative sigh to end a perfect event. I walked closer to get a better view of this surfer and I caught sight of a full wetsuit encasing a lean body with revealing curves and the swish of multiple plaits grazing her shoulders. A face, definitely feminine, turned towards me. A face, but no name with it. Ah, never mind, so. This is Ireland. That face would have a name soon enough. I moved to catch up with Mon, who was already strides ahead, his eyes scanning the water. I turned again to the woman, but she was gone.

4

———

LUKE

My hair was still soaking, but I felt alive. Mon stood beside me, grinning and laughing like we were lads together just after doing some silly prank at school. The wave we'd just ridden had been a slippery one, the type that promises much at first, and then goes all sly like, before erupting and punching you in the gut. The #crazy type of experience they made memes of on social media. Mon had nearly lost it once, an amazing thing and if I hadn't had a few lucky misbalances and a completely unplanned hoppy sequence, I would have been eating salt at least three times. As it was I slipped in the water a few moments before Mon, laughing so hard I could hardly right myself. It was the laughter that got me and I was glad for it.

We headed up the beach, boards in hand and a group of people crowded in around us, shouting, laughing and full of the great tease. We were "circus team warming up", "lads, did you need a pee?", "is that a new skill you two were working on – twats on boards?", and of course "lads, I didn't catch that on film, can you do it again?"

They were Mon's friends, some I vaguely recognised from

my few prior visits here. Both of us usually got together in Galway, in winter for the best waves and occasionally in summer. But this beach, this place was his base.

Mon laughed and shoved, clapped and jabbed them all back, his own banter whip quick. I detected an Aussie accent and maybe a trace of an American as well as I listened in and watched.

Mon turned to me, the laughter still in his eyes, his arm now slung around my shoulders. "Lads, you remember Luke, now, yeah? Luke, these are the lads."

There were four of them, standing and slouching around us, eyes alight with high five and fist bump humour that was more dude-like to be just "lads".

I smiled and gave a nod. "*Na laddaí*," I said, making a play on the Irish to give a sense of the plural of lads.

Mon gave a burst of laughter and squeezed my shoulder hard. I knew he loved the little ins and outs of my word play that were in some ways meant only for him. Working words in a manner only a brother would know all the levels of meaning they contained. I was reminding him, assuring him, that I would always have his back and he would always have mine.

Lad number one on the far left had laughed hard too. Obviously Irish, though the ginger hair, high cheekbones and lanky frame may have given it away. There were a few snickers from lad number three as well. He was dark haired, but had the translucent fair skin, blue eyes and sprinkling of freckles that also marked him as a Gael. He was even working the Cillian Murphy *Peaky Blinders* look, I noticed. Definitely Irish.

The others, lad two and lad four, were more the blond and brunette any-way-it-goes hair that reflected my own sympathies. But all of them were fit, muscular and I was certain experienced surfers if Mon allowed them in his company.

Lad number two, the blond one leaned forward and put out

his hand. "Name's Mud, man," he said in the Aussie accent I'd heard earlier.

I nodded, raising my brow. "Bad boy?"

He laughed. "Yeah. Real name's Madison, got mutated along the line."

"Mutilated, don't you mean?" said Mon.

Mud snorted. "Yeah, well, nothing to live up to with that name."

Everyone sniggered. The others seemed to take their cue from Mud. Lad number four, the blond, was called Jake and his American mother had claimed him from here when he was young, but now he was his own man, as he put it, he lived where he wanted, and lately that was in Ireland. Peaky Blinder grinned and lifted his chin as his introduction. "Alex."

The others turned to the ginger haired one, who gave a startled look. Mon laughed. "This is the witless one, Eoin. I think you met him a few years ago. But he may have been shorter and even more witless then."

We all acknowledged the messing with our respective grins that easily excused my lack of recognition. If Mon said I met him, then I must have. But any time I'd come here it was a "lick the wounds" type of visit that didn't include headspace for new friendships.

I shoved the thought aside into the press where all thoughts like that are put. My own "put to bed" place so crowded and full to bursting, but that door still shut, which suited me.

"You staying the summer, then?" asked Jake. "Mon says you're rad on the board."

I looked over at Mon. "Rad, eh?"

Mon shrugged. "Oh, dude, you know how good you are."

"Thanks, dude," I told him, the emphasis of the dude there in my eyes, if not my voice.

"Ah, cop on yourself," said Mon, digging my side.

"The usual tonight?" asked Alex.

"Yeah, sure. I'm up for a few pints," said Mud.

A few other nods and there was consensus. My evening planned, my press firmly shut and locked with the key. Just the wide open space of possibilities.

THE LIFE BUOY. Blond wood. Slate grey and blue, the paint so new I could smell it. That summed it up. I sighed as we walked in. I didn't even have to look to the window for the obligatory sailboat, the anchor planted somewhere on a wall or mantle, or some bits of rope unused and beautifully knotted, draped, nailed or stuck on a board.

I looked at Mon, wondering for a brief moment if this was a wind up. "Avast me hearties," I mumbled, just to see.

Mon turned, narrowed his eyes and then burst out laughing. "You'll see. It's new. It's great craic."

I looked around slowly, taking in the distressed wood tables, the mismatching benches and the wood beams placed against walls and ceilings, determined to belong. The people on the benches and standing near the bar at the front were a variety packet of visitors, holiday makers and curious locals. But one group did stand out and I followed the others to them. I didn't need labels to know they were surfers, or surfer friends. It might have been the salty look to the hair and face or the loose limbed manner in their stance that seemed more at home with one foot slightly forward and twisted at the waist. And it wasn't just lads, either. Plenty of girls too, though I supposed Mon would call them "babes".

The group opened ranks when we arrived and absorbed us like some amoeba, integrating us into mass. I heard the introductions, nodded to the others and noted the speculative glances and glints from some of the girls. They were young enough, and right now, I was feeling old. I started to check for drinks and made my way to the bar once I had the orders.

I placed the orders and a moment later Mon was behind me. I studied him. Something wasn't right.

"The Life Buoy?" I asked. "Is that what it's about? The life, boy. But is it?"

Mon plastered a grin on his face. "Ah, you know. The lads are great. They like it here. The babes, well, you saw... they're babes."

"Yeah, they're babes," I said dryly.

He looked away. I placed a hand on his shoulder.

"What? Is it your father?"

He shook his head. "Ah, no. I'm grand, he's grand. Usual shite."

"Is it her?"

Mon's head whipped around, his eyes narrowed. "What do you mean?"

I cocked my head to the side, the "ah come on" look evident in my face.

"Does she still come around? Do you see her, have you spoken to her?"

"Maybe."

"Maybe, what?" I said, full of patience for this brother, filled with a life of hurt. Another thing we shared, though my hurt was of a much different colour. He'd witnessed mine, but I hadn't even done that for him. No, I'd been too caught up in my prowess, my herodom. Hero doom.

"I heard she was around," he said softly. "A while ago."

"But you haven't seen her?"

He shook his head. "No."

"And you haven't asked your father about it or asked for his help?"

He gave me a sharp look. "Of course not. I would never do that. Never. Once was enough."

"It's not your fault she left," I said quietly. He knew that, but I said it anyway, just as I'd said it time and time again. But time didn't help. I knew that too. It hadn't helped me.

"She wouldn't talk to me even if I did see her," said Mon, the pain in his voice nearly cutting me.

"Ah, now, maybe not. After all this time."

He stared at me, a tiny glimmer of hope in his eyes. I winced inwardly to see that hope. It was just too indicative of the torment he'd put himself through and would continue to. How to say to him, how to tell him, in a way that he would hear and act on, that he should let it go. But I couldn't let my own hurt go, so how could I tell him to do that? I had no glimmer of hope, nothing and I still couldn't let the hurt and longing go. I was still who I was and nothing could change the past.

Mon's phone buzzed. He dug it out of his pocket, swiped, tapped and frowned.

"For feck's sake," he muttered.

"What?"

He looked up at me and made a face. "Dad. Wants me to hare it up to Donegal for some shite."

"Dad?" I asked, my brow raised.

Mon snorted. "Yeah, he hates it."

"He does of course." I laughed, knowing too well how my foster father's imposing and formal manner would balk at the use of the term, "Dad".

"Not 'Da', 'Daddo', or even better, 'Daddio'?" I asked. "I'm sure he'd love that."

Mon gritted his teeth and shook his head. "Sorry, couldn't manage that far."

"Still, brave man, you."

"Pitiful. Silly. Petty," said Mon, his tone bland. "But it gives me joy, dude. Gives me joy."

I patted him on the shoulder. "So why does he want you up in Donegal?"

"Feck if I know. He says he'll explain when I get up there."

I nodded and suddenly felt deflated. My summer interlude, my "lick my wounds" visit seemed to be evaporating.

As if sensing my thoughts Mon grabbed my arm. "But that doesn't mean you have to go, Luke. You know you can stay at mine. For as long as you want. As long as you need."

I nodded and wondered if I would. His "laddaí" weren't really my "laddaí", but maybe I could tolerate them for a while.

"When do you have to go?" I asked.

Mon frowned. "Soon. I should go now, but I won't. He can feckin' well wait. I'll go tomorrow." He looked at me and grinned. "After a bit of practice."

"Practice?"

He lifted his arm and swished the air a few times. "Yeah, practice."

I shook my head. That shake wasn't at his antics. It was a resounding "no".

I STILL DIDN'T KNOW how it happened. How my resounding "no" somehow translated into my presence here in this shed behind an old hardware shop at the edge of the town, a sword in my hand.

It was some feckin' unreal time in the morning when no decent people are up and all the less decent people hadn't gone to bed yet. The sweat was pouring off me and my breath was coming in pants. Mon was circling, our swords having clashed several times and his advantage nearly making mincemeat of me several times.

"Janey mac, Luke, when did you last practice?"

I shrugged, my eyes still fixed on his eyes and in my peripheral vision, the rest of him. It had been longer than I wanted to admit. Probably since the last time the two of us had sparred. I knew Mon practised most days, if only because his father would ensure that he did involuntarily, if he didn't manage it himself. I contented myself with jogging and surfing when I could.

"'Janey mac', are those your fighting words?" I said, teasing in my voice.

"Oh feck off."

He advanced forward, trying a sudden undercut, but I parried and advanced a little. I hated that the sword felt good in my hand, hated it almost as much as the fact that I was here, practising a skill that I no longer valued, a skill that I wanted to lose, if that was possible, yet my love for Mon wouldn't allow me to abandon, because he wouldn't allow it.

Suddenly he attacked, moving with force and increased skill. There was nothing lazy about this and if I didn't know better I would have said it was born of an aggressive anger, and one that I couldn't place or reason with. I fought back suddenly, all my instincts kicking in, my mind going blank and the steps, swings turned into attacks and not parries, the clang and clash of the blades ringing loudly in the shed. Mon was all fierce concentration, giving no quarter and no revealing emotion.

It was all over in a few minutes, his blade skittering across the concrete floor. I halted, reining in my body from the adrenalin surge that had me in its power and the instinct drove my limbs.

Mon stood apart from me, bent over, his hands on his knees. His breath came heavily, his chest heaving with the effort. I stood there watching my own chest rising, still puzzled over his angry aggression. After a few moments he stood up and made his way over to me. He pushed me in the chest and I fell back a few steps with the force of it.

"There," he said. "It's still in you. It is you, Luke. Stop rejecting it. Accept it. You are a warrior born, Son of a warrior, grandson of a warrior, and don't you forget it."

I turned away, my own anger simmering and ready to erupt. "Son of no one. Grandson of no one."

Mon shoved me again. "A warrior born."

I looked through the glass of the large sliding door to the waste ground beyond. That was me. Waste ground. I dropped the sword and heard it clatter as it hit the floor. Outside, a crow landed and began to peck the ground for food. It looked up and I stared it right in the eye, daring it. Waste ground.

5

SAOIRSE

Saoirse heard the voices around her, but the words only ebbed and flowed like a tidal white noise. She watched her fingers make intricate patterns with each other, a kind of jiggity jig with a polka twist or two. She watched them dispassionately, observing their timing, almost agitated grace. Agitated, yes that was it.

"Bríd."

Saoirse looked up. An almost sigh escaped her. Why did she insist on calling her and everyone else by mythic names? Anu stared at her, willing her presence. And did it matter what she thought? She had nothing to contribute. She remembered nothing as Bríd, supposed goddess. She knew nothing of her. And her only gift, her only magic, she had no idea how to summon, or control. All she knew was what Smithy brought forth from her, and she wasn't even sure that was still there.

She looked over at Smithy and found the usual guarded expression. He reached for her hand and squeezed it, but then withdrew again, just as he had since he'd returned.

"What do you think, Bríd?" asked Anu, her voice ever patient.

Saoirse looked at the rest, hoping for clues about what she was supposed give an opinion. Maura sat sprawled in her chair, slightly amused as always, the sleeves of her black shirt rolled up, revealing a small crow tattoo on her forearm. Beside her, Finn gave Saoirse an uncertain smile, his kind eyes conveying a message she couldn't read.

"I'm not certain Saoirse really knows what Lugh looks like, or much of his history, anyway, Anu. She was gone before Lugh arrived at Tara, if you remember."

Saoirse gave him a grateful smile and looked at Anu and shrugged. "I wouldn't know anyway. I don't remember anything from before."

Anu nodded. "I understand that. But you mustn't discount the memories in your soul, in your body. After all, you and Goibhniu..."

She left the words hang in the air and Saoirse gave her a weak smile. She understood the point, but the point was gone, blunted by something she didn't understand and Smithy wasn't about to explain to her, even if he knew. She sighed again.

"But it might help if you did know about Lugh," said Anu. "You knew him best out of all of us, Goibhniu, didn't you?"

Smithy sat up quickly, caught out. Caught out of what, Saoirse could only speculate, his face shuttered as it always was lately.

"Ah, I suppose." He looked around at the others. "What do you want to know?"

"For Bríd's benefit, tell us about him. Generally. His likes, talents, describe him as a person."

Smithy gave a sour laugh. "Person? Him?" He looked at Finn. "What would you call him? The ultimate warrior? He bested you, the king's champion, enough times."

Finn looked down, a wry smile on his face. Saoirse stared at him. He was a man who wore the sword awkwardly. But then, thinking back to the short time in the Otherworld when the fighting was thickest, Finn was there, cutting, slashing and killing the enemy with the fierceness only a seasoned warrior could. What had happened?

"A hero god," said Finn.

Saoirse blinked.

"Yes," said Smithy. "Exactly. He is the ultimate hero. There isn't anything he can't do. And when he does it, it's the best. No one can beat him. 'Lugh of the Long Arm' has all the talents."

"Ah, please." The words escaped Saoirse before she knew she'd uttered them.

They all looked at her. Maura laughed. Finn smiled and Smithy frowned.

"You think it's a joke?" said Smithy.

She gave him a puzzled look. "N-no. It just seemed so extraordinary to describe someone like that. As if he was some kind of..." She reddened, caught by her own words.

"Mythic hero?" said Finn softly.

"Super god? Sun god?" said Smithy, his sarcasm clearly detectable. "That's because he is. Why do you think he's been able to avoid us for so long? He can plunge deep into the land, become part of the scenery, the people. Take up any talent, occupation, whatever he wants and make it work."

"But, but..., really?" said Saoirse. "Why doesn't he want to be found, then? Maybe that can give a clue to where he is?"

They all exchanged glances. "He killed his grandfather," said Maura after a few moments. "What would you call that – grand patricide?" She laughed again, laughter that rang out loudly as the rest remained silent, frowning at her.

"Enough, Morrigan," said Anu.

"No, sorry, should I have said regicide, instead?" said Maura. "Balor was a king, after all."

"What?" said Saoirse, trying desperately to take in all that

Maura had stated. "Balor of the Evil Eye, was his grandfather? And he killed him? But...how did that happen? No, wait. But Balor is still alive, isn't he? Isn't he the person we're trying to stop? The person who's making it his mission to poison Ireland and the rest of the planet as much as possible?"

Maura laughed again, but after a dark look from Anu, she stopped. Anu turned to Saoirse.

"All of those things are true. Lugh is the son of Cían, a Tuatha de Danann, but his mother was Balor's daughter, and therefore a Fomorian. He came as a Tuatha de Danann, though, to the Hall of Tara as a young warrior with all the talents Goibhniu described. Later it was because he took out Balor that we were able to defeat the Fomorians."

Maura cackled. "He took out his eye with a slingshot and the poison sprayed his own men."

Anu gave Maura a look and her laughter subsided. "It's only in this past while, when Balor's energy company appeared, that we discovered Balor hadn't died. Or if he had, something, someone brought him back."

Remnants of this old tale drifted through Saoirse's mind from the overwhelming long one from the myth cycle that Anu had recounted to her a while ago.

"Why doesn't Lugh want to be found, now? Is he fearful that Balor will want revenge? Or does he even know that his grandfather is still alive?"

Anu gave her a sad look. "I don't know. I can only speculate that Lugh does know that his grandfather is still alive."

"What about his father," she paused a moment searching for the name. "Cían. Have you contacted him? Maybe he knows where Lugh is. Or is he in the Otherworld?"

"Cían is dead," said Anu quietly.

"Oh." Saoirse looked at the others, but their expressions held nothing but resignation. "Well, I don't know where to look. You would have better ideas about that. I don't even know what he looks like."

"I'm not sure that would be helpful," said Smithy. "A glamour could alter his looks enough."

"A glamour can only go so far," said Maura. "But even then, this is a large island with enough people on it that it isn't the easiest prospect. Tall, fair and handsome isn't enough. I've sent the crows out a few times in the last several months and nothing. Dublin's the worst. Too crowded. And the cousins aren't particularly helpful."

Anu nodded. "I'll try Manannan. He was his foster father. He might have an idea and he might be willing to tell me. Or Mongan. I just need to discover which part of the sea, Manannan has decided to inhabit for the summer."

"What about Lir?" asked Finn.

Anu shook her head. "Lir might be the high god of the sea, but Manannan as his son is de facto ruler. Lir spends most of his days in contemplation and conserving his energies. Some sections of the sea are just too badly contaminated and it's affecting his health."

"Feck it," said Finn, his fist clenched tight. "This is such shite."

Anu sighed. "Yes. But we need to concentrate on what we can do. Balor is the best focus. We know how to deal with him, once we have the right pieces in place. That main piece is Lugh."

Maura sighed. "I'll send out the crows again. Maybe I'll even go myself."

Saoirse looked at the others, wondering what it was that the rest of them were supposed to do. What she was supposed to do.

"I'll send out word through the musicians, again," said Finn. "Maybe someone's heard of a remarkable talent."

Smithy rose. "I'll see what I can do at the forge. Maybe create something that might lure him out of hiding that way. Or maybe issue some kind of blacksmith challenge."

Saoirse heard their suggestions and still could come up with nothing that would be helpful. "I'll keep an eye out for anyone who seems like a super hero," she said in the end.

Maura grinned at her. "You do that." She turned to Smithy. "Come here, Smithy. There's a session on tonight down at the village. Fab musicians, a 'cannot miss' event. You coming? Finn says he will."

Maura looked at Saoirse, a question on her face. Saoirse lit up at the thought, suddenly cheered.

"I will of course," he said.

THEY COULD HEAR the music from the car park. Wild, generous and very foot tapping. By the time Saoirse walked in, wearing her old Converse for a change, the weather being cooperative, she was already feeling her inner jig. Her legs were bare, but her skirt was flippy and loose at her calves with just enough warmth and protection for the season. She was her old self, her Saoirse self.

Saoirse soon felt the humming in the tips of her fingers and was anxious to play. She passed through to the main room. It wasn't a session, it was a Gathering. Definitely capitalised. Everyone and then some were here. The "then some" were not quite locals and not quite visitors, all anxious to partake in the event, the air of "special" already on everyone's lips. That so many had heard already was testament to how special it was. A spontaneous gathering of touring musicians after the official concert in the Ionad. An "after concert concert", whose possibility had spread on the thread of connections that was more efficient than any elusive superfast broadband. It wasn't

Murphy's Law, it was Zen Murphy at its most zen. All night and into morning. It was in the air. And she was here, in the heart of it.

She moved forward, conscious of Smithy dragging his feet behind her. She shoved that thought aside and put it in a bag with the other worries and tucked it away. This was not a night for worries. This was a night to feel the music. She tried to adopt her "whynot" mood, but the "why" slipped away and the "not" became knotted.

She stared at the musicians, the jaw dropping for a moment when she saw who they were. Feck me, but were all of the *Gradam Ceoil* award winners here? She knew at least one of the local top musicians, a local shouldn't be totally unexpected, but to have these others. A flutter of nerves caused her to start and then a hand on her arm, calming, reassuring reined it in. She looked over and saw it was Smithy. Of course, he knew. Of course, he understood. He flashed her a brief smile, but then it was gone, his hand withdrawn, his work done.

Some stools were kicked out to their direction, no doubt recognising Smithy and perhaps Maura and Finn as worthy of a seat close to the main table. The high table, in her eyes and she only hoped she could measure up.

She sat on one of the stools, and unpacked her flute, the music flying around her, the glasses on the table nearly ringing and dancing with the joy of it. She let it enter her, calm her and before she knew it she had her flute up to her mouth and she was blowing. Blowing away the cobwebs of fear, doubt and unreason. Beside her, Finn's sure mastery of the guitar led her on, creating the drive for her to follow the rest. Fiddles, concertinas, boxes, thrown in with flutes, a mandolin or two and a bouzouki. And even an uilleann piper, one of the high table greats. On her other side, Maura's bodhran created a great underbeat that complemented Finn's guitar. Saoirse strained to hear Smithy's fiddle amid the jig-reel-polka that immersed them all, but the roar and blend of it all was encompassing and bliss in its own end. Zen indeed.

They moved sideways into one of the local compositions, one by Himself, the quirky jumper-wearing Gradam Ceoil musician, a great, funky set of tunes that had become absorbed into the local legend. A tribute to him and his talent, and Saoirse listened carefully, only generally familiar with it and its background. The greats knew it well and then she was off with it too. Again, she stretched to find Smithy, to feel him and his connection – because he, surely more than any other, would help her find the core of these tunes. It eluded her. He eluded her. Whether it was the large number of musicians, or the press of the crowd and the distance between them, she didn't know, but she couldn't sense him in any way at the moment.

She looked over at him, saw the strokes of the bow against the fiddle, his body move in its unspoken knowledge of the tunes, but his eyes were elsewhere. She gave a puzzled frown.

The tunes ended and the group shared the grins and the joy and the spin of the tunes that still buzzed around them, lingering and not letting go. She joined them all, her own face near to splitting with the width of her smile. Ah, the pure joy of it.

The uilleann piper struck up a drone, its mournful sound calling all to attention, but gently, persuasively in its effort, to create that transition to the flying madness of the previous set to the calm and gentleness of the next. It was an air. *The Dear Irish Boy*. A few musicians joined the piper eventually, lending discreet support, a fiddle, soft guitar, and a hint of concertina. She looked to see if it was Smithy on the fiddle, but he sat there, his eyes on the piper, his fiddle across his lap. Finn had his guitar in place, ready, but not yet active, his eyes glinting in appreciation.

The last echoes of *The Dear Irish Boy* eased into a run up to *Sí Bheag, Sí Mhór* and Saoirse laughed at the sound of it, picked up her flute and away she went. She could feel and hear the humour in Finn's guitar and Maura's bodhran. She looked at each one and shared the fun, and oh so funny. Maura was nearly cackling, her crow tattoo in a gentle jig with the movement of her muscles as she struck the tipper against the drum. A little inside joke that they all shared and she was part of it. She knew and understand the wicked undercurrents their playing attached to it.

She looked back at Smithy, but his eyes didn't join in, or return the favour, and she couldn't hear or detect his playing among the others. He stroked his bow against the strings with a dogged determination. Or was it anger? He wouldn't look at her, now. And when they were alone together he hardly even managed a smile. Was it something she'd done? Increasingly he'd seemed distant. She turned away. It was about the music now, she wouldn't allow anything to pull her out of that. She turned back to Finn and he winked at her, added a little flourish to his strum pattern, a bit of a pick at the strings, to give the tune a little spin and she laughed and answered with her own flourish on the flute. The tune ended and the laughs, smiles and whoops were all that was needed to lift her up higher than before.

Finn shoved against her. "Grand stuff, eh?"

She nodded, words were redundant.

A shout rang out and Finn turned at the sound of his name.

"A tale. A tale. Give us a tale, Finn," said the dark bearded man who called out his name.

He laughed at them. "Sure, you're a tale all in yourself."

The dark bearded man roared with laughter. "Ah, come on now, lad. You'll give us one, so."

Finn grinned. "I will then, but only to keep you from bleating at me."

Fascinated at what she might hear, Saoirse watched him stand and place his guitar on his stool. This was a side of Finn she hadn't yet seen.

He opened his tale in the manner of all good seanchies, those ancient storytellers still scattered across Ireland in forgotten pubs and remote households as well as condensed and preserved or, some might say, pickled in the annual Oireachtas competitions and local *Scór* groups.

"*Fadó, fadó, fadó,*" he said, uttering the "long agos" like any good seanchie.

"So long ago it was even before your time, Paddy!" said the dark bearded man to a small and wrinkled man seating in a corner.

Everyone laughed and Finn's eyes crinkled in good humour.

He continued on, setting up the recitation, a short tale with a twist and a snicker of humour that pulled you along until you were surprised at yourself at the end. Finn told it with his voice and his face and a flick of the hand, a twiddle of finger. It was masterful and a master so full and canny Saoirse could only remain still and hope that its power wouldn't end.

When the tale had ended, the "*sine*" finish stated, all the parts revealed and gasps, giggles and nods tossed his way like bouquets for the diva, Finn took his seat, only a nod and smile to show in acknowledgment of the praise.

It was Saoirse's turn to give a shove. "Now who's the grand stuff? Feckit, you're good, Finn."

He shrugged modestly. "I do my best."

Saoirse leaned over, her voice lowered. "Not just the king's champion, but a seanchie of the highest level."

Finn gave her a studied look. "A man of words. That's who I am."

Reading modesty, Saoirse shook her head. "A man of many talents."

"Everyone has talents, Saoirse."

"But your talents are shown and used to their fullest, surely. I'm only good at music. At the flute, specifically. And only session worthy, really."

He frowned at her. "Not so. Your talents are wide, full-fledged and many. I have words, that is my power, and possibly the talent with the sword. My guitar playing, well, that's earthly with a bit of my own heritage thrown in. Your flute mastery, is beyond that. Your craft with metal, you know better than to deny that. As for healing and poetry," he fixed her with a stare, that plunged deep inside her, "I know the poetry is there and the healing talent is unfolding as we speak. Bríd." He added the goddess's name softly at the end.

Saoirse stared at him, her own words vanished. "How do you know about my poetry?"

Finn snorted. "I don't know about the poetry you've written lately, I just know it's in you, because of who you are."

She looked down at her lap, the small book she carried nearly everywhere burning through the cloth of her skirt pocket to her skin.

Seeing her discomfort, Finn squeezed her hand. "Don't worry, it will come."

She nodded and forced a smile. She picked up her flute, shook out the spit, fiddled around with it a bit more and strained to hear if another tune was in the making. But it was all talk and banter and her mood had shifted away from that direction. She put her flute on the table and rose. Air or bathroom debate ensued and she opted for the one closest, or at least easiest to reach. She made her way to the corridor and saw there was a queue. Squeezing past, the debate settled unexpectedly in the opposite direction, she plunged through the exit just beyond the bathrooms and felt the cool night air hit her.

Once outside, she hugged herself a little. She'd left her light cloth jacket inside, bundled under the table where she'd thrown it when they'd first arrived. The sheer blouse over a tank top that was entirely too tight now her body had rearranged itself into Bríd's proportions wasn't quite warm enough.

She saw a curl of smoke over near the outdoor benches and made out the features and dark hair.

"Maura."

Maura turned. "Breaktime for you, so?"

"Yes. I think my head is full to bursting."

Maura laughed. "Some fab playing tonight. Special."

"Definitely."

"What do you think of the uilleann piper? World class, isn't he."

"He is good. I've some of his recordings somewhere. Liam O'Flynn good. But not really the best I've heard."

Maura turned to face her. "No? You've heard better? Who?"

"Someone I've played with up in Dublin."

"Really? And he's better than your man?"

Saoirse shrugged. "He plays pipes and anything else you can name. Equally good at it all, as far as I can see."

"Really?"

Saoirse nodded. "It's hard to describe. He's got a chemistry when he plays, and if you're playing with him, it's like weaving yourself into his music. Well more than that. He's amazing to play with."

"Better than you and Smithy together?"

Saoirse frowned. Had Maura noticed what it was like for her to play with him? How they entered each other, became the parts of the whole that spun the tune. And more.

"Well, no. But it's different. He surfs as well. I've never seen anyone surf as well as he does. Not that I'm an expert."

"Good at everything, is he?" Maura's eyes gleamed.

"Yeah, I guess so."

"And I suppose he's tall, dark and handsome, too." There was definite humour in her voice.

"Blond." Saoirse was reluctant to follow this path.

"Tall, blond and handsome. Good in bed, too?"

Saoirse was glad for the dark that would disguise what she knew was a deep flush flooding her skin, the ginger haired lament.

Maura nudged her. "Another talent as well? Better than Smithy?"

Saoirse stared at her. "No, no. It's not like that. We, no. Smithy and I, well. We're us. Luke, he's who he is." She knew her words made no sense whatsoever and her thoughts of Luke were tinged with anger and hurt. But that was pale and wan in the face of all the things that had happened since. His abandonment of her after their few days together seemed more like a teen drama than anything she should take seriously.

"Luke? Did you say his name was Luke?" asked Maura.

Saoirse focused on Maura's face. "Yes, why?"

"And he's good at any instrument he picks up?"

"Well, any that I've seen him try his hand at."

"He surfs, too you say?"

Saoirse nodded slowly, watching Maura's expression change from teasing to disbelief. Suddenly, she burst into laughter, leaving Saoirse to stare at her.

"Oh, Saoirse, aren't you just the prize."

"What? What's wrong?"

"You've done it, you fecker. You're only after finding your man, the one we've been looking for this past age. And it's priceless, because you didn't even know it."

6

SMITHY

What the feck, thought Smithy, staring up at the trendily renovated house. The trendiness was subtle, but it didn't mean he couldn't recognise its smart exterior with the feckin' Ball and Chain colours on its trim. Brick Victorian. The fecker lived here, in this area of Dublin. Not North Dublin, Swords, or somewhere that you could rationalise the purchase. But here in feckin' The Liberties.

He knew that it wasn't house envy that had him angry. No, really, he couldn't care less about the house, or the address. It was that she knew the house. Knew the address. And that knowledge told him more than he wanted to know. More than he wanted to feel.

He glanced over at Saoirse, saw her bite her lip as she stared at the door, raising her hand tentatively to knock. That told him a few things, too, things that eased his tension and the tight knots that had seized him since Saoirse had told them all she knew where Lugh lived and would go there to see him. All the joy and hope the others had expressed when Maura had announced the discovery to everyone had centred on Saoirse's quiet statement. A statement that had brought the two of them here.

The journey up had been quiet, all the unspoken words hovering between them. Words that even the jaunty tunes he'd played through the speakers couldn't dispel. She had placed a comforting hand on his at one point and that had earned her a weak smile from him. That Anu had insisted the two of them travel together for this task seemed more than just a practical arrangement – he, to help compel Lugh, with a little physical threat if necessary, once they met up with him and Saoirse to lead him to Lugh. Well that had told him Anu knew something was amiss and this was her way of a gentle poke. And now here they were, standing on the doorstep to Lugh's house. Luke's house. It did seem the house of a Luke, the successful designer, edgy and very now. On trend. Or whatever it was they said at the moment.

Saoirse lifted her hand and knocked again. He could almost hear the sound echo through the house. An empty echo.

He cast an eye to the road. "Did I hear you mention he has a car?"

She looked back at him and then to the road and nodded. "An SUV. But I don't see it anywhere."

"Can you ring him?"

"I, uh, don't have his number."

Smithy nodded carefully. That was something, wasn't it? "Could he have gone to meet a client?"

Saoirse shrugged. "I suppose."

And there was another thing, to add to the first thing. And together they made him feel a little better. He craned to the left and tried to see into the front window. Light from the window and somewhere in the interior was enough to provide an impression of a sleek, open plan layout and not much more. He sighed, looked around at the anonymous collection of houses and reached up above the door lintel. He knew there would be nothing there, but appearances were everything.

With that gesture completed he withdrew a little cloth roll from his pocket, selected what he wanted and inserted the small metal tool in the lock. After a bit of fiddling, the lock gave way and he pushed open the door. Saoirse watched him with wide eyes, pausing on the threshold for a moment before collecting herself and following him through.

"Why?" she asked. "What's the point?"

"We might be able to find a clue to where he's gone," he stated flatly. "Did you have a better idea?"

"Oh. Right. No, no better ideas, not really." Her tone was careful, neutral.

Smithy moved through to the hall, Saoirse following behind him reluctantly. The small hall quickly opened up into the large space he'd seen from the window. Light poured in from clever roofing and window placement, making the place seem bright and spacious, a look emphasised by the sleek lines, wood floors and scattered rugs.

Smithy scanned the room, noting the modern paintings and artwork carefully placed around the living room area. This was not the home of a surfer dude. Or a musician that lived only for his music. This was...well tasteful married to wealth. Designer out of a catalogue. He moved over to one wall and stared up at the painting. It was an abstract filled with bold colours, but it seemed too perfect. Too nothing. There were no other homely touches that he could see, except for a lap blanket draped over the sofa.

He moved into the kitchen. Everything clean, put away. He opened the fridge and found a few non-perishables. The bin was empty too. Very tidy man, he thought. He found the wine rack in a cool spot just off the kitchen. Nothing special there. There were a few bottles of whiskey on a nearby shelf. He was surprised to see one of them was Powers. Did that mean that Luke was in Cork enough to enjoy it? Or was it just a coincidence?

He went back into the kitchen and found Saoirse staring at the photo on the wall opposite the kitchen sink. He came up behind her. The photo showed two men, surfboards in hand, standing with joyful smiles on their faces.

She pointed. "That's Luke."

Smithy stared at the photo, saw the blond hair, the handsome chiselled face, the deep blue eyes and the well-muscled body. All the details that together and apart meant a man that any woman would want. Every woman would want.

"Do you recognise him?" she asked.

He shrugged. He had no idea, suddenly realising that he had no visual memory of Lugh, let alone if this man could be him. The thought shook him. Jaysus. Would he ever get a grip?

"I don't know. Maybe." He picked the photo off the wall. "We'll take it to Anu. If anyone can tell, she can."

Saoirse gave him a puzzled look and then nodded. She glanced around again. Frowned.

"The surfboard. It's gone."

Smithy looked around the kitchen, hall and living room. "He kept the surfboard here?" It seemed hard to believe, given the designer feel to the rest of the place.

"He loved that board. It was special, so yeah, he kept it here." She pointed. "Over there, against the wall."

Smithy glanced over to the blank wall space where she'd indicated. It looked empty, as if something had been there. Still.

"Could he have put it elsewhere? Upstairs?"

He didn't enjoy asking her these questions and liking the answers even less. The answers told him more things and he'd had enough of that already. Her relationship with Luke was taking on more depth, the threads weaving in tighter, becoming a pattern. And the pattern said serious, said meaningful. Just when all the threads that were running through their tapestry, his and Bríd's, Saoirse's seemed to be loosening, unravelling.

"I don't think so," she said. "But maybe."

Those few words gave him permission for a little smile, a little lift. "Let's check. There might be other clues to his location."

They climbed the stairs, Saoirse leading, and he did understand that she knew where to head, where to find Luke's own bedroom and that it was to the left of the spare bedroom. They spent little time in the spare bedroom, which looked as unused as it smelled, but they lingered in the main bedroom. That too was neat and tidy, the duvet draped with care along the bed. Smithy didn't like where his mind travelled, and he turned to the wardrobe doors, opening them and scanning for signs of this person's life and current destination.

The suits, the shoes, the shirts all seemed to belong and looked comfortable in the presence of each other. No extreme neatness, but certainly not in disarray. The drawers gave up little as well. Eventually Smithy made his way to the en-suite bathroom, glancing around at the basic toiletries and all the rest that meant this bathroom is for comfort and pampering.

"Some toiletries are missing," said Saoirse a few moments after following him into the bathroom.

"Oh, right. Okay." Smithy said, the neutral tone he'd adopted sounding dead. "That's something."

"Well, I think they're missing. Look, no toothbrush, toothpaste. That kind of thing."

He nodded again. "Anything else missing? Up here? In the whole house?"

Saoirse paused then shook her head. "I don't know. I don't think so. I'm not that familiar with the house." She walked out into the bedroom and scanned the room again. She stopped suddenly.

"Ah, now. Wait." She turned to look at Smithy. "His instruments. You didn't see them anywhere did you?"

Smithy shook his head. "No. But let's check again to be certain."

They searched the upstairs and the downstairs but could only find an old battered bodhran and case of whistles. There was no trace of the guitar, uilleann pipes, violin, mandolin and possibly bouzouki Luke had in his possession. Or was it a banjo? Saoirse was vague and the fact that she didn't know with any certainty gave rise to a smile from Smithy.

"Are you sure you're a musician, Saoirse?" asked Smithy.

Saoirse laughed. "I only glanced over at them, you know. When I was putting my own instruments down near them. Sure, I've only ever been here the once."

Smithy nodded, but took it in, supped it up like a good whiskey and savoured the taste of it, the aroma and the way it felt going down. Warm, happy.

"Right, so," said Saoirse after a few moments. "We know now that he's gone for a while. And he has his surfboard and his instruments. That means he's gone somewhere he can surf and play traditional music."

"Good," said Smithy. "The coast. A pub. That really narrows it down in Ireland."

HE KNEW it was a bad idea even before he agreed to it, but the knowing had just snaked around slyly while he basked in the whiskey glow of Saoirse's claim not to really know Luke or his place. Or was it just his place? At this point he was too panicked to know. Because now they were entering The Mangle Pit, the local pub Saoirse used to go to and play in the weekly sessions. Just his luck it was this night, their only night in Dublin. He had no idea how he was going to spend the night here, let alone get through the session.

The pub was noisy, filled with the nothing special décor that marked a local and as he followed Saoirse across the floor, heard the welcome given to her and by default to him, he felt his nerves ease a bit. There was a crowd, a "I come here all the time" mass of people who shoved and bent their elbows on a regular basis. The tables, chairs and places at the bar all marked and won through years of acquaintance.

He gripped his fiddle case handle tighter and looked towards the back where he could see the musicians playing. The tune seemed familiar and he tried to hope for the best. He'd had no choice coming here, he knew that. Any objection he might have raised when they'd talked to Anu on the phone earlier to update her would have made it all worse. Provoked questions. When had Smithy ever turned down a chance for a good session? One that presumably Lugh had played with. One that he could give his perfect ear towards and pick up any stray strand of tune or air that had its origins in the Otherworld. It was a sound idea, Saoirse said when Anu had mentioned it to add another layer on the possibility the two of them might discover from the musicians where Luke had gone. And it did have great merit, except that it discounted the fact that he wouldn't know a stray strand of anything Otherworldly musical if it stepped up and announced it with a jig and hop and a diddly dee.

But he might be able to hold on to the simple tune tonight. There, amid all the musicians gathered there now. Just enjoy the craic, relax into the ahhness of it all. Have a bit of fun. Stroke the strings, never mind what came out, because sure, who would notice a bit of ole scraping and screeching when the accordion and concertina he spied got going, or the other fiddle got playing?

They arrived at the group and Saoirse gave out a few hugs, nods and "how are you's", only pausing in front of the accordion player. "Donal, is it? Sure I haven't seen you in an age."

And then Smithy was introduced to Declan on concertina, Patrick on guitar, Mícheal on bouzouki, Eileen on fiddle and Cormac, the leader, also on fiddle. And there was Jilly, seemingly a special friend from the longer hug and glint in the eye, who played the concertina as well. An all-round large group, a good group to get lost in and Smithy gave them the full nod. A nod filled with relief, mixed with a little bit of hope that he could enjoy this night. Banter with strangers, sure, he could handle that.

The two of them sat on their stools and unpacked their instruments. Smithy kept an ear out for the tune, the rhythm, mentally taking his bow and fingers through the paces in determined "I will pick this up" mind frame. And so it went. He raised the fiddle to his chin, twiddled and tweaked the pegs and got to what he thought and hoped was the perfect tuning, fingers crossed for the best.

The tunes flew at him and he thought he coped. "The Quaker" was merrily kissed, "The Pilgrim" soundly on its way to Blarney, or maybe he was full of blarney and didn't he know that, so? All the tunes they mentioned and played on felt familiar and he played easily. Not well, not top shelf or even middle shelf, but he got there and who would know his point and time of arrival with Eileen? He realised what a prize she was about halfway through the first set and was glad that he'd sat next to her. Jingle jangle jiggidy jag was her tune, her style a blend of misplaced bangles on her arm beating time and confusing strokes across the strings. Declan seemed to tolerate it with a tired smile, but your man, the bouzouki player looked daggers and Jilly rolled and raised her eyes so much that he feared for their health. Accordion man seemed oblivious, lost in his own world and sound of his box, listening only to the pitch and pull of the buttons and myriad reeds. His own fiddle was drowned amid the scrapes and jangle bingle. Sure, who would know? Who would know indeed? Miss jingle jangle had all the bad moves and his slipped inside and alongside.

Smithy moved his own bow with a bit more confidence, a little flair and do-see-do that seemed to work and even made him smile. Next to him, on the other side, Saoirse's flute played lovely lilting notes and he took his cue from that as much as he could. He would and could. He would and could.

Sets ended and new sets began. Smithy fell into them all, slipping and sliding around the playing, finding the corner that would allow him to breathe and give a little "sure, why not" flair, but not too much of course. He couldn't be having that. Couldn't be risking that. And now and then he felt a little hum, so, but nothing consequential. Just enough to give a wink to Saoirse. There was a smile back, but then an unreadable quirk of the head and he was all back to concentration.

THE BREAK ARRIVED with a few nods and eye contacts. Your man Declan, good with the feel and rub of the group, called time and said all the things to be said and a warning for songs to be sung soon. Smithy stole a glance at Saoirse, wondering what might come and hoped to all those gods that might be friends that he wasn't included in that. No, he didn't feel like he sang. No songs in his bag of tricks. There was nothing in his throat, his head or his heart that matched those words. No favourite or might be favourite song that came to light. Feckit, this shite was exhausting. He needed a drink. Or maybe two. Whiskeys. Now they felt right and familiar, that wasn't a memory that had deserted him. No, that memory was true and constant. *Uisce Beatha*. Water of life.

He placed his order at the bar and turned to see Saoirse motioning him outside. He gave a nod and collected his drink and hers, one he hoped she wanted and based on what he'd seen in front of her at her table and made to follow her. Outside, the din of the chat was nearly as strong as that inside, all the talk and banter that had been held during the session pouring forth now the break was in play.

He joined Saoirse and saw that Declan, Jilly and Cormac were there as well, a circle of smoke hanging around Declan. Smithy handed the Guinness to Saoirse and was relieved to find that everyone else had a drink in their hand. Saoirse looked at hers a moment, quirked a brow and then took a sip after the old *sláinte* was muttered in all directions. Then, without ado, she took his own glass of whiskey, drank deeply and handed it back with a grin. He was told, so. He laughed. Yes. He was told.

"I was hoping to see Luke here tonight," said Saoirse.

"Luke?" said Jilly, her eyes narrowing. She glanced over at Smithy. "Um, aren't you in touch? I-I thought. Well, the last time you two were here, you seemed to be...."

"Together?" said Declan. He gave a laugh, scrubbed his beard with his chubby fingers. "Ah, Jilly, now."

Jilly looked at Smithy again. "I didn't mean to put my foot in it. Sorry. Luke hasn't been back since the time the two of you were here."

"Oh, shame," said Saoirse.

"He didn't say anything to you then, I mean after the two of you left together?" said Jilly.

"Uh, no," said Saoirse. "We didn't part on the best of terms. Misunderstanding."

"But when you texted me the next day...." Jilly reddened this time. "I'll just shut up, now."

Everyone laughed except Smithy. He felt frustrated, unsettled.

"Ah, no, you're grand, Jilly," said Saoirse, breezily. "I just wondered if anyone knew where he was. I stopped by his place earlier to make it up and introduce him to Smithy, but no one was home. He seemed to have gone away. There was post, you know. Uncollected."

Declan looked at Cormac who shrugged. "He didn't say anything to me about any particular plans." His deep voice was calm but with a note of curiosity.

"Would you have any idea when he might be back? Based on past experience?" asked Saoirse.

"We talk from time to time, nothing much, so I can't say I know him well enough to tell you," said Cormac.

"Doesn't he have a brother or cousin, or something he goes to see now and again?" said Declan. "They surf, I think."

"Oh, right. That will be it, then. He'll have gone to see his brother," said Cormac. "Probably. He's a hoor for the surfing." He looked at Saoirse. "But then you know that, I think."

Saoirse flushed, Smithy noted. "Do you know where they surfed?"

Cormac frowned. "Let me think. Was it Clare, Galway?"

"We went surfing in Galway," said Saoirse. "He had a house there."

Smithy turned to look at her, too astounded to speak. Why the feck were they standing here, then, while he struggled and had to listen to the others spill details of Saoirse's relationship with Luke, and not in Galway?

"That will be it, then," said Cormac. "At least if he's gone surfing with his brother."

Saoirse gave a weak smile. "Yeah, that will be it."

"Do you know his brother's name?" asked Smithy.

Cormac glanced at Declan. "Con, Connell? Don?"

"Something like that," said Declan.

"Fab," said Saoirse, her smile bright. "I think I know, now. We'll try him there, at his house."

There were nods and smiles, glasses raised with the banter and the good humour all around. No ripples, just smooth waters and smooth smiles. But Smithy could feel her next to him, there was no need for that extra connection he yearned and despaired for, she was uneasy.

So, when the break was over and they headed back in, he wasn't surprised to hear the excuses from her lips, the "have to hit the road too soon in the morning to stay" excuse and then they were gone from The Mangle Pit, heading down the road towards the car that would take them to her place.

The drink was in him, but his limit, even in his mockery god state, wasn't what anyone could measure in a glass or many glasses. Still, he paused when he was behind the wheel and turned to her.

"Where do I go? You'll have to tell me the way."

"Do I, Smithy?" said Saoirse, her voice serious. "Do I need to tell you the way? Because, if I do, you need to explain to me what's going on. Why, for a start, you play the fiddle like a ten-year-old discovering their first jig?"

7

———————

LUKE

I walked in and blinked against the dimness after the bright sun outside. I didn't have to see anything to know. "This is more like it" messages cluttered all my senses, sight coming last. The chatter, the tuning instruments, the smell of spilled ale and Tayto crisps and the taste of a good plate of chips already in my mind. I blinked again and my path was clear. I headed to the music.

There were a few vaguely familiar faces, but in this land of summer visitors and locals who came from miles away to play, that was grand. I was grand. I nodded and they nodded back. There was an inquiring "Luke" and I "howareyou'd" him back and thought to place the name Calum to him. He had his box resting on his lap, lazily tapping the buttons as though to warm up his fingers. His smile was sly and suggested good banter and I suddenly attached a very witty exchange to his name and face that had occurred between the two of us the last time I was down.

The group was a fair size and the other faces didn't have names, but that was grand, too because it was about the music and sure, I was only a visitor myself. The instruments looked encouraging overall – besides the box, there were a couple of guitars, a flute, and a fiddle. I was glad I'd brought the mandolin and the fiddle, which would complement the selection well. I could switch off between the two, as needed. The uilleann pipes could be for another night. I'd see how the others fared.

The mandolin spoke to me first, so I got her out and tuned while the others tried a set. Calum was session leader and I was soon thankful for more than that as he led these ones through a basic set beginning with the Kesh and onward out from there. The buzz was minimal, but there you are, that's the give and take and it could easily improve as the night wore on. I joined in and gave support and flair where needed and earned a grateful smile from Calum. Once the set was done I asked about drinks, though I could see all of them had glasses with only a few sips missing. Still, the offer was on for anyone game and there was only the taker from the female guitar player, who looked well able for the pint she asked for.

I made my way to the bar, noticing the cluster there, though few seemed to be ordering. When I squeezed my way to the edge and looked for the person to place my order, the reason for the male only composition of the cluster became apparent. The curves, the face, the hair were all that you could want. She, the owner of it all, was filling a pint glass at one of the taps, head bent. I didn't have to see her face to know who it was. I recognised the curves, the numerous plaits of her hair. Though I'd never really seen her face, not up close. I'd only seen that body, undulating in perfect harmony with the waves. She was my surfer. I knew it in my gut, my head, and every other place it counted.

She turned her face to me, her eyes catching mine and she winked. Eyes of such vibrant blue, wide and lash lined. Hook, line and sinker eyes. I broke into a slow grin, taking her all in as I watched her place the pint on the bar, take the money, ring it up and head towards me. Sexy and hot with her winding tattoo that started on her right hand, worked its way up her arm to disappear into the strap of her sleeveless top for a brief peek before it was covered again at her back, but then surprisingly, appearing again at her right thigh, where her short jeans skirt ended, to travel down those long, shapely legs to her sandal clad feel. Oh, intriguing. The face was classic and so was the figure, but the tattoo added the something that just took me.

She stood waiting and I grinned wider.

"Just collecting my eyes from the floor," I said.

"Oh, good," she said. "Eyes like that shouldn't be in danger of being trampled. Can I get you anything, now they're back in place?"

"There's plenty I could ask for, but I wonder if I would get it."

"I'm sure there are no worries on that front."

"I saw you surfing earlier today. Great moves. You're clearly experienced."

She smiled and her eyes lit up. "Thanks. Do you surf, then?"

"I do. But not here usually. Mostly up in Galway or Clare. I'm visiting someone who has a place here."

She nodded over to the musicians. "Surfer and musician, I am impressed."

I grinned again. "Ah, you noticed then."

"Well, I can see the daggers being sent this way from herself there, the guitarist. I presume either she's your girlfriend or you were supposed to get her a drink?"

"Drink," I said. "Definitely not girlfriend. I don't even know her name."

"Does the 'definitely' mean you're not inclined to ask her name?"

I shrugged. "I'm not sure I'd remember it. She's probably a visitor anyway."

"Would I get a 'definitely', or do you want to know my name?"

"You'd get a 'definitely' as in 'I definitely want to know your name and I hope you definitely want to know my name'.

She laughed. "Clio."

"Luke."

"Now, Luke, can I definitely get you some drinks?"

"You can. And maybe your number? So we can hook up. For the surfing, like."

"You can have my number. For surfing. And the like."

"Good."

"Good," she said. She withdrew her phone, and I recited my number. A moment later I heard my own phone go off. She smiled, winked. "There. All done."

"Come see me during your break," I said, the words out before I could think.

She tilted her head. "Maybe, we'll see. You could be busy there in your corner. Can't interrupt the master player."

I laughed, loving her inference and how she could pick her own tune with her words. What a woman.

THE SESSION, as I'd hoped, improved as the evening wore on, with me sparing the occasional glance over to Clio working busily at the bar. A young lad from a local Ceoltas, or so Calum said, joined us and his skill on the flute was good, considering his young age. Under twenty, in any case. Fresh faced, dark curls and shy enough. He added a bit of direction and cohesion to the efforts of myself and Calum and the music took on a livelier character. For the sheer devilry and for the lad's skill and energy, I slipped in a short tune, one of my own from long ago and far away, the Otherworld tinge to it just evident at its fringes. Calum raised his brow and gave a small nod of appreciation as he caught it up and the young lad followed his lead. The fiddle was in hand at that point, though it could have just as easily worked on the mandolin, but fiddle was where it came from and the reason it just hopped out of me. I moved us on to another, well known tune, keeping my tune tucked and warm against any curious onslaught or elaboration. Calum took over then and we all got behind him, the lad's foot keeping time, lost inside it all.

I appreciated such feeling and joy of it all, so I did. What a lad and full of promise. I saw his trainers, his mop of hair, hoodie and jeans and wondered what the world would offer him. Calum, there, I knew owned the local furniture shop and traded by day in an affable and half-hearted manner, enjoying the banter more than the sales. A good life, so. A good life.

The music halted and I grinned at the lad. He smiled back tentatively.

"That was a mad tune, you played," he said. "What was it? It's not one I've heard."

"Ah, that one. Well, *Gan Ainm*, if you must know," I said. It was a joke, and convenient, because it translated as "without name" and was the title of many a tune in the Irish traditional music repertoire. It saved further questions about inspiration, had I composed others and how unusual it was.

The lad laughed. "Ah, of course. I should have known."

"You have it now, so work away with it. It's all yours to make it your own."

"I will so," he said and grinned.

I nodded, glad to have him take it and feed it back into the music with his own bits and pieces added. It was how the music grew, evolved and stayed alive.

"Eoin, lad," said a familiar voice.

I turned to see Clio ruffling the young lad's head fondly. "No farm chores to keep you busy?"

Eoin turned bright red. "No, not tonight," he mumbled.

"Did your mam bring you over, then?"

"Dad did," he said. The flush on his face deepened.

"He's a grand player, this one," I said, taking pity on the lad. "Real skill."

"Oh, I know he has skill," said Clio, her eyes twinkling.

I pulled a stool over from the next table. "Will you sit for a moment? You're on your break?"

She nodded and gave me a cocky smile. "Ah no, you have your music. I only thought I would come and say hello. I'm just off out for a breath of air and that."

"No worries there," said Calum. "We're on our own break now."

I stood, not deterred. "See there now? I'll just come with you, then. For my own breath of air and that."

She shrugged. "If you like." She nodded to the others. "Enjoy, lads."

I followed her as she weaved through the tables, towards the back and then out through the back door. It was a staff door, meant for deliveries and bins, I gathered, but she didn't seem to mind as I took up a place beside her, my pint of lager in my hand.

The night air was cool and above a few stars peeked out, startling and bright in the moonless sky. Clio took my pint from me and drank deeply, licking her tongue across her lips and ending the motion with a sigh that sunk inside me. I stared at her, intrigued, aroused and so wanting to plant a kiss on those lips.

"That tasted so good," she said, staring into my eyes.

"Will I get you a pint for yourself?"

She shook her head. "No, don't bother. By the time you get it my break will have ended. Never mind, though. I've got this." She pulled out a small spliff from her pocket along with a lighter. "It's my little treat. Gets me through the rest of the night."

I nodded and watched her, mesmerised, as she put the spliff in her mouth, raised the lighter, flicked it and a flame erupted at the end of the spliff, her hands cupping the area. She inhaled deeply, sensuously, held her breath for a moment and then gradually blew out the smoke, her eyes closed in appreciation. The smoke came across me, surrounded me and all I could think of was her, her mouth and having it against mine.

She placed the spliff against my mouth. "Come on, big boy, inhale," she said in a low throaty voice.

I inhaled, from surprise, from desire, my lungs and body on fire with more things than just a spliff. It was a narcotic all of itself, a cannabis that left me burning with more than a cannabis high. She took another long drag on the spliff, that seemed to roll around in her mouth, before she leaned up and placed her mouth full on mine. I parted my lips slightly in surprise and she blew the smoke into me, followed it with her tongue and the heated exchange became more than just tongues, but smoke that set my whole body aflame. I reached for her and pulled her against me, pressing hard, unable to help myself. She pushed forward, aligning her body with mine.

My arms went around her, closing her in tighter, wanting to feel every last part of her against me. It was all instinctive, uncontrolled, my hands wandering up under her shirt, feeling the soft skin. I found my leg between hers and she leaned in against it, the message clear. I kissed her neck, tasting it, and needed more, nibbling, biting and kissing again, until I was panting. She pulled back a moment, took another drag on the spliff, held it to my lips and I followed suit. She breathed out right next to my ear and the fire inside burned darker, stronger. My hands found her breasts, stroked, rubbed. She chuckled soft and low against my ear, the smoke still teasing the fine hairs nearby.

"Ah, aren't you a one," she said. "A gorgeous, lovely one." She pulled back, kissed me quickly and moved away, tamped the spliff and put it back inside her pocket. "This was a good break," she said, her eyes darkening, unreadable. "Now, it's time to get back to work." She winked, turned and disappeared inside. I stood there, watched her until she vanished, feeling like I'd been hit by a whirlwind.

8

———

LUKE

The flames rose up, small sparks shooting with the crackle. I stared at the flames, hypnotised for a moment and allowing it to briefly take me back to other places, other times, careful though to guard against making it too real and too unreal. In the distance the waves lapped the shore. The tide was out, but the gentle whoosh was still audible, even above the sound of the partying and the roar of the bonfire.

Someone nudged me and handed me a bottle.

"Here ya go, mate. Get that down you."

I nodded my thanks to Mud. "Thanks, mate," I said, matching his Australian accent and phrasing.

He grinned. "Great party, yeah?"

"Yeah," I said.

Someone started playing music from their phone blue-toothed to a speaker and heads started to nod. It wouldn't be long before some were up and dancing, or singing to the latest of whatever was in the charts. Rather than strain to hear it, I tried to focus on the sound of the sea.

Mud nudged me again. "You out surfing tomorrow? Meant to be good, dude."

"Yeah, maybe," I said.

"You were fierce yesterday and today. Despite the waves. Shame Mon wasn't here, though."

I nodded my acknowledgment of the praise. I had enjoyed the surfing, though the waves were only mediocre. But no one would argue with the weather and so I wouldn't even comment on the waves. Three star, fine. My lack of enthusiasm I conceded, though, was more from the lack of Clio's presence than the surf conditions. The truth was I felt frustrated. A few texts had only elicited vague evasions or simple answers. I was certain she would have been here on the beach at least once in the past few days, but she hadn't. And the sole reason for my presence here tonight was in the hope of seeing her. Sad bastard. I couldn't explain why I really felt so compelled to meet up with her again, but I did. She'd caught my attention. I wanted to see her again. Had to see her again, if only to figure out why I wanted her so much. I could still feel her legs, her mouth on mine, her tongue. Jesus on a cross, what was I like? This was nothing like Saoirse, or rather Bríd, so no danger there. I silently thanked Mon again for warning me up in Galway. I know I'd never met Bríd before, but still, I should have known better. The music. She had the music in a way that could have only come from one place.

"Hey," said a voice, low and throaty.

I turned, a slow smile forming on my face. She was not Bríd, she was very beautiful, but so very earthy, sensuous and something indefinable. A siren in any other tale. But this tale, I was determined to taste her again.

"Clio," I said. "Good to see you again. I was wondering if you'd make it."

She smiled and shrugged. "Got lucky with my hours. I've

been working hard the last few days, but I have a few days off, now."

"That's fortunate." I looked over at Mud, still at my side. "Clio, don't know if you've met Mud."

Clio nodded at Mud. "Aussie. Right? I think you've come into the pub a few times."

Mud beamed at her. "Yeah, that'd be me."

The many "how to get rid of unwanted gooseberry" ideas crowded my head to accompany an overwhelming desire to talk to Clio. On my own. To test her feelings towards me, to persuade her my company was the only thing she wanted. To touch her, to taste her lips and anywhere else she might allow.

"Do you mind if I have a word with Luke, a moment?" asked Clio her tone full of apology, persuasion and promises later.

Oh feck me, what a woman. Just hearing those words sent a rush of feelings through me. I wanted those promises, though.

"Oh, yeah, sure," said Mud. "See ya later, then. Or maybe I'll get you a beer, if you're not going to be too long."

"Maybe a beer later, Mud," she said with a wink. "Much later."

He flushed and nodded. "I'll see ya then." He nodded to me and then made his way over to the cooler in the distance.

"Tactful," I said. I couldn't keep the grin off my face.

"Ah, well, you know. Can't offend any punters for the pub."

I laughed. "Somehow, I don't see him being a regular there."

She shrugged. "You never know. Things change."

"As long as I'm here, it will be my regular."

"Didn't see you there in the last few days," she said.

"I was welcome?"

"Of course. Always."

She looked at me, her lids half lowered, her thick lashes nearly obscuring her eyes. Obscuring the flash of desire I saw there. I felt my own pulse quicken.

"Your texts seemed to suggest not."

She placed a hand on my arm. I could feel the heat of her hand through the long sleeved T-shirt I wore.

"I was busy with work, Luke. The place is full of visitors."

I nodded, not wanting to sound desperate, like a child. "Of course. No worries. I've been surfing a lot, in any case."

"Yeah? Any good?"

"Not bad."

"I will see you surf sometime. I've promised myself."

"Ah, you will. Maybe tomorrow? It's meant to be good tomorrow."

"Perfect," she said. "We'll do that. Just text me the time."

I nodded, my earlier poor mood dispelled.

She took my hand. "Come with me."

She led me away and I followed – all eager puppy, besotted lover and every other cliché that could be named. She led me across the sand, already cool as it slopped and sprayed up against my bare shins while we made our way along. I was wearing board shorts, the breeze suddenly cool on my legs and the back of my neck now that we were away from the heat of the bonfire. Clio seemed not to mind it, though, wearing the same short jeans skirt I'd seen her in the other night. But this time she had on a zipped hoodie over her shirt and she pulled up the hood after a moment.

When we reached the edge of the beach, and the shelter of the cliffs that edged the coastline up ahead, she stopped.

"There," she said. "That's better."

"Better for what?"

She pulled out a spliff from her pocket. "This," she said, lighting it quickly. She took a deep drag. "And this."

She leaned over, nudged my lips open with hers and poured the smoke in my mouth. I inhaled in surprise, but managed not to cough. The smoke was soothing, if anything and it swirled and filled my head. Her mouth stayed on mine and I deepened the kiss, tasting her as thoroughly as anything I might have imagined in the past few days.

She pulled back slightly, pressed the spliff to her mouth and took a long drag again, this time pulling it back inside her. She held the spliff to my mouth and I did the same, wondering at the soothing sensuous feel of the smoke inside me, and the elusive taste and smell that was unlike any other cannabis I was familiar with. We danced this slow, melodic rhythm, our bodies twining and tangling like two vines, or two snakes rising from a basket, winding and twirling. It seemed to go on in a timeless place, the whoosh of the waves the only sound beside her delicate moans and my deeper ones.

Our hands wandered and wondered over each other, finding bare skin, making skin bare. Until it became impossible not to be inside her. She sensed the need, shared the need and took my hand, pulling me away from the cliffs.

"Come with me," she said.

And I did.

THE DOOR CLOSED BEHIND US, pushed by a foot, an elbow, something to create the click and snick that told me it was shut. She took my hand as if she needed to lead me again. But there was only one place to go in this small room of a bed, a chair and a door to the bathroom. There was only one place I wanted to go anyway. No leading required.

I stopped her at the bed's edge, caught up her chin and kissed her deeply. She responded immediately and I had no doubt about her desire matching mine. Clothes were shed and we were quickly skin to skin, falling onto the bed, falling into our desire. My mind spun, weaving circles around the rest of my body as each new place on hers sent stronger shoots of desire in me. We were two, we were one and it was all that I could have imagined of her and more. The more kept coming, even after our initial desires were sated and she stroked and kissed me to a further meeting of mind and bodies in a never-ending circle of one.

The time passed in peaks and desires, just as our bodies and the night was over, but I wasn't. Lost in her, I ploughed on, delighted and so aroused at the never-ending energy and wonder of this woman.

But eventually, as the sun found our bodies, and the thirst and hunger overtook us, we roused and rose. I kissed and stroked her even as we showered and dressed, needing to touch her, any part of her, always.

A café, a table, plates of food. It was all there and I sat, ate, drank, all the while touching her face, her hand, her fingers. Her eyes held mine, I held hers. It was ridiculous and unavoidable. This desire, unexplainable, but there you are.

"You are an incredible woman," I said, playing with her fingers.

"Ah, no, just a woman," she said.

"A special woman."

She laughed and I smiled back. "So poetic."

I reached over and tugged one of her small braids with its beads and feathers. "So beautiful. The hair, it's like Cleopatra's. My own Cleopatra."

"She had black hair, I think. So not quite."

"Oh very much quite. Quite beautiful, quite Cleopatra mine."

"I'm yours, am I? In your dreams."

"Always in my dreams." I picked up her fingers and kissed them. "And by my side. As much as possible."

"As much as possible? Possibly, then. Possibly."

She leaned over and brushed my hair from my face. "I'm your Cleopatra. I can braid your hair like this. And you could be mine."

"Your Cleopatra?"

She smiled slyly. "Or maybe just mine."

"With beads and feathers?"

"Of course. Like mine. My beads and your beads, my feathers and your feathers would make music and twine together whenever we did."

I laughed. She was too much. She was everything. She filled me up with laughter and so much more.

"We'll make even more music, then," I said.

"We will, Luke." She took my forefinger, leaned forward, put it in her mouth and sucked for just a brief moment before releasing it. "You had a bit of sauce on it," she said, grinning cheekily.

"You have plenty of sauce on your own," I said, with a mock groan, my level of arousal difficult to ignore.

"Are you finished?" I asked, glancing at her nearly empty plate.

"With my food, yes."

"Will we go back to your place?"

"Oh, I think so."

9

—————

SAOIRSE

The day was warm and Saoirse could hear the bees buzzing in the distance. Just a slight breeze disturbed her hair. It was one of those rare, fine summer days that had everyone finding all excuses to be outside. She certainly was no exception. She closed her eyes for a moment, letting the sun warm her face. Even the flat rock that she sat on felt warm beneath her.

Just a short distance away, staring out along the valley and the mountain beyond, were Smithy and Finn, their broad figures painting their own story. Saoirse watched Finn rest his hand on Smithy's shoulder and murmur a few words in his ear. Smithy shrugged, gave a forced grin and stepped away just a fraction.

"Now, so," said Anu, coming up behind her, bearing a tray filled with cups and a plate of sliced brack. "There's a cup of tea here for the lot of you and some cake."

Finn moved towards her and took the tray, resting it on the grass beside Saoirse who scooted over to make way for Anu to sit down. The two men found a place in the grass and Anu handed out the cups and passed the plate of cake to Smithy, who paused and then took up a slice from the plate. It hovered outside his mouth uncertainly, as uncertain as his expression.

Saoirse started to open her mouth to question him, but shut it almost immediately. She sighed. Evasions, deflection and any other behaviour that meant she hadn't been able to discover what was going on with Smithy was all she'd experienced from him since they'd gone to Dublin. At first she thought it was because he discovered that she'd been with Luke. She felt her cheeks flame just at the thought of it. But she couldn't blame that, she realised now. His behaviour had been strange since his return from the Otherworld. Had something happened there that he hadn't revealed? Or was it the other type of "returning" he'd experienced. Coming back from a death could affect anyone badly, she would imagine. But then she realised she didn't have to imagine, or was that correct too, because with no memory of the before or the immediate after, was she even qualified to compare herself to Smithy? All she knew was that if her "before" feelings for him were anything like her "after" feelings for him now, she had some right to be concerned.

"Sorry, sorry," said Maura, stalking down to them through the grass, breathless. "I got held up." She made a face. "Your man there, Dennis, wanted help with his cows."

"His cows?" said Finn, grinning. "Is that what they call it now?"

"Oh, feck off, you," she answered. "He's sixty if he's a day."

"Don't fancy younger men then?"

"Hah! I am as young as I feel, you gobber, and as I look."

Saoirse laughed. Maura certainly looked no more than thirty with her black hair, slim but shapely figure. Her dark eyes may have centuries and more in them, but the rest of her was pure prime woman.

"Ah, now," said Anu. We were only having a cup of tea, so you've missed nothing." She handed Maura the spare cup and offered her the plate of cake. Maura grabbed a slice and took the cup, settling down next to Smithy.

"Now," said Anu. "I thought if we all heard about the trip to Dublin together, we might glean more to add to what we already know."

"That Lugh, no excuse me, Luke, has flown the coop? Again," said Maura.

"We're certain that it's Lugh?" said Anu. She looked over at Smithy.

Smithy looked at Saoirse, shrugged and nodded. "Yes, pretty much."

Saoirse stared at him. He wasn't certain? If he wasn't certain, why didn't he show them the photo? Didn't Smithy know what he looked like? But he must do, he'd made swords, shields, a spear for Lugh, hadn't he? She opened her mouth to speak, but shut it. Again.

"He's a surfer. Blond hair, shaggy. Very blue eyes. Well built. He's very talented at music. We looked around his house and his surfboard was gone, along with his SUV and some clothes. The lads at the session seemed to think he might have gone to visit a cousin or a brother. Another surfer. He has a place in Galway, as I mentioned. On the coast. He might have returned there after he...," she trailed off, caught out. She cleared her throat. "Dropped me at the railway station in Galway, but he said he had to head north."

"Wait," said Maura. "You were at his house in Galway?"

Saoirse glanced at Smithy but he was staring at his cup of tea. She nodded. "Not long. Just a night and part of a day. We did a bit of surfing."

Maura gave a roar of laughter. "A bit of surfing. I love it." She turned to Finn. "You can put that in your book of 'what they call it now'."

Saoirse stared at her feet and gave herself a good talking to, all rationale and reason. Girleen, you have no call to be embarrassed or fearful about what Smithy would make of it. The fecker had broken it off, called time on them and their brief relationship, well the one in the "after" that made up her world at the time. She'd had every right to go with whomever she chose at that point. But sadly, her heart wasn't paying attention and it chased reason and rationale out the door.

"Oh, hold your gob," said Finn. "You've not the notion in your head about what anything is called. Only how it's done, and how often."

"For someone who is the God of Eloquence, <u>Ogma</u>, you're sadly lacking," said Maura.

Saoirse looked over at Finn. She saw the kindness and compassion in his face as he returned her gaze.

"Eloquence isn't needed when it comes to you, Morrigan," said Finn, a hint of edge in his tone. "In war, it's seldom valued."

Maura stuck her tongue out at him and he laughed, Saoirse and Anu joining him. Smithy gave a weak smile.

"So," said Maura. "He said he was heading north. Was it planned that he go there all along do you think, or did he get a text or phone call that may have prompted this?"

"It wasn't planned, no," Saoirse said, recalling their heated desire that had suddenly disappeared on the morning after she'd watched him surf. "There was no text or phone call. At least I don't think so. No, it was sudden, I think. Just after he went surfing and chatted with this other lad on the beach."

"Other lad?" said Finn.

Saoirse nodded. "Yes. He was another surfer. They obviously knew each other well."

"What did he look like?" asked Anu, her eyes suddenly intense.

Saoirse tried to recall. "I only saw him in the distance. He was well built like Luke, but not as tall. Maybe a little more sinewy. And he had blond hair. Really blond. Almost white."

Finn exchanged looks with Maura. "Mongan," he said.

"Mongan?"

"Well, maybe. I mean, it sounds like him. He's Lugh's foster brother. He's the son of Manannan Mac Lir of the Seas."

"The seas?" asked Saoirse.

"His power is over the seas," said Finn.

It rang a vague bell to Saoirse. But so did all of it, and when she tried to recall everything, all of it, she felt overwhelmed. She'd even refrained from googling it. Or searching out a book in a bookshop or those diddly idly Oirish gift shops.

"So you think that Luke could be back in Galway with Mongan?" Saoirse said.

"It's worth a try," said Maura.

Saoirse looked at Anu. "Do you want me to go to Galway, then?"

Anu paused and shook her head. "Not just now. But if you can explain to Maura where the house is she can go and see if anyone is there. Mongan could be there, but it's possible he might be a few other places. I'll check with Manannan. Or perhaps Daghda can. He might be more likely to talk with him." She took a deep drink from her mug, filled with milk, rather than tea. "And that comes to my next point. The treasures. Daghda has the cauldron still, but we're still missing the Nemed's magic sword. That leaves the slingshot and spear of Lugh's."

"Doesn't Lugh have those?" asked Saoirse.

Maura and Finn exchanged glances.

"No," said Finn. "He tossed them away after the battle."

Saoirse looked at Smithy. How did he feel about the careless manner Lugh had treated weapons that she presumed Smithy had fashioned? He avoided her eyes, studying his cup of tea.

He'd hardly said a word during this conversation, remaining impassive, uninvolved, as if he didn't care.

"I've only recently received news that the spear and slingshot have been located," said Anu.

Saoirse looked back at her in surprise.

"That's great news," said Finn.

"Balor has them."

"Not so great news, then," said Maura, her tone sarcastic.

"No," said Anu. "Admittedly I could have hoped for anything but that. At least we know, though. And that's to our advantage. At this point he thinks it's a secret."

"You want us to get them back," said Smithy flatly.

Everyone looked at him, the interest on Maura's face clear, as was the concern on Finn's. Saoirse tried to suppress her inward alarm.

"Wouldn't Lugh be the best one to do that?" asked Saoirse. "I mean, he would know him the most, and they are his weapons." She knew how ridiculous the statements sounded the moment they left her mouth, but they had just tumbled out, inspired by anxiety, and so many other feelings she didn't want to sort through.

Maura gave a hard laugh. "Not the best choice, no."

"We can't ask Lugh, now, obviously," said Anu. "And though I have plans regarding their retrieval, I want to discover more about where he keeps them and any other bits that would help us when we do retrieve them. In the meantime, we'll keep it in mind whenever we have any dealings that concern Balor."

Saoirse breathed a small sigh of relief. Delaying such a project gave her hope that it might not be needed. Something could resolve it, something that didn't involve what she suspected was a dangerous task. She didn't like the thought of dealing with Balor in any way and she didn't like the thought of Smithy being involved in it either. Not when there was something wrong. More than just forgetting tunes, or inability to create the music in the manner that had been an essential part of him. She looked at him again. This time he studied Anu as she mused about the potential places Balor might keep the weapons. Smithy's expression was wary and a little worried. She would have to force him to talk to her. She wouldn't stand for any more deflection.

"But we'll leave that for now," Anu said, after a few moments. "The final matter I wanted to raise concerns the rogue Tuatha men who were working with Balor."

"The traitors, you mean," said Finn, darkly. "How many were there, in the end? Have we caught all of them?"

"It's impossible to know if everyone has been caught, but we believe so," said Anu. "Ten are being held, though."

"Ten?" said Finn, his tone angry. "That many?"

Anu sighed. "I'm afraid so."

"Scum," said Finn. He looked at Smithy, who returned his stare and nodded slowly, his expression impassive.

"Well scum or not, Daghda is mediating, but he asks that Ogma, Goibhniu and Bríd attend, since they were involved in the incident that brought the treachery of these men to light."

"Fine," said Finn. "I'm happy to help."

Saoirse blinked and looked at Smithy. The alarm on his face only fed her anxiety and concern. "M-me?" she said. "What can I do?"

"Daghda will lead you through it," said Anu. She patted her on the hand. "There's nothing to worry about, child."

"I'm not sure there's anything I can add to it that Finn and Saoirse wouldn't be able to handle," said Smithy. His tone was reasonable, but Saoirse could hear the panic underlying it.

"Don't be so foolish. There's much that you can recount and discuss that neither of those two can comment on, Goibhniu," said Anu. "You journeyed on your own through the woods and then you were captured. We need you to recount all that in detail."

Smithy paled and nodded. He mumbled something that sounded like acquiescence and turned his head away.

"When does Daghda want us to go?"

"Soon. Maybe a day or so," said Anu. "I'll let you know exactly when."

They all nodded. Anu rose. "Now I must get on and do the milking."

Rising, Maura laughed. "Ah, you love it. You and those cows. And the bees."

Anu gave a rare grin. "I do, of course. I love it all. It's part of me. And I'll do my best to keep it that way."

10

LUKE

The morning light slanted into the room, draping itself across the floor and then the bed. Beside me, Clio's face was in shadow, but the rest of her body was bare, open to the light. Her skin so pale against the dark ink that wandered in beautiful circular curves up her arm, over her shoulder, down the right side of her back, and along the side of her leg. I traced my finger lightly against the ink at her hip and followed it down her thigh. It depicted waves, stylised in swirls and curls that rose and fell, following the swell and dip of her waist, hip and thigh. It was beautiful and stirred me, filled me with desire.

In the two weeks since I met Clio, I'd found myself finding as many opportunities as possible to be with her. On the days I didn't meet her surfing, I ended up sitting on one of the bar stools while she served the drinks, one of the cluster that made up her cluster. But I was the only one she took with her on her break out to the back, sharing the quick smoke, the deep kisses and on occasion a bit more, if there was time. The taste of her. It kept me coming back. And the wonder of her, her eyes when they held mine, those long limbs, even the beaded and woven hair that hung sensuously around her head, swaying with her movements. I watched her always, drawing the pints, filling the glasses, mixing, wiping, a slow smile on my face while I nursed my pint, coffee, whiskey. Whiskey was for the late evenings, before closing, so that she could taste it on me, and I would taste her back in my bed, or in hers.

She stirred in the sheets, her eyes fluttered open and she stared at me. I smiled. "Good morning, beautiful."

She smiled and the smile reached her eyes. She sat up on her elbows. "Is it?"

"Oh, yes. Very good." I leaned over and kissed her lips.

"I'm not complaining about it so far," she said.

I began to trail kisses over her, slowly, languidly, my hands leading the way, brushing, stroking, finding the sweet spots. I arrived at her hip, licked the swirls of the tattoo ink, resting my hand on her thigh.

"Don't stop," she said with a little moan.

"I'm getting lost in your waves," I told her.

She sighed. "You're getting lost in my story, then?"

"Willingly. I love your story."

She moaned, low. "Good. I want you in it."

Later, when I brought breakfast to her and she sat cross legged on the bed, she drew her canvas bag to her, the one with the essentials she brought with her when she spent the night at my place, as she'd done last night. After a few moments searching she withdrew something.

"Come here a minute, Luke."

I placed the small cup of tea and toast on the bedside locker and sat on the bed. She took my left wrist and tied a woven leather thong around it.

"I made this for you," she said, her blue eyes shining.

I fingered it carefully. It was dark, with three thick flat strands that had been tied off at each end with a thin thong.

Each flat strand had a design carefully etched on it, swirling, rolling marks that curled gracefully at each rounded curve of the weave.

"The waves," I said, marvelling. "The sea. It's beautiful, Clio, thank you."

She leaned over, kissed it and then my wrist. "I'm glad you like it."

"I'll keep it on all the time, I won't take it off."

She smiled. "Good."

She held up her wrist. "I have one for me, too. One for the surfer boy and one for the surfer girl."

I SAT NEXT to Clio on the sofa, weaving my fingers into the plaits of her hair. We hadn't seen each other enough this past week, a bout of design commissions for me and increased hours for her. A few nights only and they left me hungry for more. This time, though, we'd managed to steal the night and the day together, here at my place.

The afternoon was grey, the rain promising its arrival and casting a dim light into the room. An old film flickered on the telly, something to murmur to us as we murmured to each other.

"Did you do the plaits yourself?" I asked, leaning towards her. I lifted some of the plaits and kissed her ear, one for each stud that decorated the edge.

"I did," she said. "And the studs in my ear. It's all part of my story."

"It's a lovely story, a beautiful story."

She gave a throaty laugh. "Parts of it are." She turned to face me. "You said you wanted to be part of my story, will I make you part of it?"

I smiled, nodded leaned over and kissed her mouth. She kissed me deeply. Eventually she pulled away.

"Stay here, so," she said.

She rose and went over to her canvas bag. She withdrew a small case and sidled back over to me, the long T-shirt she wore dipping and shaping until it ended at the beginning of her shapely legs. I watched her, intrigued, as she pulled out a fine-toothed comb, some beads and a few paper packets and set them on the coffee table in front of us. A little while later I found myself sitting on the floor in front of the sofa, my head resting on her crossed legs while she combed my hair.

She stroked and combed, her fingers gently pressing and brushing against my scalp. I could hear her singing softly under her breath and I found it soothing, almost like a lullaby. She carried on singing and combing and I dozed lightly, the flickering light of the black and white film adding to the mesmerising quality of the moment. My eyes closed and mermaids came, sirens sang. The water lapped and rocked my body, gently, so gently, as I floated on the water. The waves whooshed and encouraged, pulled me into the sea, the deep water swirling, promising, enfolding.

I woke to a kiss, light and cool on my lips. My eyes fluttered open and Clio greeted me with another kiss planted on my nose.

"There, sleepyhead, I'm just about done."

I pulled her down into my lap and closed my arms around her. "I'm only just beginning."

"We're only just beginning," she said.

I leaned down to kiss her amid a shower of plaits, mine meeting hers and for a moment I was startled. I laughed, delighted and nuzzled her neck, shaking my head slightly. Beads met and made their own kind of music and desire rushed through me. I could feel the plaits, now, given weight by the beads scattered among them. I was surprised at how they felt, the goodness of it, the rightness, but also how they seemed to connect me with Clio, made her more part of me. She'd done this for me.

"Thank you," I said, suddenly filled with emotion. "This is special. You're special."

"You're special," she said softly, looking up into my eyes. "You're special to me."

She hugged me, tight and hard. "You're mine, so you are. All mine." She pulled back and laughed. And I laughed with her, all pure joy.

We were still laughing when a text came through. Both our phones, almost at once. We looked at each other, all raised brows and amusement. I looked at my phone, looked up at her. "Mud?"

She nodded and laughed again. I opened the text while she did the same, and the surprise and excitement grew as I read. I looked over at her and saw matching emotions.

"Will we?" I said.

"How could we not?"

I rose and held out my hand to help her up. Together we left the flat to fetch our surfboards and go meet these raging waves that were building out at the beach.

THE WAVES WERE MAD. THE "LADDAÍ" were half gone with fear and exhilaration when we arrived, wetsuits donned, boards in hand. Jake straggled in, just as we made our way down to the water, the wind whipping at us.

"Wicked," he said, breathless, his hair plastered. "But it's knackering. I wiped out half way. You may want to rethink going out. It's getting worse."

I looked over at Clio who was still, eyes glittering as though readying for battle. I could feel her energy rising up, powerful focused.

"Ah, we're grand," I said, putting my arm around Clio's shoulder. "But thanks anyway."

"Mud's still out there," he said and pointed. "That's one crazy dude."

I looked and I could see Mud, crouched low, struggling to keep his balance as he rode the curve of the wave, a defensive move for a tricky wave. A moment later it took his board and he flipped, disappearing under the water. Seconds passed, and we watched, waited, until eventually, we saw a head pop up some distance from where it had disappeared.

Jake shook his head and looked over at us again. "See what I mean?"

I nodded. "We get it. No worries. We'll be careful."

I took Clio's hand and led her to the water. I would do my best to protect her, to guide her to the best wave. The best for her, and then the best for me.

The wave, when it came, took us both, not what I'd planned. It wasn't safe, but it was done and I held on, steering, leaning, gripping, trying to feel its direction, its power, while all the time wondering at its anger. It grew before it diminished and I started to sway, fighting it. I uttered a few words, ancient and seldom needed and for a moment the wave calmed. Until it didn't. The calm, the tiny lull, was my "more fool you" moment, for it surged back and flipped me, plunging my body deep, deep to the bottom.

I fought my way to the top, bewildered and struggling. Moments piled together passed, stilled and passed again, the sea talking to me, angry, insistent. The sirens were gone and so were the mermaids. It was only rage.

My head burst through the surface and I swung around, looking for Clio. The beads of my plaits banged around me, reminding me of her, of our connection. She would be all right, I told myself. She would be fine, so.

The water churned and I caught sight of my board, still attached. I had my board. I at least had that, if I needed it. I grabbed hold and hoisted myself onto it, straddling my legs to help maintain its stability. From that perch I scanned the sea, looking for her, or any sign of her. Raging waves stretched into the distance. I squinted, surveying the shore. A few people dotted the beach, but none that marked Clio. I looked to my right again, where I last saw her, but there was nothing. I felt fear rise up and was about to jump into the sea again in a foolish attempt to search for her under water when I heard a splash behind me. I looked over and saw a head just above the water. Clio, her face full of fury, coughed and spat water. I grinned. What a woman.

Back on the beach, I was chafing her wrists, hugging her and kissing her in succession, my fear and joy blended into the need to touch her and ensure that she was fine. The light and laughter was just returning to her eyes when Mud and Jake joined us, the others not far behind.

"Dude!" said Mud. He clasped me in a one-armed hug and raised his fist. I bumped it with my own, unable to help my accompanying grin.

"Wild, man. That was wild," said Jake. He mirrored Mud's fist gesture and I happily returned it. "Hey, Clio. Good save."

"Yeah, that was a shit hot ride from the both of you, no doubt about. I thought you were goners, for sure."

"Those waves were really odd, altogether," I said. "Weirdly unpredictable."

"That was the magic of it," said Mud. "So cool." He shook his head and grinned suddenly. He reached up and tugged one of my plaits. "Cool hair, dude. And the stud and nose ring."

I stared at him a moment, uncertain he meant me. Clio had

the studs and nose ring, in addition to the plaits. I nodded anyway.

Jake touched my ear. "Yeah. Stud looks good, bro. Thought about getting one myself. Or maybe a nose ring."

I reached up to my ear, feeling the place where he'd touched. I was almost unsurprised when my fingers found the stud. I fingered my nose, at the septum, where Clio had her tiny nose ring. The thin gold metal felt strange under my touch. I looked over at Clio and her eyes danced, humour and something else filling them.

She leaned up to me and spoke in my ear, so only I could hear. "While you were sleeping, I worked my magic with my numbing ointment and a needle. Welcome to my story, Luke."

There was only one thing I could do. I leaned over and kissed her.

11

SMITHY

He stared at the photo, two young men in wetsuits, squinting at the light, arms on each other's shoulders, surfboard in the other hand. A common enough photo among surfers, he was certain. Nothing remarkable in that way. Behind the pair he could see a stretch of beach, pale against the light of the sky. There was no "jump at him" moment when he regarded either face, even though he examined every detail.

He tried another tack and looked for signs of the Otherworld, something that would mark either one of them, or both, as part of Anu's people. But what would he look for? He'd no idea what marked them out and he dare not ask Anu.

He sighed, ran his hand through his hair. What an eejit. He should have just thrown the photo on the table and said, "there". Let them exclaim or say something that would clue him in about the identity of the lads in the photo. It seemed that as well as losing his memory he was losing his presence of mind. He tossed the photo on the kitchen table in disgust. Rose from the chair and went into the sitting room. The afternoon sun poured in through the side window, spilling across the floor, just missing the fiddle case that he'd set there a week ago, after they'd returned from Dublin. He idly went over, squatted and opened the case. The fiddle lay there, innocent, filled with potential for so much. He ran his hand along the strings and he could hear that, after so much neglect, the tuning was off.

He picked it up along with the bow, went over to a chair, and for the next half hour messed with the tuning, twisting, turning, plucking and occasionally bowing. He used his ear to tune, forgoing any assistance, and at the end of it, when he thought it was as good as it could be, he lifted the fiddle to his chin and stroked the bow across it. The sound pleased him, nothing jarring, nothing slightly flat or sharp.

He started to play a tune, something simple, nothing too testing, too tricky or round the houses. It flowed well, the tune, and after a few tentative sections he flowed well on the repeat. He played it again and again until it was almost as if the needle was stuck and doomed to play the same phrases, but his needle had increasing confidence born of hope.

Eventually, the hope in full bloom, he lowered his fiddle. Perfect. Ah, now. He raised the fiddle again, and on to the next tune, adding a little lilt, a little this and that, but halfway through the stumble came, that ball in the air dropped, and so did all the other balls – all crashing down on hope. Hope fled the room, the fiddle went into the case and Smithy turned his back. Leave that there, he thought. Leave it there. For now? The now was definitely out of the question, but doing it for later? Well, that that was a faint possibility, so it was.

Hope hovered at the door, deciding whether to return.

Smithy paused outside Maura's gate, the good idea that seemed so bright in his mind turning to the dark side where bad idea held court. Maura was Morrigan after all, and you just couldn't chance your arm with someone like her. She would know, and it's what she would do with that knowledge that got the dark side whispering to him now.

"Smithy," said an amused voice.

The decision was taken from him, or at least the stage where he approached her. There was still some back-up room, some "eh, how's it going just calling in for a bit of a chat" room that meant banter and no real substance.

Maura emerged from her house, her dark hair blowing in the breeze. Above her, one of her crows gave a squawk and she looked up and laughed.

"Ah, now, give the poor man a chance. He's clearly trying to decide how to handle it." She moved forward, her hands casually stuck in her dark jeans.

"What will you decide to say, Smithy, I wonder, when what you really want to say is so clearly burning to come out?"

Smithy narrowed his eyes. "Oh, feck off, Maura. You know next to nothing about me and my thoughts."

She snorted. "Problems, you mean. But there is a specific one now that you want my help with?"

She left it as a question, but Smithy wasn't sure if that was just a tease. That really, she did know his problems, maybe not this specific one, because how could she? He looked up at the tall fir trees, to her henchmen clustered in branches, her men at arms. They stared back at him, beady-eyed.

"Don't mind them, Smithy. They won't tell."

Smithy grunted and forced a casual shrug. "Sure, there's no mystery, sure there isn't." He withdrew the photo from his back pocket slowly. He fingered it a moment and then plunged on. "We picked up a few things at Luke's house and I found this among them. It looks like Lugh and I was wondering if the other lad was Mongan. You would know better than I would. Sure, I hardly met the man."

It was a bluff and a bit of a "chance yer arm" move, but it was the best one he had. He held out the photo to Maura and she took it, but not before a gleam of mischief shot through her eyes. Oh, feck.

She studied the photo, turned it sideways, squinted, pulled it back, squinted some more, until Smithy was nearly screaming with annoyance.

"For feck's sake, Maura. Give over, will you. I know you're winding me up."

She gave him an innocent look and then burst out laughing. "Just giving it my best." She held up the photo beside her, facing out. "Now, so, what do we see? A pair of surfers. Serious ones, judging by the confidence of their pose, the manner they handle their surfboards. Very athletic, nothing slouchy about their build." She raised and lowered her brows in an exaggerated manner. "Very hot, altogether."

"Just answer the question, Maura."

"Well, you see Smithy. I have a few questions for you, first. Why didn't you show this to all of us earlier? Why now? Why just me?" She gave a roar of laughter. "Oh, to be fair, not just me. You have thoughtfully included my lads, too."

Smithy reached over and snatched the photo from her, turned and began to walk away. Definitely gone to the dark side, that idea. Eejit. No other word for it. The idea. Himself. Oh, himself belonged in the first-class section of that eejit train.

"You've got your answer, Smithy," shouted Maura. "And I've got mine."

Smithy stared out at the mountains in the distance. The evening was quiet, little peeps of fuchsia beginning to show on the horizon as the sun sank behind it.

"Have you ever done this before, Smithy?" asked Saoirse.

They were both leaning against the wall that enclosed his yard, enjoying the evening. At least that's what Smithy had hoped would happen. Just a few moments to treasure, to savour against what was to come. To rest his leg, which had given him a dodgy moment there when he made his way to the wall, a plan that had originally been to go up into the field, but halted by the gate.

"Done what?" Smithy asked cautiously. "What had he done", echoed in his mind with its irony and truth on all levels wrapped up together, entwined.

"Given testimony, or whatever it is we're doing."

Exactly. What was he doing? He turned and gave her what he hoped was an encouraging smile. "You'll be grand. Daghda will be there, he'll explain it all to you and help you if you need it."

"Will you be there, Smithy? Will you help?"

"I will," he said. "I will, of course." He reached over and grabbed her hand, squeezed it.

"Will they come to get us, or will we go there ourselves?"

"Did Anu not tell you?"

She shook her head. "I didn't ask, to be fair. She probably didn't think to tell me, it's so much a part of her world." She looked up at him, caught his eyes. "It's not a part of mine, not naturally. But I'm trying."

He lifted her hand to his mouth and kissed it. She tasted good, tasted right, but the coil of sadness was still there in him. It was a taste only, and taste could only go so far. He sighed.

"We'll go ourselves, so. In a few moments. Anu will come to see us off."

He was glad he could tell her that much and thankful that Anu had seen fit to tell him the detail, knowing he would guide Saoirse through it. So much unsaid and unknown. And his cowardice, denial preventing him from finding out as much as he could to be best prepared. "A wing and a prayer" and "chance yer arm". He was still on that eejit train and had no clue how to get off.

He took one last drink of his cup of tea, wishing it was whiskey. "Come, we'll go inside, gather our gear and head down to the river."

She nodded and followed him silently into the house. Cups in sink, a small pack on their backs and that's all there was. It was time.

The path through the woods was dimly lit and Smithy used the torch from his phone to show the way, for Saoirse's sake more than his. He still had his keen sight, thankfully immune to the rigours of the forge or his temporary death. Saoirse followed him silently, and he was grateful. Chatter seemed too much to bear at the moment, when he needed to gather himself, focus and have all his senses engaged.

They emerged into the open grass eventually and headed towards the river. There Smithy could see Anu in the dusk shadow, her hair woven into a single long plait that hung over her shoulder.

She greeted them both softly and patted Smithy's arm when he came alongside her. Saoirse, she embraced, made encouraging noises and smoothed Saoirse's hair, also woven in a plait. They both wore dark clothes. "Serious clothes," Saoirse had called them.

"You'll give Daghda my warmest greetings," Anu told Saoirse.

"I will," Saoirse said.

"He'll look after you," said Anu.

"Will he?" she asked. The tone was uncertain, hopeful.

"Of course, child. Why wouldn't he? You're his daughter."

"Daughter?" Saoirse looked at her, shocked. She frowned, glanced at Smithy. "I'm his daughter? But I thought...." Her voice trailed off weakly.

Anu gave a soft laugh. "You didn't know what to think, I'm sure. So, he didn't tell you?" asked Anu. She stroked Saoirse's head again. "Ah, that man."

"No, he said nothing. I was with him all the way to the well. He said nothing." Smithy could hear the anger gathering in her voice.

Anu took her hand and held it tightly. "He may have felt the time wasn't right, then. Don't be hard on him. You are in this world, he is in the Otherworld. Since we brought you back, he's had only glimpses of you before this. Allowed himself only that, I suspect."

Anu turned to Smithy. "Look after her, Goibhniu."

Smithy nodded dumbly, his own shock from the news resonating through his mind. Daghda's daughter. And she was in his care. In the care of a feckin' eejit that couldn't get off that train.

Anu hugged Saoirse again and softly intoned the words that summoned the boat. Smithy strained to hear and commit them to memory. The first step of many in the "chancing yer arm" scenario he'd brought on himself.

The boat came and they drifted off to the other side. The Otherworld and whatever awaited them and Smithy's "chance yer arm" strategy to survive it.

12

———

LUKE

I studied the laptop screen, at the small desk in Mon's flat, examining the angles and curves of the logo and frowned. It was for an Irish whiskey export company, a Celtic Tiger company that had floundered in recent years but was forging new ties with the Chinese as well as the Japanese. It had to be a logo that would persuade, would woo them away from the Scotch whisky and bring them firmly into the Irish camp. I wanted an Asian flavour to it, all puns intended and I wasn't yet satisfied with the result. There was the curve of the harp, and the diddly idly swirl of the fiddle shaking hands with an angular fragment of a Chinese character, all in abstract.

Behind me the door opened and I rose, smiling. I didn't expect her today. Working a double shift, she'd said, so I decided to mark time with some of my own work. I was glad she let herself in with the key. I'd pressed it on her a few days ago, wanting her to feel part of my world as much as I felt I was becoming part of hers.

"Dude," said Mon. "You do actually work."

"Mon?" I said. "I wasn't expecting you."

He gave me a funny look. "Who'd you think it was?"

I shook my head. "Never mind, what are you doing here? I thought you were with your father?"

Mon snorted. "Five weeks is long enough with my father. Even then, he wanted me to stay longer."

I looked at him, catching up with the surprise at his appearance and the fact that it had been five weeks since he'd gone. A sudden thought struck me. "You did tell your father you were leaving, didn't you?"

Mon shrugged and laughed. "You know me too well, bro."

I joined his laugher, shaking my head. "He'll find you again."

Mon gave another shrug.

"What did he want with you anyway?" I asked.

Mon frowned. "Mostly shite stuff." He looked at his phone. "I'll tell you later. To the pub, I think."

I'D FORGOTTEN that Mon's notion of a pub had transformed into trendy nautical notions of sea life and I found myself sitting in The Life Buoy sipping a watery excuse for lager and waiting on fish and chips. In the background some anonymous music aspired to hip and cool. Mon gave a nod to a few familiar faces across the room and turned back to his lager and took a deep drink.

"I've missed this, all right," he said.

"No pubs up in Donegal?" I asked.

He grimaced. "Ah, now there's a joke. I saw no pubs."

My face darkened. "No pubs at all?"

He shook his head. "We were a long way from pubs, dude."

"The other side of the water?" I asked, glancing around for listeners.

Mon shrugged and nodded. "We had meetings. Or, he had meetings and took me with him."

"About what?" It was like dragging out a state secret.

"Mostly the usual shite. Danger coming, blah, blah, blah. Anyway," he said and grinned widely. He leaned forward and brushed his hands at the ends of my plaits. "What's this all about? You becoming more dude than I am?"

I laughed. "Feck off."

"Oooh," he said, touching the nose ring. "And the nose ring and a stud, in your ear, too. Is this a competition? If so, I'd say you've won, hands down."

I elbowed him away. "Get away, so. It's nothing."

He caught my wrist in his and laughed, until his eye caught the leather band. He fingered it a moment, raised his brow at me and then pulled it closer to examine it. His grin turned into a frown and he looked up.

"Where'd you get this?" His tone was careful, neutral.

I shrugged and couldn't help the sloppy smile on my face. "Clio, my girlfriend." It was the first time I'd said "girlfriend" aloud, though I'd been thinking it for weeks. A girlfriend. Something steady, regular exclusive. It didn't bother me, it felt right. Together. I was ready to do this, live in the now and take what the future would bring, as it came.

Mon stared at me, a slow smile on his face. "Girlfriend. You? The king of no commitments, the kiss, shag and shrug off person?" He started to laugh. "You're having a laugh, right?"

"No, there's no kidding." I shoved at his shoulder with my hand. "I know, I know, but Clio, she's different. She's like no one else. Amazing. Beautiful, witty, intelligent. And she surfs. You'll like her."

"She sounds too perfect. What's the flaw?"

I shook my head. "No flaws, I'm telling you. Ask Mud, Jake. All of them."

"They've met her?"

I nodded. "A few times. When we've been surfing." The few

times I'd been with that group had been on the beach or surfing, preferring to keep company with the lads at the session or with Clio. Mostly Clio. Almost always with Clio.

"So, is this the reason for the transformation?"

I shrugged. "I like it. She was happy to do it for me."

Mon nodded and snorted. "You've got it bad, dude."

I gave another shrug. I didn't mind his teasing. I knew he understood how it was to be so caught up in someone, you could hardly see anything but that person. But I wouldn't want to remind him either of the time he was in love like that, and the loss that went with it, when it all went badly wrong. The fact that he lived here, near where it fell apart, told me he had his own penance in place and I certainly didn't want to make it worse.

"Where's she now?"

"Working. She's on a double shift. She tends bar at O'Sullivan's."

Mon nodded, a warm smile on his face now. "Do I get to meet her, this perfect woman? Or are you going to keep her hidden?"

"Not at all," I said. "You'll meet her soon enough."

It wasn't until after our meal and three more pints that I remembered there was still a little more to discuss about his meeting with his father.

"Other than 'danger, blah, blah, blah,' did the meetings reveal anything more? You said it was mostly shite. What was the other bit that wasn't?"

Mon looked up from his pint and stared blearily at me. "I didn't know how to tell you this, man, but they're looking for you."

I paused, considered his words and eventually shrugged. "So? We know that. I've been avoiding them for years."

"Yeah, but they're looking. Really looking. They realise that you and I still see each other. That's why my father dragged me along to the meeting. They know you surf. They know I surf. They wanted to know if I knew where you are."

"What did you say?"

"I told them no, of course. What else would I say?"

"I know you wouldn't tell them. Did you say anything else?"

"Well, I don't think they believed me. My father certainly didn't. He didn't say anything. Not that he would. You're a son to him, you know that. I just knew that once he got me alone, he would get it out of me somehow. So I left."

I nodded, the relief soaring through me. "He didn't tell them you live here most of the time, did he?"

Mon shook his head. "But they're not stupid. It won't take them long to piece together possibilities." He looked down at his hands. "They know my story. They know my father's involvement."

"But that's exactly why they wouldn't suspect here, or anywhere near Glandore. Because of that. Who in his right mind would come back to the scene of the crime and stay here all this time?"

Mon snorted. "Are you saying I'm not in my right mind?"

"Only when you sing, only when you sing." I punched his arm again. "No, of course not. They'll just think it wouldn't be your first choice to hang out."

Mon nodded and looked into the distance. "You shouldn't stay here too long, though. Just in case."

My heart sank. I knew he was right, and the thought had already lodged, unwillingly in my mind. But could I go? I still had a bit of time, surely. Time enough to perhaps persuade Clio to come with me.

"And you shouldn't trust anyone," said Mon. "You understand that, don't you? Not anyone."

I frowned. "Yes, I know."

"I mean it, Luke. Be careful. Because...." Mon pressed his lips together. "There's something more I found out. The danger. It's real. And most dangerous for you."

"Me?" My mind raced, trying to fill in the danger spaces of the statement. "Why me?"

Mon took a deep breath. "It's Balor. The danger is Balor. You know Balor Energies, or whatever it's called?"

"Vaguely. I really didn't take much notice. It's some kind of petroleum company now, expanding into fracking, I think. Terrible logo. Whoever designed that piece of shite needs to return to design school."

"Balor, Luke. Balor. The danger is Balor. Your grandfather."

I stared at him. "You must be joking. He's dead. I should know. I was there."

Mon shook his head. "No. Somehow he isn't. And he's Balor Energies. He has a headquarters here in Ireland as well as the US. His company business is his tool to poison the land, the sea. All of it. He doesn't care about anything else. Except you. If he finds out where you are, he'll go after you, until you're dead, you can be certain about that."

I started to scoff, but stopped. I was no longer the warrior I had been. I wasn't anything I used to be. Now, I was a logo designer, reputable, yes. I was a surfer, top man on local waves. I was a musician, talented, of course. Good on any instrument you put in front of me. Oh, yes, a man for these times. But nothing more.

"Feck," I said.

Mon just nodded.

I SAT THERE, watching her pull the pint, laughing and chatting with the man in front of her. She gave me a sideways glance, and a sideways smile that was my smile, a private one, meant only for me. I knew its meaning so well, now, it sang and whispered "only you" in my ear, over and over.

A few moments later, she came over, placed a glass of whiskey in front of me. "A whiskey night, I think."

Most nights were a whiskey night. Or the nights when I came in here, waiting for her, watching her while the evening wore away and my nights slowly turned to the night ahead. She loved the taste of whiskey on my lips and tongue, said it was the best way to have it. I grinned at the thought and took a deep drink from the glass. It was a Jameson's and I had no complaints. None at all. In the background the noise of the night had quieted, leaving just a few on this weekday night. Not long now. And I needed it, especially after talking with Mon. His words had rattled me and I wanted to stop thinking about the danger, thinking about who I could trust.

The "not long now" became "now" a half hour later when the doors were shut, the tables wiped, and glasses all sorted. The rest could wait until the next day. The goodbyes were soon done and we were off, walking down the road, my arm on her shoulder, placing a kiss on her temple. One of the few people I knew I could trust. I knew it deep inside me.

"Will we go to mine?" she said. "There's something I want to show you."

"Ah, right, of course," I said. "That actually suits."

Mon was with the lads at The Life Buoy tonight, but even so, it wasn't a comfortable idea if we went to his place. He'd return soon enough and it wouldn't be the same. With Mon back in the flat, Clio and I would most likely be confined to her room in the future. My thoughts followed a new direction. A direction I'd never explored or considered with anyone before. Sure, we could. Why not? We were together, why not live together? It was a question I could discuss with her tonight. I felt confident I knew her answer.

Back at her room, unable to wait any longer, we explored the whiskey taste just inside the door. After a little while she pulled away and retrieved one of her special spliffs from her bag. She led me to the edge of the bed and we sat there, exploring the taste of that, smoking and kissing. We didn't smoke that often, but it was nice for a change and I loved how sensuous it made her feel under my touch, her breasts fuller, her toned body even more rounded.

When the spliff was finished I began to take my exploration further, gently pushing her back against the bed, but she pressed a hand on my chest.

"Wait," she said. "Let me show you something."

I watched her walk across to her bag, the short denim skirt rumpled up high on her long legs, and marvelled at her grace. She returned shortly, a piece of paper in her hand.

"Here," she said, holding out the paper. "I drew this. I thought it was the perfect for you. It's our story."

I took the paper and looked at it. It was a beautiful, stylised rendition of flowers circling and entwining with a sun, all of it surrounded by curling waves, the waves the same design and style as the one on the leather band on my wrist.

"This is really something," I said, and I meant it. I could see where it came from, the place of her and the place of me, together. I leaned over and kissed her. "You're very talented."

She took the kiss, deepened it and then moved back a little, her eyes twinkly. "I have many talents." She placed her hand on my cheek. "Will I ink your arm with it? I think it's perfect. I can put it on my story, too."

Warmth, joy and so much more spread through me. Ah, now. It felt settled. Right. The "yes" was there in my mind – a "yes" so loud and full of all that I felt and shared with her. And then it was said, even louder than it was in my mind and my hands cupping her face and kissing her again, planting the "yes" inside her. She was hugging me, kissing me back as the "yes" filled both of us.

Eventually, she pulled back, the joy and excitement in her expression lighting me up inside.

"I have the equipment here. We can start right away," she said.

"What? Now?" I asked, startled.

"Yes, why wait? I want to do it now, I can't wait to see it on your arm."

I looked at her, felt her excitement and realised it was mine. "Perfect," I said.

The time passed but only on the clock. I had no idea what amount or where it went when it did pass. I was wrapped up in Clio, her face, her mouth, the way it pursed or softened, her eyes, how they glittered, steely with focus as she etched our story on my arm. Her gloved hand held my arm steady, the skin taut while the other gloved hand skilfully wielded the inking tool. All the while she sung softly under her breath, her own music to work by.

When it was finished I looked at it. Reddened at the lines, it still was undeniably beautifully rendered. It wasn't overly large, disc shaped. Perfect. I looked up at smiled at her.

"Do you like it?" she asked.

I reached for her, gave her my answer with my lips, my hands and the rest of my body.

I WASN'T certain this was a good idea. The weather was damply indifferent, the waves uninspiring, and there weren't many people bothering. It certainly fitted my idea of not bothering, but Mon wanted to do it, his laddaí were here to support it. He'd had this crazy notion that the waves, which promised more than what they were showing would rise up once we got out there. "Crazy" was what Jake called it, but they all came anyway. Mon was their magnet and they followed him anywhere.

"What's going on anyway?" I asked in a low voice.

We were changing by his car in the car park, slipping off our clothes, our trunks on underneath, and pulling on our wetsuits.

"Nothing," said Mon, his eyes twinkling. "I just want to try something out. And besides, I haven't been able to surf for too long. I'm not fussed about the conditions. I just want to get on the water."

"Get on the water, or in the water?" I said with a grin.

"Oh, ha ha." He squinted at me. "Hold on there. What's that on your arm? You getting some strange disease I need to know about?"

I glanced over at the tattoo, still slightly red at the edges, but improving all the time. I loved it. Loved how it looked and what it meant.

I smiled widely. "Ah, you're just jealous. Clio did it for me. It's our story."

Mon pulled back and whistled. "Oh, now. Excuse me. 'Our story'? What does that mean?"

"Oh, feck off, I like it, so you can just shut it."

Mon came closer and pulled my arm towards him, examining it. "Well, she certainly knows how to draw. And tattoo. I can't argue with the skill." He narrowed his eyes. "What did you say it means?"

"Our story," I said. "What?"

He frowned and shook his head. "Nothing. It's just weird, dude, that's all. All those waves."

I shrugged. "That's obvious, surely. The surf, the waves."

"Yeah. I suppose." He looked up at me and forced a smile. "It looks cool. Cool tat for the cool dude."

"Oh, go on with you," I said and gave him a little smack on his head.

He gave a grin this time. A genuine one. "So, when do I get to meet this Clio? You keep promising."

"Soon, soon. We'll go to the pub where she works after this."

"Good."

"But," I hesitated, trying to find the right words. "It will be a quick meet, Mon. She told me last night she has to take a quick trip back home, for a few days to Galway. She...she asked me to go with her and I told her I would. We'll leave directly after she finishes work. I meant to tell you earlier after I got back from hers this morning, but well, with one thing and another, I didn't get a chance."

"One thing and another?" Mon said, his brow raised. "Is that wise, going away with her? You hardly know her, Luke."

A spark of anger rose. "I know her. I know enough that I would trust her with my life."

"That's what you will be doing, you realise don't you?" His voice was serious, full of concern.

"Yes, Mon. I am well aware what the risks are, but I promise you, Clio is sound. Besides, if anything, from what you say, it will be good to get away from here. It won't be long before they realise I might be here with you."

Mon frowned and sighed. "I can't argue with that, but I have to say it doesn't feel right. Something about this is off."

I placed a hand on Mon's shoulder. "I know. It's hard to trust anyone. But I trust Clio. And you can trust her, too."

"Maybe," he said, but his voice was full of doubt.

I looked over to the "laddaí", to Jake, Mud and the others. "That lot, there, any one of them could easily be an informant, ready to tell Balor all he knows."

Mon looked in their direction and snorted. "That 'lot'? I don't think so. But it's possible. Anything's possible when it comes to Balor. Anyone is possible, dude. Don't forget that."

"Except you," I said.

"Except me."

I STROLLED UP THE ROAD, Mon at my side and tried to calm the nerves that were surprising me. The two people who mattered most to me right now were going to meet, so I suppose it was natural. It just wasn't natural for me. I was the "lad of good times, great craic" just as Mon was, or at least tried to be. But this commitment, this tie I felt with Clio seemed perfect. So it needed to be perfect between the two of them.

I had decided to take him now, before the noontime crowd got going and Clio had no time to chat. But it was already later than I planned, our damp squib of a surf session having played out to be something of a marvel, which Mon just couldn't shut up about, even now that Mud, Jake and the others had headed off.

"It was perfect," he repeated. "The pure drop."

"Pure luck, though, you mean," I said.

"Nothing lucky about it, but all pure," he said.

"You wish."

"No, man. I told it would happen, didn't I?"

"And what, you just arranged it?" I gave him a sceptical look. "I think your father would have something to say about that."

"No, man, it's true. I cast out to the sea and it answered. I promise you. Finally, it's worked."

I stopped and stared at him in wonder. "No."

Mon's eyes gleamed. "Yes. I mean it's only a small thing, but it worked."

I was speechless for a moment. "Feck. What does this even mean?"

Mon nodded slowly. "Yeah. I know."

"Playtime over?"

He shrugged. "Maybe. I don't know. It's only a small thing."

"How do you feel about it?"

Mon sighed. "All right. Maybe. For years I've wanted something. Not just the abilities to be in and on the sea, but more. But now, now that it's happened...." He straightened his shoulders and gave me a wide smile and nudged me. "Now I can give us masterful waves."

"Cool," I said in a mocking tone.

"You're damn right."

I studied his face and could see the little traces of anxiety. "Does your father know?"

He returned my look carefully. "I don't know. Possibly. But if not, he'll know soon enough."

I put my arm on his shoulder and squeezed. "It'll be grand. Not a bother at all."

He smiled wryly at me. "Yeah, dude."

"Now, let's meet my babe, dude," I said and punched his arm lightly. "Just in here."

I opened the pub door, blinking against the dim light, Mon right behind me. After a few moments I could see there were already people milling at the bar and seated at tables. Oh well, maybe a quick hello and a pint at the bar might steal a few more moments for us. I started heading over and Mon pulled me back.

"Wait," he said.

He tightened his grip on my arm and dragged me towards the toilets, out of sight of the bar.

"What?" I said.

"That woman serving at the bar, is that Clio?" His voice was strange, almost strangled.

"Yes, why?"

"Feck. Tell me you're joking."

"Why would I joke?"

He looked at me, and I could see a mixture of pain, sorrow, grief on his face. And something more. Anger. He stared at me a moment more and then turned and walked away, back through the pub and out the door. I looked at his retreating figure – too stunned to speak, let alone move. With only a glance in the direction of Clio, I made my way out of the bar. I caught sight of Mon walking rapidly in the direction of his flat. I chased after him calling his name, but he didn't stop or even turn around.

I caught up with him just a short walk from the flat and grabbed his arm, forcing him to face me.

"What is it? What have I done?"

"As if you don't know," he said, his tone cold.

"I don't, Mon. I don't."

He shrugged off my grip and kept on walking. I came alongside of him.

"You have to tell me, Mon. How am I going to make it right if you don't tell me?"

He kept on walking. "You can't make it right. It's too late."

He unlocked the door to his flat and headed up the stairs to the living area. I followed and when I reached the top of the stairs, he turned to me.

"Well, now you're here, you can just pack and go. You were leaving anyway."

"I'm not leaving until you tell me what's going on. What did I do?"

He looked at me in disgust. "Of all the women, you had to feckin' pick her. Why would you do that to me?"

"Clio? Why would you be upset about her? What's wrong

with her?"

"Clio?" He raised his brow. "Don't tell me you didn't know. After all I went through, suffered and still do. Something I only told you. You, who were a brother to me."

His voice was threaded with such anguish and I could only stare at him dumbfounded.

"Mon, you know I wouldn't hurt you. Never."

"But you have, you dim fecker. And you can just get out."

"Why? Please. At least tell me."

"Oh, Lugh, the hero. The clever golden god who can do anything. But you're telling me you didn't know that she's Clíodhna?"

"Clíodhna?"

Mon gave an impatient nod. "Yes."

"You mean Clio?" I shook my head. "No, you're wrong, Mon. She can't be Clíodhna?"

"You're telling me I wouldn't recognise Clíodhna?"

"No of course not. But Clio can't be her. It's impossible."

He folded his arms across his chest. "And why's that?"

I stop, unable to find the words. "It just isn't." It's the best I could come up with.

"Well, you stupid ass, she is."

He moved over to me, flipped my braids and gestured across my body. "And all this? This shite you've got going on since you met her? She's bound you to her, weaved her spell."

I could only look at him, the denial screaming in my head blocking out his words. "But I never met Clíodhna," I finally whispered. "I wouldn't have known her."

He gave me a look of disbelief. "Ah, sure, and after all I've said. And the name didn't give you the slightest clue?"

I shook my head slowly, horror starting to take hold of me.

"Now, so. What was I saying?" Mon said, his cold tone returned. "Oh, right. You can leave. Right now."

13

SAOIRSE

She opened her eyes reluctantly, her mind still caught in the "if onlys" that had swirled around in her mind on the journey across to the Otherworld and added another one to them. If only she could stay longer in the Time Between Time. In that "if only" she would be able to absorb the words Anu had spoken before she left the bank. The possibility of their truth was more impossibility in her mind. More impossible than the likelihood that Seamus Donohue was her father, which at the moment seemed the likeliest of all likelihoods. It was normal, it made sense of her boarding school existence, her mundane holiday celebrations, the hidden books, the secret love of trad music and the few sullen exchanges she'd had with her father. Or the man she knew as her father.

That it wasn't him, that it couldn't be him was just unimaginable, now. The notion that he'd adopted her had been far-fetched enough and one that she had begun to explore, but now, all that faded into the farce of what had just been presented to her. Daghda. A god? She was the daughter of a god – and not just any old god, but one of *the* gods and the granddaughter of the mother goddess, if Anu was to be believed. She couldn't contemplate its implications for her and who she was. It was one thing to accept that she was Bríd and together with Smithy was able to forge some unique weaponry, beyond anyone's imagination, but quite another to accept her supernatural status. What had she been told her powers were? Smithcraft, healing and poetry. Hardly healing. She'd done nothing for Smithy when the need was great, so how could that be so? The thought oddly gave her comfort.

Smithy nudged her and she turned to look at him. "It's time," he said softly.

He stood up carefully in the boat and made the short leap to the bank, before turning to assist her. She took his hand and followed him onto the ground. Figures hovered above her. She raised her head, put her hand to shield her eyes from the glare and made out Daghda at the front, Finn behind him, and a group of others she didn't recognise.

Questions for Daghda filled her mind but she silenced them and gave him a brief greeting. He stepped forward, placed his hands on her shoulders and kissed her head quickly before turning to speak to Smithy.

"You've come just in time. The judgement will start soon."

Saoirse looked at Smithy, Daghda questions crowding her thoughts. Smithy steeled himself and nodded.

"Don't worry, Bríd, you'll be guided through the proceedings. There is little enough for you to do, really, but observing the traditions is important."

She nodded and tried to be satisfied with those words.

Smithy moved ahead of her, joining Finn, while Daghda walked beside her. The silence between them seemed to hang and she suddenly found herself at a loss for words. Or at least how to begin.

"I didn't know," she said finally. "About you. About us. I mean, I don't remember. I only now learned it from Anu."

Daghda grunted. She waited for more, but nothing more was offered. "What shall I call you?" she said finally. Of all the questions that clambered to get out, this found voice first, though it was the least of her concerns, weighed up against all the others. And maybe that was why it found its way to her lips before the others.

"Daghda," he said, his tone even. "What else would you call me?"

What else indeed, she thought. "Of course. It was a stupid question. Sorry. You'll have to excuse my silliness, it's from my lack of knowledge. Well, my lack of memory..." she trailed off when she felt his hand on her arm.

"It is what it is, Bríd. There's nothing that can change it, so we must make our way the best we can and be thankful that we have you back."

It was only at the last words that a softening came to his hard expression and she couldn't explain the tears that formed, made her blink and look away. "Thank you," she said.

They had lagged behind the others, groups of men passing the two of them, but Daghda moved forward, his long strides catching them up. She hastened after him. She could see Smithy and Finn in the front, still, chatting amiably. A man tapped Smithy on his shoulder and he turned, a puzzled look on his face as the man addressed him. The look disappeared quickly, replaced by a neutral expression and a careful nod with a shrug shortly after. The man laughed and clapped Smithy on the shoulder. She didn't understand what was said because the man spoke in the old language and Smithy in Irish. One of the questions that was in her mind at the very first, from the time she learned Daghda had requested her presence now came to her.

"How will I be useful if I can't even understand what they're saying, let alone the proceedings and my role in them?"

Daghda shrugged. "Someone will translate for you. Ogma or Goibhniu."

She was about to ask who Ogma was, when she realised he meant Finn. Ogma. The name echoed in her mind. Anu had called him that, she remembered. But of course, he'd always been at the meetings, had defended her boldly not so long ago. She searched her mind, trying to recall the tale that Anu had told her of her people. Ogma, one of the three men, along with Daghda and Smithy who went to negotiate with the Fomorians. Wasn't that it? Had Ogma – no was Ogma a god? It seemed difficult to imagine someone as full of the craic and music to be a god. But they had said it. Maura had. The king's champion. And had she said more? She couldn't remember, but it was a question for later.

Up ahead another man caught up to Smithy, shouting in the old language. Smithy didn't turn immediately but when he did, the man still talking, there was a momentary look of absolute panic that alarmed Saoirse more than any other action that Smithy had made to cause her concern. She glanced over at Daghda to see if he'd noticed, but he was too busy talking to a man on his other side. She would have to confront Smithy, there was no getting around it. The time for gentle prods and sensitive questions was over. She wouldn't let him deflect or put her off as he'd done over the music. Something definitely wasn't right. Many things weren't right.

THE LARGE STONE and timber beamed hall was filled with people, men and women, their faces containing a mixture of curiosity, anger and sorrow. Saoirse entered behind Smithy, using him as part shield, part comfort under the scrutiny of all those people. She remembered to keep her head high, and though she was dressed in jeans, Doc Martens and a long-sleeved top she tried to carry herself in the manner she imagined any goddess would. The thought nearly made her burst into hysterical giggles. No that wouldn't do, would it, she told herself. What would her father think? As soon as she heard those words in her head another fit of giggles threatened to seize her. Oh, feck, feck, she thought. She decided to concentrate on Smithy instead, blocking out the ripe aromas of bodies mingled with unfamiliar perfumed scents that suddenly assaulted her as she made her way in front of the men and women seated, to the empty chairs placed just in front of them.

She sat down beside Smithy and Finn sat on her other side. There were a few men who took the remaining seats at Finn's end and she recognised them from the battle. At the head of the hall Daghda stood, another man beside him dressed regally in finely made trousers or something along those lines, and a jacket and a sumptuous cloak draped over his shoulders. A gold torc was at his throat. The king?

This could be a ballad, a *Sean Nós* song that went on for ages. The Fairy Queen at court. The Fae Court. The tune would nearly shape itself. And words, rhyming within lines of lines of lines as was proper, so. A pure drop of a song. One for the big events. One for the prizegivings.

Finn leaned towards her. "This is serious. The king himself is here."

Well, there you are so, Saoirse thought. Question answered. *Sean Nós* song here you are, just do your thing. "Does that mean he'll be in charge, not Daghda?" she asked, in an effort to be sensible. All sensible, very sensible. Full of sense. But the sense somehow slipped into sentiment and there she was back at that *Sean Nós* song, the verses piling, the meanings layering. Her leg jigged up and down and it was all she could do not to slap it. She crossed it with the other one at her ankles.

"No, Daghda is still presiding. The king is here to lend his authority, though. Treason is a serious offence."

She nodded, trying to remember the question she'd posed that had prompted the answer. Oh, yeah, fine. "He wouldn't normally be present for judgements, then."

"No, not the ordinary sort. But times are strange, there is danger in the air. Look around you, the unease and tension is pretty plain to see among the clan nobles."

"Clan nobles." Saoirse blinked. Oh, now, here was the song, rising up to again, taking a new shape in all the "clanness" surrounding her. This was no touristy "I'm in the Murphy clan" shite, this was real clan. Clan in its old meaning that was heavy with obligation, blood ties and so much more she couldn't even speculate. It left her numb, with the song still humming distantly.

"There seem an awful lot of people for one medium-sized fairy mound," she said, in an effort to echo the little joke Smithy had made some time ago. The "is this a big fairy mound or little fairy mound" question she'd posed to him the first time across, playing on the translation of the *Sí Bheag, Sí Mhór* tune. Her attempt to joke now was an effort to lighten the mood. Something she had to try, if only for herself, her mind that was suddenly alive again and so out of control. The "make a song of it" impulse needed to be seized again, if only to give her focus, so she didn't either high tail it out of here, or puke on her own feet. Finn gave her a puzzled look at first and then chuckled.

"Oh, right," said Finn. "I remember Smithy telling me the joke. No, this is no medium-sized fairy mound here. This is Tara, a very big mound."

"Tara?" Her voice echoed loudly and she drew a few curious looks. "We're in Tara?"

Why hadn't she realised that when she'd caught sight of the great hall from her horse? The journey from the bank hadn't taken long, but she'd come to understand that no journey in this world took long when in the company of Tuatha de Danann. At least not in her experience. Mother of God. Tara. All the tunes, the airs about Tara crowded her mind, a jumble of sounds like one chaotic session containing brass instruments and screeching fiddles. Janey.

"Yes," said Finn. "Where did you think we were?"

She faked a shrug. Words couldn't manage themselves. They were all caught up in the airs at the moment and the Sean Nós song that suddenly had no care that it wasn't in Irish and somehow took on *Tam Lin* ballad proportions. The Hall of Tara, the seat of the Irish kings of legend, where so much of the drama of Irish myths had taken place. Even she knew that.

She looked around her for distraction, to find a grounding connection that would get her out of her head and settled on Smithy, who was surveying the room intently, his expression guarded. She nudged him. "All right then?"

He gave her a distracted look and nodded after a moment.

"Tara," she said. He would understand how it made her feel, the awe, the confusion, the disbelief.

"What?" he said, blankly.

"Tara. We're here in the hall of Tara. It's hard to credit, you have to admit."

He frowned, glanced around again. "Oh, right. Tara." His expression darkened. "Feck me," he muttered.

"What's wrong, Smithy? And don't tell me that there's nothing wrong. Everything about you tells me that's not so."

In the centre of the hall, Daghda cleared his throat and began to speak, but Saoirse wasn't to be deterred. "What is it?" she whispered fiercely.

He looked over at Daghda and then at her, the panic clear in his face. "I can't understand him. I don't remember the old language," he whispered in a ragged voice.

SHE MANAGED TO NOD CALMLY, at least she thought her actions and expressions shouted "I am the poster girl for calm" as Finn translated Daghda's words for her benefit. She was sitting so close to Smithy she was practically in his lap. It was the best she could do so that he could hear Finn's translation, her only idea to combat her own panic and get them both through this ordeal without anyone discovering Smithy's secret. How they would cope if Smithy should be called upon to speak, she hadn't a clue. The ballad *Tam Lin* had nothing on this. Ah you Scots, listen up now to the *Tara Ballad*, or maybe she would call it *Clueless Cailín*.

Up until now Daghda had been the only one to speak, first calling the captives to be presented for judgement and then moving on to the charges. There were a significant number of gasps as the various traitors appeared, especially at one well-dressed person that Saoirse didn't remember from her own encounter. Finn later explained that he was a small petty king, head of a major clan leader, who was disgruntled and had taken Balor's bribes and promises. The two she did recognise had apparently revealed him as the leader of the rebel group, so Daghda had ordered him seized to be held to account.

With all these various entanglements unfolding, Saoirse could only hope that neither she nor Smithy would be asked to recount their version of events. She could only imagine what she would babble through nerves and sheer disbelief over the situation. She watched and listened anxiously as the next steps were revealed. Daghda requested that the four little men who used to appear to her out of nowhere, whom she called "the Watchers" and Smithy labelled the "twa corbies", come forward. She relaxed a little, safe in the knowledge that at least for now it wasn't either Smithy or her that was called.

In the middle of their very confusing and contradictory account of minor things, which Finn did his best to untangle in translation, Saoirse found her mind caught up in her own diddly idly tune of worries, Smithy and situation taking lead tune in that set of worries being played out. It was no ordinary worry tune, it had major phrases that were no A and B switch back and forth played three times like any other trad tune. This was a "pay attention tune". The man couldn't remember his own original language. One that he had spoken easily when he was here, in the Otherworld, before. But was language loss his only problem? Looking over the past few weeks since his return, it was clear it was something more. She looked at him, but he was focused studiously on the "twa corbies", though she knew he was listening intently to Finn's translation.

The questioning continued and other people stepped up to give their account of other tangents and other aspects to the tale of treachery. Then it was Finn's turn. He looked at her apologetically.

"You'll have to rely on Smithy to tell you what I say," he said.

Saoirse smiled and nodded. That was a small worry tune next to Smithy's complex big one. She wouldn't know what he'd said but she knew Finn's tale. She'd been there for most of it. And she wasn't certain that what she didn't know was vital anyway. The alarm that was rising was purely to with the certainty that it wouldn't be long before they were both were called.

Finn took his place near Daghda and the questioning began. Saoirse leaned over to Smithy.

"What will you do?" she asked in a low voice.

"Don't worry about it. I'll be fine."

Saoirse frowned. "So you have a plan?"

"Of sorts. It will do."

"What? What is it?"

"All in good time," he said. He turned and gave Saoirse a severe look. "You'll say nothing to anyone about this."

She drew herself up. "Of course not. What do you take me for?"

His face softened a moment. "A good person."

"Not a goddess?" she said, her tone teasing.

He gave a sad smile. "That, too."

Finn's account continued and each moment that passed served only to make Saoirse's nerves increase. By the time he bowed and made his way back to his seat, her palms were sweaty and her heart was beating rapidly, the worry tune taking on a whole new layer of complexity.

Her name, when it was called a few minutes later, was muted by the sound of her heart and the roar in her ears. Smithy squeezed her hand and released it.

She looked down at Finn. "Will you come up and translate for me?"

Finn glanced at Smithy, who shrugged. Finn nodded and the two of them made their way to where Finn had stood a few moments ago.

Daghda spoke, his words solemn in tone and Saoirse surveyed the people lining the hall. Oh feck. That Tara ballad had stuttered sideways and comic notes and words crept in. Would she giggle? Then she noticed some leaning forward, while others shuffled and looked uncomfortable. Discomfort over what? She knew Daghda would be mentally noting all of this and had no doubt would be much better placed to make conclusions than she was. Was the comic overtone slipping sideways into tragedy like any good ballad should? *Clueless Cailín* indeed.

She was startled out of her thoughts when Finn began to

translate the words which were more or less an explanation of who she was in relation to Daghda and the rest of the Tuatha de Danann, and her recent return to the living. People exchanged glances filled with wonder, curiosity and unease. She supposed she was a wonder to them in some ways, an unknown in others and she didn't know herself what she was and would be. They couldn't imagine how much a wonder they were to her, how all of it was – this hall, this place, everything. She smashed the giggle impulse with the words from the ballad rising up. A woman so silly. No brave. She was brave. Brave woman, oh but that was a shite opening that sounded more like an opening for some American Indian thing. Or maybe some nostalgic Scots film that was more like *Not Braveheart*. No, she was brave. She'd fought. She could wield a sword. Well, she could wield a knife. She'd make Smithy show her how to fight with a sword, so she would.

When Finn finished the translation, Daghda spoke again and she realised it was time to give her account of how she came to be crossing over to the Otherworld and the events that occurred. She tried to gather her thoughts, as she had before, preparing what she would say and how she would say it.

The words came haltingly at first, all giggle impulses firmly tied down by the brave woman who was wielding a sword in her head, well at least that's how she thought she would wield a sword, and her tale unfolded. She began her tale with her arrival at Anu's and her encounter with Smithy. She had to keep correcting herself when she said Smithy's name, using Goibhniu, but eventually she found her stride, pausing occasionally while Finn made the translation for the hall.

She was just about to embark on the moment when she and Smithy had fashioned the blade, omitting their intimacy, the love, the absolute connection they'd formed both in and out of bed, when a clatter sounded across the hall. She looked over and saw Smithy collapsed on the floor.

"Smithy!" she cried. All words fled her mind and she rushed across the hall to his side.

Other shouts joined hers and people crowded around her as she knelt there. A bigger roar rose and it caused Saoirse to turn. The man who Finn had described as the small petty king had broken free of his guards, seized a dagger from someone and was holding it at Daghda's throat. The hall fell silent and, beside her, Smithy stirred. Saoirse took his hand and he squeezed it. A ruse? The squeeze reassured her, but her eyes remained fixed on Daghda and the sword at his throat. Alarm filled her at the thought of the violence, especially since she'd so recently wielded a sword in her mind, but also at the fact that Daghda, the man who she'd only recently learned was her father, was now under threat. Nothing could happen to him now, surely? She had only just begun to know him. And what did she know of him, what could she say about him in any case? Not even a twitter message worth of impressions, #mydad.

Finn approached the man, his hands held up to signify he had no weapon to hand. Finn spoke in the old language, his voice calm. The man replied, his voice angry, threatening. Daghda shifted and the man pressed the dagger against Daghda's throat, drawing blood. Finn spoke again, remaining calm, but Saoirse could see the concern in his face. The man demanded something and Finn looked to Daghda and then the king. The king sighed and said a few words, first to Finn and then to the man. The man made his way to the door, dragging Daghda after him, his eyes darting around the room at those who might prevent him from leaving.

When he disappeared through the door, silence held everyone motionless for a few seconds only and then Finn was out of the door, followed by others. Saoirse was surprised and secretly gratified to see Smithy not far behind, his collapse all but forgotten.

Saoirse made her way after them, unsure and anxious about what she might see. But she didn't get far beyond the door before the crowds prevented her from moving forward. She had no way of getting them to let her through, other than pushing and shoving. She hesitated a moment and thought, feck it all, and got her elbows out. Her elbows got her as far as Smithy. He put his arm around her and that action alone made her fear the worst.

"Don't worry," he said. "He'll return shortly. As soon as your man lets him off the horse."

"The petty king?" she asked.

"Yes. Colm, I think his name is."

"You think? You don't know?"

He looked down at her, his eyes clouded with frustration and anxiety. "Don't, Saoirse," he said. "Not now."

Saoirse sighed and nodded, allowing the comfort of his arm to be enough. For the moment. But she was determined to make the "not now" become "now" soon.

She stood there, waiting for sight of Daghda, the crowd of people murmuring around her, lost in their own speculation and comments of which she understood not a word. But then he came, his bulk that was becoming familiar striding angrily down the track in the distance.

It was only later, when he had the three of them, Finn, Smithy and her alone, that she discovered the reason for his anger wasn't just that Colm, the petty king, had escaped.

"That bastard has the sword," he said.

"The sword?" asked Finn.

"*The* sword. The treasure."

"He does?" said Finn. "How do you know?"

"Because the fecker told me, after he threw me off the horse and was galloping away. Shouted it out like it made little difference that I knew."

"Do you believe him?" asked Smithy.

"I'll find out soon enough. And if it's true, I'll have it back. And his head on a platter."

14

SMITHY

"Daghda is furious," said Finn. "He wants to act now. Rise up."

Smithy nodded. It was the best he could do, since he seemed to have left all his words across the water. It wasn't that he couldn't speak, it was that he felt choked with all that he would say, could say and should say. But all the "says" together seemed to have come up with one big nay. He was just grateful that Finn hadn't left his side, creating a buffer between him and the world. Between him and Saoirse.

He could feel her concern, frustration and anger at him simmering, even though she clasped his hand as they stood by the milking shed talking to Anu. It was where they'd found her on their return, knowing they had to tell her immediately about everything that had happened.

"That's out of the question. We're not ready to rise up." Anu sighed. "Come inside. We'll go over this in detail."

Smithy nodded, liking the idea of a break, but decidedly unhappy with the phrase "in detail". Anu looked tired and that surprised Smithy. He'd never seen signs of fatigue or real age on her, not in the usual sense of it. But now, examining her closely, he could see a grey tone to her skin, fine lines around her mouth, brow and eyes. The observation made him uneasy and the benefit of going inside, sitting down seemed to take on a different meaning. This was more than his own troubles, it was Anu's and the effects of all Balor's actions. It was thoughtless of him not to have realised, or noticed any of this before, but Anu had always seemed ever present, never changing. Indestructible? It was a witless and stupid concept and he knew better, really, but he'd never examined it closely. They weren't immortal, he'd never thought that. Time moved differently for them, the Tuatha de Danann and those from that Otherworld time. Perhaps that made him subconsciously believe Anu would always be with them. She'd always be there, always present.

Inside, they found seats at the table, the seats they selected seeming a ritual now in these increasingly frequent discussions about Balor and the events surrounding him. Maura's absence was soon rectified when she sauntered through the door.

"What did I miss?"

"Helping with cows again, Maura?" said Finn in a playful tone.

She batted her eyes in an exaggerated manner. "Why? Did you need me for something?"

Finn gave her a mock grin. "Ah sure, sometime maybe never."

She shrugged. "I was out and about, only got back and saw your message."

"Did you see anything?" asked Anu quietly. She carefully set the mugs on the table. Saoirse suddenly rose and took over.

"Let me," she said.

To Smithy's astonishment Anu nodded and took her seat while Saoirse finished making the hot drinks.

"Not a thing," said Maura. "There's no sign of him in Galway that I can see. Nothing in Clare either."

"Daghda says Manannan doesn't know where Lugh is either," said Anu. "Or Mongan. Manannan asked him."

"Would Mongan say?" asked Maura. "Those two were close. They're foster brothers, after all. And the photo. That says something."

"Photo?" said Finn. "What photo?" He looked at Anu.

Anu gave a slight shake of her head. "There's a photo?" she said.

Maura looked at Smithy pointedly. "Ask Smithy, he's the one who has it."

All eyes turned to Smithy. He shrugged. He struggled for the words and finally he managed a few, though they were close cousins to the "would, could, should" says. And maybe because it wasn't directed at Saoirse. "I showed it to Maura. She's seen it."

"The one we took from Luke's house?" asked Saoirse.

"You knew about the photo?" asked Finn, his face puzzled.

Saoirse flushed. "Yes, I did. But I didn't know if it was Lugh and I certainly didn't know the other man in the photo. I-I left it to Smithy to show you."

Finn gave an impatient snort. "But somehow he forgot."

"I showed it to Maura," Smithy said again.

"Do you still have it?" asked Anu.

Smithy slowly retrieved the photo from the inside pocket of his light jacket and held it out to Anu. She examined it carefully and nodded, passing it on to Finn, who frowned and looked over at Smithy, his expression dark and disapproving.

Anu turned to Saoirse. "Is that the man you saw with Luke at the beach?"

Saoirse took the photo and studied it briefly before nodding. "Yes, I think so."

"Now, so. Maura has a point. Do we trust Mongan's word, since clearly the two of them still have a close relationship."

"So, this is Lugh, then," said Saoirse.

Anu nodded. "And Mongan beside him."

Saoirse looked at Smithy, her expression puzzled and annoyed. He shifted under her scrutiny. Yes, he should have known, should have told her. More of those "should" and "says" to add to the pile. She wouldn't understand that instead of the "should have said", the real story was "didn't know".

"Why didn't you show us all?" asked Finn.

Wasn't he just a dog with a bone, thought Smithy. He assembled a neutral expression. "I showed Maura."

"Let's move on from that," said Anu. "It's not important in the greater scheme of things. It's more than likely that Mongan knows where Lugh is. If we work with that assumption, does it give us any more ideas?"

"Well, we were narrowing it down to surfing beaches and pubs before," said Maura. "I don't know if we can get any more specific than that."

"Have we tried all the surfing beaches? Where does Mongan surf?" asked Anu.

Finn shrugged. "I don't surf."

Maura rolled her eyes. "No one imagined you surfed. But you know how to use Google don't you?"

"Here," said Saoirse, looking down at her phone. She held it aloft. "It says there are surfing beaches here in Cork. One in Barleycove and one in Inchydoney."

Maura exchanged looks with Finn. Anu put her head in her hands. "Of course. Inchydoney. That's near Glandore, isn't it?"

"Near enough," said Maura.

"Clíodhna. Of course, he'd want to be where it all happened. Near her. The question is, will Lugh be there with him?"

"Smithy."

Smithy didn't turn. He had hoped no one would find him here after he'd left Anu's place. Had hoped she wouldn't find him, he admitted. He remained standing there, on this small rise in the hill, off the track, furze, bracken and bog all around him. He fixed his gaze on the two mounds in the distance. Mounds that represented nurturing, healing. If only. But perhaps it was more than if only.

She came up beside him and slipped her hand in his. Without thinking, his fingers closed around hers and he was surprised to feel some comfort.

She stood there silently for a moment, following his eyes, and laid her head gently against his shoulder. For some reason the gesture choked him with emotion. How the feck was he supposed to do all this. To guide her, protect her in all her innocence and to prepare for the upcoming turmoil that would surely change them all forever?

"Smithy," she said quietly.

He turned to look at her, knowing the questions were going to come now and he still didn't know how he would answer them. Would he answer them? Would he have the words?

"I want you to teach me how to use a sword."

"What?" He was so startled by what she'd said that the word just slipped out through the choked throat around all those says, shoulds, woulds and coulds.

"There's a battle coming, maybe even a war, and I want to be able to help, to fight. I have to. I-I don't want it to be like last time, where I stood by and did nothing. Like some limp damsel in distress."

"You...you don't know that's what happened," he said quietly, convinced she meant before, long ago and not a short time ago. The words came now, allowed passage since they bore no resemblance to the woulds, coulds, shoulds and the says. He made an attempt at a grin. "You may have been out wielding that sword somewhere."

She raised a brow and grunted. "Would that have been before or after the sexual assault?"

Her tone was bitter and it made Smithy wince. Her ancient story, rape, and death after giving birth to triplets conceived during that assault. He squeezed her hand again. "I'm sorry."

"So will you teach me?"

He looked at her, brushed from her face the hair which had escaped the long plait that fell down her back. She hadn't worn her hair in a coronet style since all this had begun, and for some reason it made him a little bit sad. Her clothes were more subdued in colour and style. The Doc Martens were still there, but he hadn't seen the fuchsia-coloured tights, the bright corduroy skirt for some time. The pixie bouncy girleen that had charmed him that first time was now enveloped in a different Saoirse. A Saoirse who still meant the world to him, regardless of how broken he was. A stronger Saoirse. But he would still protect her from his own demons. It would only break her heart to know that she had failed to heal him. And he knew what that kind of failure did to a person. Sure, wasn't he carrying around that exact same guilt?

"I'll teach you," he said.

"Now," she said.

He frowned. "Now?"

She shrugged. "No time like the present. I know it will take more than one lesson, but we can start now."

Smithy sighed and nodded. "Right, so. Now it is."

HE COULD SEE the muscles in her forearm flex and strain to hold the sword in place. She was growing tired, but her face was filled with determination. He gave a small snort, recognising the stubbornness that caused her jaw to set and her shoulders to straighten.

"We'll finish now," he said. "That's plenty for the first time."

"No, I'm fine to continue. I want to."

"We'll stop," he said firmly. "It doesn't matter what you want. Your body needs time to get used to using those muscles, to absorb what you've learned. I don't want you to injure yourself, either. It will only set you back before you're even started."

She opened her mouth to argue but then shut it. Eventually she nodded. "Right. Yes. It makes sense."

She reluctantly handed Smithy the sword. He took it from her, walked towards the house. He could hear her slightly panting as she followed him and swallowed a smile. She was still feeling the workout, though he knew she was trying to hide it from him.

Once inside the sitting room, he took up the cloths and wrapped the swords in them, ensuring that the oil in the cloth still was sufficient. Once wrapped, he placed the swords in the narrow chest on the floor. He'd put the chest away later.

"Cuppa?" he asked.

She nodded and followed him to the kitchen and took the mugs out while he filled the kettle and turned it on. Tea bags in place, milk out. She was nearly doing it all while he looked on, watching her face, still reddened from the work out.

"Feeling okay?" he asked.

"Grand out," she said and gave a sniff.

"Make sure you take a hot bath when you get back to Anu's," he said.

She waggled her brows. "You could give me a massage," she said.

He laughed. "You don't want me to give you a massage. Your muscles would end up mangled."

She smiled. "Ah, no. I'd not object to any mangling you'd give me."

He snorted but decided not to respond. The kettle boiled and he took over, glad for a task that kept his hands busy and his mind focused. But before he'd completed it, Saoirse spoke.

"Let me help," she said quietly.

He stilled, his back to her, her words about more than making tea. She reached to get her mug, still clutched in his hand where he stood by the worktop. She placed her other hand on his shoulder.

"I'm a healer, Smithy. Let me help."

Slowly he turned to face her. "What do you mean?"

She knitted her brows. "I know something is wrong. You said yourself that you couldn't remember the language of the Otherworld. And you didn't recognise Lugh and Mongan in the photo. And the music. Something's not right there is it?"

He stared at her and started to open his mouth to refute her words, but she placed a finger on his lips.

"Don't deny it Smithy. You know it's true. I know it's true. Let's now look at what can be done."

Her face matched the solemn tone she'd used and Smithy looked away, unable to bear it. But that slight glimmer of hope had been lit and he cursed it. "There's nothing you can do."

"How do you know that? You don't. And it can't hurt to try."

He sighed and looked back at her. "Where would you start? You remember nothing, Saoirse. How would you know how to be Bríd the healer?"

She bit her lip. "We have to try, Smithy. I want to. We found the magic before, the two of us. Who's to say we won't find the magic again, for this?"

He snorted again, but found the hope unfurling in his chest. "How? What would you do?"

She took a deep breath and shook her head. "I don't know."

She paused. "The music? We could start there. That's where it began before."

He looked down and gave a bitter laugh. "That was when I had the music. I don't now."

She gave him a stricken look. "All of it?"

He shrugged. "The parts that matter."

"What else, Smithy?"

"What else, what?"

"What else is gone?"

He shrugged. "It's as you said." The words were more choked, he was more choked and he looked up to the ceiling and tried to swallow. But no more words would come. He shook his head.

Saoirse wrapped her arms around him. "Oh, Smithy."

He stood there, allowed the arms, but wouldn't respond. She pulled away after a few moments.

"Has it happened all at once?"

He looked at her and sighed after a few moments. Then he shook his head.

"Gradually, so."

She took his hand. "Come on, We'll try for a gradual return. With the music."

He allowed her to lead him back into the sitting room, thinking of the tunes he'd managed recently. A "perhaps" and "maybe" entered his mind and did a careful jig.

"Your flute?" he asked. "Did you want me to take you to get it?"

She shook her head. "I'll sing, you play."

He nodded. He could possibly pick up the tune, it would be slower, but not necessarily the usual patterns he felt were now learned that all the dance tunes possessed. Still. Still and all.

He drew out his fiddle and tuned it up, his fingers slow and meticulous in their actions. He could feel her hand on his back, a slow rubbing motion that soothed him. He felt a knot loosen.

She began her song, a *suantraí*, a lullaby, and it was soft and delicate, unwinding its melody slowly. He played along, the tune simple enough and felt it wrap its warmth and reassurance around him. Her hand was still on his back, rubbing up and down in a hypnotic motion and inside he swayed and turned to the music, to her voice as she mesmerised him, like the motion of the leaf cast adrift in the wind, floating to the ground.

While he played, he felt the ease of it, the beauty of the music and the beauty of her. They enveloped him and it gave him hope.

She ended her song, leaned down and kissed him. Her lips felt soft and sensual, they felt right. They felt home. He opened his eyes and she opened hers. They stared at each other, not daring to say a word until he blinked. The blink was enough, and he realised she knew, though he'd tried to keep it hidden from her. To keep the sadness that he knew was there, in the depths of his eyes.

She rested a hand on his cheek. "Gradually, Smithy. It will come."

He nodded and resisted a sigh. The comfort, the warmth had faded now, along with the careful jig of hope. The song was beautiful. Her voice was a balm, a joy and so much more. But it hadn't been enough. For a few moments only he'd felt the surge, but it was gone now and he wasn't sure what he'd felt was anything more than wishful thinking.

15

LUKE

I stared at the surfboard now strapped to my SUV roof, my mind still reeling. Though I'd planned to pack my bags this morning in preparation for heading off with Clio, I still couldn't believe that they were there now, in the back of my SUV and my board already on my roof. I'd watched in horror as Mon threw all my belongings in my sports bag, saying nothing and then, when all my things were inside, shoving it into my arms. He'd marched me to the door, shoved me out and followed me closely with the surfboard. When we'd arrived at my SUV he'd put the board down beside it and without a second glance, turned and walked away.

Wordlessly I'd put the surfboard on the roof rack, but now, as the recent conversation came flooding back, I could only stand and stare. Stupidity didn't even cover it. Feckin' Eejit times infinity came a little closer. Dumbest fecker in both worlds sounded okay. I could think of a few in the Hall of Tara who might get a good snicker out of it. Social media for #Sídhedum-dum. Down beat. A "beat me up beat". Sounded like the right beat, the only beat for me at this moment in time. Beat me up please and one and two.

I shook my head. This would get me nowhere. I had to get somewhere. Anywhere away from this. From her. I needed to think. Too much was going on, too much had happened and instinct told me there were rumblings. More than what Mon had relayed to me about Balor and the other Tuatha searching for me. I took a deep breath and conceded that I needed some answers first, before I went anywhere. That's if I could get them.

I LEANED against the wall outside the pub, but a moment later I straightened when I saw the familiar figure emerge. She spotted me and grinned. I blinked, unable to force a smile. I nodded to my SUV.

"I'm just over there. Come on."

She leaned up and kissed me on the cheek and gave my arm a squeeze, but I headed off before she could do more. We crossed the road and got inside the SUV. She chatted away, ignoring my bad mood. I could feel myself softening at the sound of her voice, wanting to pull her hand to me, to place it on my thigh. Wanting to pull over. Feckin' eejit I thought. Shee dum dum. Shee dum dum. I kept up the words, the rhythm, and beat it out softly on the steering wheel as I drove down the road. Soon we were out of town and headed towards the beach.

"Did you want to stop there?" said Clio. "I thought you already surfed with Mon this morning."

"I did. I just wanted to check something," I said, making my tone even. It took effort. Talking and keeping that beat going in my head. Keep it going. Keep it going. Shee dum dum. Shee dum dum. You dumb fae fecker.

I managed to keep it up, to my surprise, perhaps my years of training oh so long ago weren't lost to the mists of time. I found myself parking the SUV, getting out and moving down to the beach, Clio trailing behind me silently. She knew something was going on, but I wasn't quite ready yet.

I found the place, the set of dunes with tall grass, nearly wild off to the side on the way down to the beach. There were few enough around now anyway, the weather gone a bit wild. I noted that detail subconsciously, but now I wondered if Mon had anything to do with it. Whipping up the waves, angry and roiling like he was. The thought hardened my resolve. I turned to her.

"Why? What do you want from me?"

She looked at me in surprise. "What do you mean?"

"No pretence, Clíodhna." I spoke her name with an angry sarcasm. "Tell me why you enchanted me."

She looked at me, full of pleading. "For you, Lugh, for you. Because I wanted you. I-I couldn't risk your rejection, I wanted you so much."

I snorted. "Oh, I am flattered you thought your beauty wasn't enough for me."

She laid a hand on my chest and I threw it off. "Please, Lugh, don't be that way. I'm being honest. I wanted you. Can't you see that? How could I fake that?"

"Oh, I'd say you could fake much, if the desire was there. Or something else."

She bit her lip. "It wasn't faking."

"I don't believe you. Tell me why you did it. Was it Mon? Did you want to get back at him?"

Clio's eyes darkened. "That bastard? I don't need to enchant you to get back at him. I get back at him every day of his life."

"Why? Hasn't he suffered enough?"

"Suffered enough? He could never suffer enough after what he did. What his father did."

"Can't you learn to forgive him? He loved you. He loves you still. He regrets every bit of what he did."

"He made his father trick me. Lulled me to sleep while Ciabhan was hunting and then sent a wave to wash me away back to the Otherworld. Kept me there while Ciabhan mourned me for dead. Ciabhan, the only one I've ever loved! How could Mon have loved me if he did that? He deserves all his suffering and more."

"So," I said. "You didn't enchant me because of desire or love, then."

She opened her mouth to speak and then closed it. I took her wrist and squeezed it tight. "Why did you do it? Why now, here?" My voice held a threat and a promise.

She looked at me with contempt but remained silent.

Suddenly, I knew. "Balor. This has to do with Balor, doesn't it?"

I saw a flicker of fear, but then it vanished. "You think you're so powerful, golden boy. So talented. Such a warrior," she said with a snort. "But you're nothing. I didn't even have to work at it, and you were already at my feet. I only bound you there because they wanted extra assurance." She paused and looked at me. "I could keep you there, even now." Her face transformed, losing its anger and she smiled at me seductively. "You still want me, don't you, Luke?" She raised a hand to my cheek and brushed softly against it with the backs of her knuckles. "So willing, aren't you, so willing."

I could feel the draw, even now, after all that had happened between us. She leaned forward and placed a kiss on my lips and for a moment I responded. Shee dum dum. I summoned the beat and kept it with me, kept it going as I threw her off and marched away up the path and back to the car park. Once there, I got into my SUV and headed off. Away.

I didn't allow myself too much time to think, I knew what I had to do. I drove, heading towards the roundabout and the bypass and when I saw the petrol station, I pulled in. Once in the toilets I shut and locked the door, went over to the sink. A hazy image stared back from the clouded mirror above the sink. I pulled out my pocket knife, slid the blade open and began to hack at my plaits. It was a messy job, but I didn't care what I looked like, I just knew that I had to get them off. When I was finished, I stared at what remained of my hair. I decided a hedgehog would find me good company.

With the hair finished I turned my attention to the other mementos that remained from Clio. The ear stud was quickly dispensed of, the nose ring a little more delicate to remove but I managed it without too much trouble. I cut off the leather band around my wrist, lacking the patience to manage sea swollen knots. I wanted to sever that connection anyway, and this seemed the best approach.

Those bits removed, I gathered them up, including the plaits and put them in the bin. I took a deep breath. There was one remaining memento. I looked at my arm, the disc shaped tattoo peeking out from my T-shirt sleeve. What had seemed small when it was first inked, now seemed extremely large. Still, it had to be done.

I reached inside my sports bag, searched for a few moments and drew out some athletic tape. I used it occasionally on my ankles when I surfed but it would serve a different purpose now. A wad of toilet roll was put next to the tape, on the shelf above the sink.

A knock sounded on the door. "Hurry up, mate," said the voice. English.

"Sorry, now, I'll be out soon."

All time for hesitation or care had passed. I took up the knife and cut, wincing with the effort to hold back the moans and cries of indescribable pain as I cut out the last remaining binding Clio had wrought. The blood flowed, but still I cut, until it was done. Quickly, I pressed the thick wad of toilet roll against my arm and started winding the tape tightly around my arm. It wasn't going to last long, but it was only temporary, until I could get something better. It would get me out of here.

"Come, on, mate, there are others here who need it badly."

"Sorry, sorry," I said. "I'm coming now."

Hastily I cleaned up the mess as best as I could and tossed on a sweatshirt. That would keep the worst from showing. My arm was throbbing with pain so much that it was difficult to concentrate. I forced myself to breathe slowly and grabbed my sports bag and opened the door. I plastered on a bright smile.

"Sorry, now. All yours," I said.

I staggered away to my SUV, threw the bag into the back and got into the car. I needed to get away from here. Far away. I just didn't know where. But first, some supplies from the pharmacy. I weighed my pain, my ability to drive and how long my tight bandaging would last before numbness set in, or the blood soaked my shirt noticeably, and the distance to the next town. Skibbereen was big enough, not too far. Or would I go to Bandon? I ruled out Dunmanway, and Macroom seemed too far. I pulled out into the road and headed west. West. It always drew me, like the sea. West along the road. The Westerly Isles, Into the West.

PART II

THE WISE WOMAN OF BEARA

16

SMITHY

"You have to come," said Finn. His face was full of amusement, his wiry auburn curls more out of place than usual. "It'll be good craic."

"Good craic?" said Smithy, his tone full of disbelief. "Hunting a dangerous man with Nemed's magic sword will be good craic? I'd say it's cracked you'll be if you think that."

"Ah, come on, now, Smithy. You and me. It'll be grand."

Smithy looked out of his kitchen window to the yard, and, in an effort to calm his panic, tried to focus on the fallen leaves that had begun to clutter it. It would be Lughnasagh soon. August 1. Just a few days away. And Lugh was no closer to being found, not really. Maybe they'd find him on his feast day, he thought grimly. And Smithy? He was still…well, still. Despite Saoirse's efforts. Bríd's efforts. It didn't matter what name he gave her in his thoughts, didn't change the outcome. The music was only a flicker inside him, nothing more, and that was after numerous tries.

"You'll come then." Finn punched his arm.

"I said no. Besides, Anu told you to go, not me."

"Ah, now. She didn't say you shouldn't go."

"She might want me for something else. Something with Saoirse."

"Come on. You know you want to. Besides, it makes sense for you to come. It's a sword. You know swords, you craft them."

"Anu told you to go, a champion who fights with swords. Surely that's better."

"No, what's better is for us both to go. Someone who fights with swords and someone who creates magic swords as well as fights with them. What better combination?"

"Maybe someone who knows how to hunt the bastard?" Smithy said. It was impossible. He had to find a way to get out of this because he wasn't able for it, couldn't go across the water with Finn. He would put Finn at risk as well as himself.

"You're coming and that's the end of it."

Smithy took a deep breath. "Fine, so. We'll go in a few weeks' time. I have some things to sort and it will give us both time to prepare. To create a plan." Maybe in that time he could make some headway with Saoirse. Or find a way to get out of this mad plan to retrieve Nemed's magic sword.

"No," said Finn. "We go now. Anu's orders."

Smithy raised a brow. "Anu's orders?"

Finn shrugged. "Well, she told me to go as soon as possible."

"She told *you* to go as soon as possible."

"Same difference. Now get your sword and let's go."

"Where's your sword, your shield?"

"Oh, that's already secured over there. We'll pick it up."

Finn headed into the sitting room and dragged out the small chest from under the sofa where it was usually kept. He snapped his fingers at Smithy, who handed over the small key that unlocked the chest. The swords were withdrawn and Smithy chose one, his thoughts whirring in a spiral of feckityfeckfecks that he couldn't stop except for the occasional "jaysus", "ah janey" until he descended into "holymarymotherofgods" that was almost more bizarre to him than the situation facing him. He couldn't tell Finn. He couldn't. His thoughts, still in the spiral, wouldn't unlock the chokehold his voice seemed to be in again.

Finn clapped him on the back. "Are you set then, Smithy, me lad? Let's go find this sword."

"Are you all right?" asked Finn.

Smithy shrugged and nodded. He opened his mouth and managed to croak out a "grand" after a few moments, but nothing more than that. He'd been blindly following Finn since they'd left his house and now, trudging along the road, heading towards a small tower where Finn had his weapons here, across the water.

He kept scanning their surroundings, looking out for what, he hadn't a clue, but anything could pose a threat to him in his current state. The spiralling loop of words was still there, but not screaming down all other thoughts, and for that he was grateful. He touched the sword at side, the sword belt slung across his jeans. He wore his padded motorbike jacket as an added precaution, but still he felt naked and vulnerable to attack. Finn's clothes weren't much different, but that didn't seem to help. They both wore thick boots that were more than a match for much that was worn here. And Smithy's skill with the sword seemed intact still. At this point. He couldn't count on it continuing, and so, the sooner they located this sword and took it the better, as far as he was concerned. He'd forgo all and any craic to be had, if only it could be done quickly and simply, with harm to none.

They stopped outside the tower. It seemed deserted, but all

the same, Smithy wasn't going to take a chance. Finn didn't look pleased, but he said nothing and banged on the large wooden door. A battered middle-aged man with greying hair, stubby nose and scarred face opened the door.

"Fachtna," said Finn.

Fachtna gave a brief bow and held the door open. Finn strode inside and Smithy followed. It was simply furnished, the stone floor and walls bare except for some tapestries and old rushes strewn around.

Finn spoke and Smithy heard the words, but still had no idea what they meant, except for the mention of "Ogma", Finn's name. His real name. At least Smithy remembered that much. He bit his lip in frustration, the feckityfeckfeck loop getting louder now. Ah now, calm yourself, he thought. It'll be grand.

Finn nodded and glanced over at Smithy with a shrug. He spoke a few words to Fachtna and gestured to Smithy to follow him. Gestures, yes. He could handle gestures.

Finn led him to a small room off the main hall of the tower. There was only a chair, a bench and several chests there. Finn selected one chest, in the corner. Smithy was surprised at the modern heavy-duty padlock that was fastened on the chest. Finn withdrew keys from his jeans pocket and unlocked the padlock. Inside was an oiled cloth bundle. Finn unfolded it and withdrew a beautifully crafted scabbard holding a sword, the hilt finely wrought in silver, engraved with symbols. Smithy stared at it, longing to touch something so beautiful.

"You sure that isn't the magic sword?" he said, his tone joking.

Finn laughed. "Ah, you know yourself the magic it holds, since it was you who made it."

Smithy nearly laughed, thinking it was a joke, part of the craic, but he saw from Finn's expression that the joke was on

Smithy. He'd made that? Feck's sake. How could he ever match that now?

Unthinking, he squatted down and ran his hand lightly along the scabbard. "I'd forgotten how fine it was."

"No modesty, here, then," said Finn with a laugh. He picked up the sword belt first, fastened it around his waist with the scabbard and sword attached. He stood up. "Let's be on our way, so, Fachtna says there's no trouble."

"Where are we going? I mean where do we start? We don't know anything really."

'We'll go to Colm's holding. See if we can find out any information. What else would we do? Would you have a better idea?"

Finn's tone was just a little impatient, laced with a hint of puzzlement. What else indeed would they do? Smithy shrugged. "Grand. That's sound enough. Just checking."

Finn nodded and he clapped Smithy on the shoulder. "No time to waste, then."

THEY TOOK two of the horses from the stable and Smithy was glad of it. A slight weakness in his left leg was starting to play up and if they'd kept on foot he wasn't certain how long he could conceal it from Finn. The whole thought of it made him want to draw his sword and put an end to the leg in some way. At least then there would be no question about his fitness for retrieving the sword.

They carried on for some time, Finn leading, a fact for which Smithy was grateful. Though it was his role to be in the lead, Smithy reasoned, Anu had sent Finn. Or rather Ogma in his role as king's champion. Or was it former king's champion? Lugh had won that role, but then, he wasn't in the picture any longer. These thoughts were all in the realm of "beside the point" and just "pointless" in aim and result, but it kept Smithy from other thoughts that were very much the point. And all those points pointed. Pointed at him with accusing fingers, shaking fingers, wagging fingers and anything else that was filled with reprimand and accusatory. Just tell them, the fingers said. Just tell the truth you cowardly eejit. You'll get yourself and Ogma killed.

Ahead, Finn's horse reared slightly and halted. Smithy drew up quickly and looked ahead. Almost directly in front were a group of short dark men, spears in their hands. They looked none too pleased. One of them stepped forward and looked directly at Smithy. He spoke and Smithy sat, frozen in the saddle, unable to understand.

"We should dismount," said Finn. "It won't serve anything if we show the Hunters disrespect."

Smithy nodded and carefully slid from his horse, Finn doing the same. The dark-haired man stepped in front of Smithy and spoke again.

Smithy looked at him. Feckityfeckfeck was having a field day in his head. Smithy made a great effort to shove it aside. He bowed low and said in Irish, "I'm sorry if I have offended you, my lord." Sure, a bit of grovelling never hurt, he reasoned, all the while praying that they understood the Irish.

The leader snorted. He pointed at Smithy. "You owe us a debt," he replied in Irish.

The relief at understanding was instantly replaced by alarm. Debt? What the actual feck was he supposed to do with that? "Uh, exactly what is the debt?" He tried to sound authoritative.

The leader frowned and snorted. "You made a bargain with us. Are you so stupid that you pretend you don't remember?"

"What's he talking about?" asked Finn. He turned to the men. "Are you sure you have the right person? Smithy is hardly here. Except for two brief times. Is this a debt from long ago?"

"He bargained with us recently," said the leader. "In the forest. For safe passage. We've come to collect."

Smithy stared at them, searching for a clue about this debt. He may not remember, but he didn't need a memory to understand that this debt wouldn't be any trifling thing, and he had even more suspicion that the consequences of either fulfilling it or avoiding it wouldn't be trifling either.

17

———

LUKE

"West Along the Road". That's what I'd done all right. Gone along and kept going, stopping only in Skibbereen long enough to properly bandage my arm. It would make quite a scar, but it was no price to pay and a reminder. My arm throbbed now and I knew I needed food and drink, if only for the sake of the arm. I hadn't fancied stopping at Glengarriff, but now I regretted it. Adrigole was my next possibility and I could only hope there would be a shop open at least, though it was well past six. Sure, it was summer, everything was open, wasn't it?

Eventually, I saw the signs for Adrigole and after some twisty bends and signs that might have taken me elsewhere, I came upon a shop and pulled in. There were a few other cars and a man emerging from the shop itself. I sighed, my stomach already rumbling at the thought of food. At least a sandwich, or a packet of crisps.

I passed by the man who'd just emerged with a nod and "how's things" and his matching return, followed by the weather talk and all good things.

"That your surfboard?" he added, nodding towards my car.

"It is," I said, recognising the chat and *aon scéal* stance he'd taken. I moved to the side. His trousers were old, dirty and his jumper had that seeking a shape look. I didn't need to see the wellies to identify his profession. I grinned. This could be good.

"You coming from Barley Cove?"

I shrugged. I wasn't certain I wanted to say. "I surf all different places. Making the rounds, I am."

"The Wild Surf Way," your man said, playing on the Failte Ireland's promotion branding for the coastal roads in the west, The Wild Atlantic Way. Like the laddaí had, only with your man it was funny. His delivery, his expression, I don't know what it was, but it stirred the old bog fire of the soul all right. It was as if he could sense I needed this balm. A grounding, a reassurance that some things were still right with the world and time could be taken for the little things.

"Something like that," I said.

"You won't find much surfing this way," he said.

I laughed, going along. "Ah but this way is my way for now."

"A different way?" He raised a brow. "A better way?"

"I hope so."

"It will, lad. It will, if you make it so."

He clapped me on the shoulder and headed out to his SUV, a battered old Toyota, dusty and with a rusty trailer hitch on the back. I watched him climb in, start up the engine and then pull out. With a brief raise of his hand, he was gone, out into the road and disappearing into the distance, heading west.

I stared after him a moment, watching the road, puzzled about his words and trying not to read too much meaning in them. Had there been something familiar about him? I didn't think so, but his words, how he made me feel, were all so…I struggled for the right word…comfortable? Comforting? Calming? In addition to the grounding and reassuring elements? Or was it all the same? I just knew that the feeling of loss, shame, rage, and desire to run as far away as possible had now slowed and was so much less urgent than before.

I shook my head and made my way inside the shop. I wandered the aisles and eventually picked up a sandwich and a fruit juice, paid for them and left. Once inside my SUV, I contemplated my next steps, eating slowly.

I'd been drawn along this road, the western road and I didn't know why. I hadn't cared initially, my "just get the feck away" in full force. Now, I wanted to know why. There was nothing this way that I could think would cause me harm. No one who knew I was heading this way. There was certainly nothing that would attract Luke the surfer. Luke the musician. The scenery was grand, beautiful, nothing to doubt that. But, no. A start of a McCarthy's pub crawl from Castletownbere was certainly not going to get me in my SUV. I had never expressed interest in the Buddhist retreat centre further up this peninsula. I had a mild curiosity about it, but nothing more.

I shrugged, finished my sandwich and leaned my head back against the seat.

A while later I woke with a start. I checked the time. Two hours. I'd been asleep two hours. Feck. It must have been the blood loss along with the rest of the mess that had been this day. I shook my head to clear it and started up the engine. I hesitated a moment before pulling out on the road, but shrugged and continued to head west.

I PULLED into the car park just off the main road in Castletownbere. It was dusk by then and in the dim light I could see the lights from the harbour and the ships anchored there. Behind me the Supervalu had just closed, but I hoped that somewhere along the main street I could find something to eat.

And maybe a place to sleep. It was a plan, of sorts, but I still wasn't committed to here, or anywhere along this peninsula.

It was sometime later, after a hearty bowl of chowder and feeling "all ahoy" from the restaurant decor and the outfitted waitress, I made my way back to the SUV. No rooms to be had in this scenic town in the height of summer when the weather was good. The holiday homes filled, the friends visited and the draw of the Beara Peninsula was in full force. Sure, I couldn't argue with them, wasn't I visiting myself, though the scenery was more of a bonus than a destination.

Once in the car, I decided to make myself comfortable in the back and hoped no zealous garda would decide this was not a camping zone. My arm still throbbed, though not as badly as before. I didn't want to risk checking the bandage in the dim light that was available. It could wait until morning. And then what? I asked myself. Exactly so. A wandering pilgrim am I? Blarney pilgrim, maybe. Was that what I was going to do? The lights from the ships winked at me, like some flirty woman. Was that the answer? Board ship? Stow away? Get a job on one? Who actually stowed away, except migrants forced from their lands by war and severe economic hardship?

More to the point, what was I running from? Who was I running from? Sometimes I didn't know. All the "ride the wave" joy that had inhabited me for the last few years seeped out of me. Deflated balloon, me. One feckin' deflated balloon. Without the punch and jab of Mon's good humour that had lifted me beyond numbered times, I was deep in the realms of self pity and loathing.

"Oh, feck off with yourself," I muttered. I turned on my side and tried to find rest.

IT WAS the tune that woke me up. For a moment I thought it was outside – some busker chancing it outside the Supervalu. But it wasn't, the tune was in my head. Cutting up a storm, a mad dash across a reel and a polka, then winding down into a slide and then an air.

I realised now it had been going through my head with all its vigour and vibe throughout the night, or at least the hours I'd snatched since I finally managed to doze off sometime after two in the morning. I picked up my phone and saw the time. Feck. Just gone six.

I eased the crick in my neck and tried to straighten my cramped legs. Nothing would be open for a while, so I was best off just trying to get back to sleep. But the tune, or rather, tunes, wouldn't leave. It was the mad dash reel now, gearing up in full-fledged insanity, the tune playing out in roaring mandolin picking. I tried to identify it, but after a moment realised it was unfamiliar. Good though. Something special. I grinned. With it playing in my head all night, there wasn't a chance I would forget it. At least that was something. I sighed and folded my arms at the back of my head. I may as well enjoy the music, pick apart the patterns, the nuances, maybe add a flourish here or there.

By the time the slide was playing in my head I began to wonder. Wonder and ponder. This was no set. Of course it wasn't. Unless you called it the "No Sense Set". With an air tacked on. An air, when it started playing again, that had something in it beyond special. Not a touch of lament, betrayal or any sorrows that though common in pain, were uncommon in sound and word. Not even a *suantraí*, nothing sleepy or soothing about it. It swayed, it enticed, it "come hithered". And the more I heard it, the more I wanted to play it, to have it enter my body and fill me up.

But no.

Ponder.

The wonder, I shoved aside. I could wonder why, wonder who, but I wasn't having that. I was having to leave. Escape. I wouldn't be drawn. Not again. I was not going to be thrice the fool and more shame on me. I had enough shame as it was. Pondering done. The ponder and the wonder went back in their box and I was getting up. I glanced over at the ships. I hadn't a clue. No clue. Oh feck it.

I got out of the back of the SUV and slid into the driver's side, conscious of my arm throbbing like a Saturday night disco. I'd picked up some pain tablets in Skibbereen and I swallowed a couple of those with a mouthful of bottled water, then slipped the key in the ignition, starting up the SUV.

I pulled out into the road and just drove, veering up, heading for the hills. The road took me where it took me, the tunes fading – but the air, it hung around me, trying for the all of me. The fill of me. Ah, no, no.

I stopped in Allihies. Not because I wanted to, or the air had run its course, but because I stopped. I made it practical, discounting that my hands and fingers seemed to have done all the work ahead of my practical reasoning. So I got out of the SUV, searched for some little shop, something I could get a cuppa, or a coffee and maybe something to eat. The village was sleepy, waking slowly with an "at your leisure" kind of manner. And despite myself, or because of myself and my air, I eased my way out of the car, my own "at your leisure" matching my view and the whole idea of a sleepy Irish village in the grips of a lazy summer day.

The shop, when I found it, was all nods and "howareyous" and weather remarks, but sure, wasn't that the craic. It was, so. And I was happy to be part of it. Wanting nothing more than same old, grand old. So I could be grand out.

And maybe it was the saying it, the acting it, I became part of it and I was. Grand out. Except for the old throb in the arm. But ah, now, what can you expect? I'd take care of that in a moment.

I found a place on a wall to drink my coffee, eat my breakfast roll and avoid imponderables. Because I was grand out. The village, when surveyed from the wall, looked good, so. A place to meander, a walk around. To bide a bit of time and ho, ho, is that a B&B I spied? Maybe so. Or a room above a pub. Bound to be something. This wasn't a destination place. It was where you stopped for lunch, a break in the journey, so.

These thoughts were ponderables and I let them wander on around my mind, sipping and munching. The music, soft and hardly there became even fainter and I smiled. Ponderables, that was all it took. And food and drink.

Drink made me think of the pub and I wandered down to it, stopping outside its window. It had potential, so it did. Nothing outrageous in the paddywhackery department, nothing "ahoy" about it. Your usual. A pub. A "down the road" pub. I noticed the small board up on the wall just tucked inside the doorway. "Session every Thursday, 10pm". A small jump of the heart registered the pleasure I felt at just reading those words. Yes, this is me grand out.

But I paused on my grandness. "Take care" took over. Would I risk it, going to a session? Sure, who would be out in this peninsula? What harm, eh? I frowned and sighed. It became an imponderable. Never mind, so. Time to search out digs.

18

SAOIRSE

Maura was there by the time Saoirse arrived back at Anu's. She'd gone to Smithy's again. Third day in a row, only to find that he wasn't there. She was getting beyond impatient, she was worried. She'd let herself in with the key, noted the empty sink, the cold stove and the neglected bed. His forge appeared equally neglected. Beyond that, she could find no traces of where he might have gone. His fiddle was there, untouched in the corner, but lately, with his growing despair, that meant little. Or could mean little.

It was only after standing in the middle of the room for what might have been an hour thinking, reaching out to him and trying to feel at least the remnants of him, or lingering notes of his song, his hum, that she'd thought of something. And that thought sent a chill up her spine, a chill so strong that it might be classed and named as a hurricane. Quickly, before she lost her nerve she moved to the flat chest under the sofa and drew it out. She saw the lock, knew Smithy had the key on him, but something about it, the sheer arrogance of it as it lay there locked, convinced her that it would contain at least one item less. Still, she made herself lift it. She sighed, rose, and moved toward the forge, the key on the ring containing the house key fitted the padlock and a moment later she opened the door to the forge. The hammer was there on the worktop.

It didn't take her long, once she had the hammer. One blow across the lock and it was broken. She lifted the lid, unfolded the cloth. There, the visual proof. She hadn't needed it, but she knew that if anyone else were to be convinced, she had to confirm it. A sword was gone.

Now, as she entered the house and saw Maura talking with Anu, there was only one thought on her mind. Find Smithy.

"And Mongan said he didn't know where Lugh was," said Anu.

Maura shook her head. "Not beyond what I'd said. That he'd been there, but now he was gone. Clíodhna got her hand on him for a time, but he left a few days ago."

"Clíodhna?" asked Anu. "What did she want with him?"

"Fecked if I know. Mon was nearly incoherent on that point. Claimed she wanted revenge on him, but I don't believe that."

"Ah, well, that's understandable, so," said Anu. She sighed. "Oh, Mongan. He must reconcile to the situation. It's beyond time."

"Yeah, well, tell him that and he'll bite your head off."

"You talked with Mongan?" asked Saoirse, cutting in.

Maura turned and looked at her. "I'm just back from Clonakilty. Found Mongan there. And just missed Lugh, apparently."

"Who's Clíodhna? No, you can tell me later. At the moment, I just want to ask if either of you know where Smithy is."

Maura looked at Anu and shrugged. "Haven't seen him in days."

Anu shook her head. "I've been giving him a bit of time to himself. To clear his mind. He seemed troubled."

"Does Finn know?" asked Saoirse.

Maura shook her head. "I doubt it. He's gone to the other side of the water."

"He's in the Otherworld?" asked Saoirse. She looked at Anu. "Why?"

"For the sword," said Anu. "I asked him to go."

"The sword," said Saoirse. An ache seized her. "Did Smithy go with him?" She uttered the last words in barely a whisper.

"I didn't ask him to accompany Finn," said Anu.

"He might have gone," said Maura. "Is that a problem?"

"Is there a way to tell?" asked Saoirse. "I need to know."

"Why?" said Anu. She sighed heavily. "What's troubling him, that so clearly troubles you, now?"

Saoirse studied Anu and made her decision. "He's lost his music, some of his memory. He can't remember the old language, the language of the Otherworld. And...and I'm not sure about his physical health. His strength. He won't tell me the full extent of it, this is only what I've observed. Every time I confront him, he evades my questions. Except about the music." She looked at her hands. "I tried to help him, to heal him with the music, that strong bond we have when we play, but it didn't work. At least not enough to make a difference."

"How long has this been going on?" said Anu.

"Since we returned. Since...since we went to the Well of Slane."

Anu nodded. She looked at Maura. "See what you can find out. Meet us back here in an hour."

Maura nodded and was gone. Saoirse could hear the flap of her wings outside the window a moment later.

SHE HADN'T HELD out much hope, but still, when Maura had uttered the words she felt tears well in her eyes. But only for a moment because then it was replaced by anger. The feckin' feckless fool. And then some. But she couldn't rage here, though she wanted to, wanted to do that and more. She turned to Anu for answers, but then seeing the worry on her face, she turned again. Not to Maura, conflict loving Morrigan, whose eyes gleamed wickedly at the moment. No, she turned to herself.

She reached down deep. Looked for that goddess. The power of it. The woman who survived. The woman who gave birth, brought forth new life, inspired words and music and could forge magic. That woman. She would be that woman.

"I'll go there," she said.

"To the other side of the water? On your own?" asked Maura. "Not a good idea. Besides, Finn can look after him."

"No. He can't," said Saoirse. "He doesn't even know half of Smithy's problems. And when he does, it might be too late. Besides, I went before on my own."

Maura raised a brow. "Yes. You did. And look what happened. You can't even speak Irish."

"You'll go with her, Morrigan," said Anu.

Maura looked at Anu. "Me?" She gave a laugh. "Ah, no. I don't think so."

"You helped me before," said Saoirse.

Maura gave her a dark look. "I thought you spoke Irish," she muttered. "And I didn't think Smithy was stupid enough to be captured by a bunch of ridiculous twats."

"You know it was more than that."

"You'll go with her," said Anu, in a voice that brooked no argument. "You know what Finn's likely movements are, you know where Colm's fort is."

Maura's eyes flashed in anger for a moment, then narrowed. "Fine, so. I'll take her across. But I'm not going to take an active part over there. That's not what I do."

"You take part here, you help us here," said Saoirse. "Why not help me over there?"

Maura looked at her with cold eyes. "You don't know anything. Or if you did, you've forgotten. So it's best if you just remain silent."

"Enough," said Anu. "There's no time to waste. Get your things together. You'll leave at dusk."

THE SWORD WAS TUCKED at her side when they crossed. She knew somehow when she'd removed it from Smithy's chest that she would need it. And that she would need it because she would cross over and look for him. Like before, but not like before. This time, she was more prepared. She hoped. And she had Maura. A reluctant, surly Maura, who even now only spoke in a begrudging manner as they climbed the small rise at the bank by the river. Saoirse didn't recognise the place; it was different again to the places she'd come to before. Each time it had been different and she didn't want to ask how or why. She could only take so much of this unreal situation.

"Do you know where they are?" she asked instead.

Maura held up a hand to silence her. She stood still, staring up at the trees ahead. A moment later a raven came down to her, large and sleek. It landed on her shoulder, nearly as big as her head. Maura didn't flinch, she looked at the bird, murmured a few words. The bird rustled its feathers, uttered low guttural sounds and flew off. Maura watched the bird disappear and frowned.

Saoirse held her tongue, sensing that any probing questions would elicit nothing more than a snarl from Maura. Instead, she folded her arms and sighed. Right, so. I'll wait it out, she thought.

Maura turned to her, and still frowning, spoke. "We need to find horses."

Saoirse blinked in surprise. "Horses? Where?"

Maura gave her a sour look. "And you were going to come on your own?"

"Well I don't know where we are. I've not been here before."

"We're close to Colm's fort. But apparently, your boyfriend and that clown Finn aren't here."

Saoirse fought her surprise. "How do you know?" She saw Maura's sarcastic face and glanced at her now vacant shoulder. "Right. Of course." She sighed again. "And where are they? I presume that's where we're going now."

"To the Forest of the Hunters."

"The Hunters?"

"They're old offshoots of the Fir Bolg. You might know them as the Wild Hunt."

"I don't know them at all. But I've heard of the Fir Bolg. From Anu. They're people who were here before the Tuatha de Danann, along with the Fomorians."

"Yes. Something like that. It doesn't matter right now. What matters is that those two have managed to get themselves entangled with the Hunters."

"And I take it that's not a good thing."

"No, it isn't a good thing. They love to hunt, that's what they live for, especially the kill at the end of the hunt."

Saoirse nodded, hearing the chill of the last few words. "And you think Finn and Smithy have joined in the hunt?"

Maura laughed. "No. I think they have become their prey."

Saoirse blanched. "Their prey? But why?"

Maura shrugged. "Sport. Revenge. They don't like anyone trespassing in their forest."

"And if they catch them?"

"When they catch them. They'll kill them. Unless a bargain is struck. But that could be worse."

"A bargain could be worse than death?" asked Saoirse, incredulous.

"A bargain with them, yes."

Saoirse took a deep breath, tried to clear her head. "But they haven't been caught yet?"

"I don't know."

"But you know that Smithy and Finn are in the forest. The Hunters' forest."

"Yes. And if you want any hope of saving them, we need to move quickly."

"Horses."

"Yes. Since you can't fly."

Saoirse let the comment pass. How could you respond to that?

"Can you get us horses?"

Maura frowned. "Yes. But you have to stay here. Don't do anything. Don't move. And stay away from people."

Saoirse did a mental eye roll. What else would she do? Work on that old Tara ballad that made a lot more sense as *Clueless Cailín* who was fighting the title *Cowardly Cailín*. Not a bother, in that she would be damned if she would bother with that kind of ballad. "How far is the forest?"

"Not far. About an hour's ride on the horses."

Saoirse gaped. "That long? How long will it take you to get horses?"

"Longer, if you keep me here talking."

"Ah, feck off Maura, will you. Just go."

Maura gave her a dark look, but she turned and pointed to a small copse. "Go there. It's hidden enough. I'll return as soon as I can with the horses."

Saoirse turned and looked in the direction Maura pointed.

When she looked back Maura was gone. Up in the sky a large black crow flapped its wings. Saoirse sighed and ambled over to the copse. Already she felt nearly overburdened by this task. The sword bounced against her leg, reminding her that this was no game, not a film set and certainly not a re-enactor's playtime. Ballad turned film. Feckin' perfect. Liam Neeson? Sure trot him out. Or maybe Cillian with his old *Peaky Blinders* hair, waving a sword instead of a gun.

She settled herself down by a tree and leaned against it, deciding on a sleep. Safe enough, why not. She closed her eyes.

She awoke with a start, a hand clasped over her mouth. He spoke, but of course she couldn't understand. She tried to turn around, to reach for her sword, but her scabbard was empty.

19

———

LUKE

The session was small enough, but I had no complaints. The pub wasn't sizeable either, so the music wasn't lost in sea of conversation and clinking glasses. Local was the watchword and I certainly liked local. One or two visitors were sitting in on the session, giving it a test, so I hadn't felt alone in that. Not to say the local musicians weren't welcoming, they were all right, but also full of the elbow jabs and sly winks of people who've played together for a while.

I could interpret the language of it all and it warmed me through, especially when this young lad from perhaps Germany or maybe the Netherlands pulled up with a tuba in great spirits and exchanged glances and slight nods led them to try a tune or two and let him figure it out for himself that a tuba was best left in the back of the marching band bus it came from, or the beer garden it was destined for. A hearty clap on the back from the session leader and an offer to stow the instrument behind the bar reinforced the lad's newfound wisdom, as well as ensuring there would be no lapse in that wisdom.

It was a conversation and dance, all of it, conducted and exchanged in a language all its own, a tune that came from years and in symbiosis to the sound, the mood and the whole jiggity jig of the local's local.

It was an hour in and I was on my third pint, just settling down for the night, so I was. Getting the "ah now" going, so that it was a slide and jump and a little twist as I diddled away on first the pipes and then my mandolin. The pipes were a given at the sight of the tuba, but the "ah come on" from one of the tunes led the switch to the mandolin. I was loving it, doting on it and finally losing myself into the twists and turns, the nods and winks of it all. A few whoops and hollers and it was all polka time and then a strathspey turned up, shifting it over. The fiddle gave me a call and then the low whistle, and before I knew it, the third hour had come and gone and so had the fifth pint.

I rose for the break, the second one I think, and tried to decide between last orders at the bar, or a trip to the toilets. Toilets won out and as I made my way over a man jostled into me, his elbow finding the sorest place on my arm. I clutched it without thinking, the pain still soaring through me and I let out a curse.

"Sorry, mate," said the man, his eyes probably as bleary as mine were. "Didn't see you there."

"Ah, you're grand," I muttered automatically. I rubbed the arm and hissed, the pain soaring again. I'd have to do something about it when I got back to my room. I'd found a tiny one, but only for the night, as the weekend was booked out. Tomorrow's problem was for tomorrow.

"You're not grand, though," said a voice.

I looked over and saw a woman sitting on the bar stool. She was slightly older than me, well, than I appeared to be, or pretended to be, however it made sense. Her fair hair shone gold under the spotlight of the bar and it was woven into one long plait that hung down her back. Generous curves in all the right places, as Mon would say, were clothed in a loose linen top and trousers. There was nothing suggestive or seductive about her look though. Polite concern, a warm and caring hand put on my forearm, which I noted showed a ring on the third finger. The eyes were difficult to describe. Hazel, gold, brown. Something for a poet to contemplate, to describe. I found them compelling. Reassuring.

It was the wedding ring, though, and perhaps the seven pints (or was it eight?) that allowed just a little ease in my immediate defensive manner.

"I've a bad arm," I said.

"Hmm. I can see that," she said. "It seems really sore. Have you had it seen to?"

"It's grand, I'll live." I tried a grin.

"I'm not so sure. Do you mind if I have a look? I can see it's red around the bandage, there."

I glanced down. A small part of the bandage was visible where it peeked out from my T-shirt. And even in the dim light of the pub, I could see it was red. I touched the wound gingerly and winced again, swallowing a curse. I had felt heat there. Was an infection building? I'd given it a hasty clean when I'd arrived here, but I really didn't do much other than put a bit of Savlon cream on it and hope for the best.

"Are you a nurse? Or a doctor?" I tagged on the last bit, realising she could just as easily be a doctor as a nurse.

"Neither. But I do know something about wounds and healing."

I gave her a sceptical look, trying to see beyond the words and the touch of her hand.

"Let me help you," she said softly.

I narrowed my eyes, not trusting the words. The woman herself, well, told me different story, but I'd learned not to trust that too.

I forced a smile. "No, I'm grand. Honestly. Thanks, though."

She gave me a sorrowful look. "I know. But the offer's there. I shan't be here too long. I have to get back to my daughter."

"Your daughter?"

She nodded, took a sip of her drink. It was a glass of cider, hardly touched. "She's ten and her gran is there, but still, I don't like to be too long."

I nodded, noting the omission of a husband. Divorced? Widowed? She looked too young to be a widow, but tragedies happen at any age. And why was I even bothered?

"What's your daughter's name?" I found myself asking. As if I needed to know or it would even mean anything to me five minutes from now.

"Bláthín." She smiled when she said the name, her eyes lighting up.

"Flower," I murmured. "Is she like a particular flower?"

"Like all the beautiful and sweet-smelling ones."

"She is of course," I said.

Why was I still bantering with this woman? I swayed a little on my feet as all eight pints (surely not?) and the mad pace of the session caught up with me.

"Whoa," said the woman.

"Your name. Are you a flower too?" I asked.

"Ah, no, nothing so lyrical. I'm Kayla."

"Luke," I said.

"Luke, I think you need to gather up your instruments and get that shoulder tended."

I cocked my head and looked at her. "A glass of water and I'll be grand. Maybe a packet of crisps, too." I turned to signal the man behind the bar but he was in full "last orders" mode, as was the girl beside him.

Kayla slipped off the stool and gently took my good arm. "I think it will take more than that to make you grand, Luke."

She herded me back to the stool where my instruments

were. I frowned at the disarray in which I'd left them. The pipes were in their case, but it was still open for any stray pint to splash or person to trip over. The mandolin leaned up against the table leg and the fiddle was on top of my stool. Feck's sake, you gobshite, I cursed myself.

With studied care, born of my state that could only be down to my arm, for inebriation was not so easily won, given my origins, I packed up my instruments. Why had I brought so many? Only a braggart or a fool would have done that, no matter that at the time it had seemed a good idea and the craic had proved it so. But the "proved it so" evaporated as I gathered them up and minded my arm in the process.

Kayla, took the fiddle off me, so I'd only the mandolin and pipes then to bother with and I ended up managing them both with the one side. I followed her out of the pub, already feeling like a sheep trailing the shepherd. She took me to her car, an old battered thing that had all the markings of the farm and then some. She loaded the instruments in the back and I crawled into the passenger seat in the front. By this time my arm was on fire and I had no notion to talk, let alone argue about where she might take me.

"It's not far, Luke. Only a bit longer."

I nodded and closed my eyes. If this arm wasn't a reminder to be on my guard, I didn't know what was. I'd let her treat my arm and then get her to take me back to my room. An hour, tops. The thought reassured me enough that I allowed myself to close my eyes. Just for a moment.

It was the car door shutting that jolted me to my senses. I looked around in alarm. Kayla came to my side of the car and opened the door.

"Come, now," she said. Carefully, she helped me out of the car.

I felt a little dizzy at first, but then I righted myself after a deep breath. She took me in the back way, to the kitchen which felt warm and comforting, like her presence. It was small enough, fitting a table and two chairs, and the sink, and small fridge, cooker and presses on the other side. But even with the overhead light there was something cheering in the pine presses, the scarred wooden table and the tile floor. Nothing trendy, nothing bespoke in the Dublin way, like my house, just...average. Rural average. An average that settled inside me and eased some of the tightly curled tension.

"Sit there," she said, in her soothing voice.

I sat on the chair she indicated and rested my arm along the table with a wince. She frowned. She studied me, and I know she was noting everything about me, from the clammy skin, the slightly dilated pupils I knew I had and everything else that told her the story I'd been denying for the past hour.

After a deep sigh and a brief shake of her head she left the room for a few minutes. I could hear her murmuring to someone in the other room and a grunt in response. When she returned she had a large chest which she set on the table beside me. She washed her hands, pulled up the other chair and sat down on it.

"This isn't going to be easy for you, but it needs to be done," she said. "There's going to be pain."

I gave a shrug with my other shoulder. "No bother. I can do pain."

She raised a brow. "A hero, is it?"

I flushed and narrowed my eyes. "Hero, no. Not a hero. Just used to pain."

She nodded and began to ease up the sleeve of my T-shirt. I tried not to wince. Just the mere touch had become agony, but I was damned if I was going to let her see it.

She started to remove the dressing, gently pulling on the

tape. I bit my lip and turned my head away, trying to think of something to say to take my mind off of it.

"Is your daughter asleep?"

"She is."

"That was your mother you spoke to, then?"

"It was."

I nodded and searched for more conversation until I heard a humming. It was a tune, coming from Kayla, soft and feathery, just touching the air, wafting about until it slowly surrounded me, settling down on me. A song upon me, like a sorrow, only better and full of something so warm, sweet and soothing. She was humming it, whatever it was, and I didn't know if it had words that made it a song, but somehow I knew. *Tá amhrán orm.* A song upon me.

I hardly knew what she was doing, whether it was the song, her deft skill, or the numbness of the drink finally doing its thing, but the arm was probed, cleaned and balm from her chest applied, all in the presence of that song and the soothing calm. The bandage she used was wound around, wound to the music, with the song and filled with its rhythms.

When she was finished, she washed her hands and packed up the chest. There was no lock and she left it on the table while she boiled the kettle. She took down a couple of mugs from one of the presses and, returning to the chest, retrieved a small packet. Once the kettle had boiled, some of the contents of the packet was emptied into the mug. She stirred it around, let it steep for a moment and then strained the liquid into the other mug.

I watched her complete these tasks with just the slightest suspicion, a suspicion that grew when she handed it to me.

She saw my expression and touched my shoulder. "It's just something to ease the pain and take away the inflammation and any fever. Nothing else, I promise."

The touch, the words and the credibility of her remarks led me to nod. My ability to resist and leave was low, so I took the mug and drank it when it had cooled. She watched me for a little while and then began tidying up the kitchen and took away the chest. By the time she came back, I'd finished the drink which had a slight bitter taste, but other than that not much to speak of.

"Come with me," she said. "You're in no fit state to be on your own for the night. You can sleep in my bed and I'll go in with my daughter."

I nodded and rose. I just hadn't the energy to insist on anything else. The ordinary quality of this situation soothed me, along with the song, which echoed in my head and through my body. The arm's ache had eased, but so had my fear and tension.

I followed her through the sitting room, nodding to the woman who sat on a sofa near the fireplace, a few embers still red in the hearth. An old crane was still in place and held a kettle there.

The summer was past, gone on the tail of Lughnasagh, my feast day, and in the old ways, it was time to think of autumn harvests and the needs of winter. That's what the hearth told me, and the old woman sitting on the sofa with her penetrating hazel gold eyes, her grey hair pulled back in a bun and the shawl that was draped across her shoulders.

She gave me no greeting, but a small nod in recognition of my own and maybe more. But I was tired and wouldn't contemplate the "maybe more" aspect that had struck me with her look. I would leave "maybe more" for later. For tomorrow, with the rest of the things to think about.

20

SAOIRSE

Saoirse's captor kept a good grip on her arm as she struggled against him, his other hand still clasped over her mouth. He dragged her to her feet once it was clear she couldn't understand his words. Now they were heading away from the copse to a small track up ahead. She could see riders there, about four or five, and she presumed they were with her captor.

It was only when they drew closer, just a few metres away, that she recognised the familiar shape of one of the riders. The brawny muscular figure, the fair hair and strong nose. His startled eyes when she was shoved towards him told her that he hadn't expected to find her here. Her heart gave a small uncertain lurch at the thought that this soldier, this warrior, was her father.

"Is Maura not with you?" she said, trying to distract the direction her thoughts had taken.

"No," said Daghda from his horse, a puzzled look on his face. "Why would she be?"

Had she detected a slight defensiveness in his tone? She

dismissed it and focused on the problem at hand. "She was with me, but we needed horses so she left to get them?"

"Why do you need horses? What's brought you here?"

His tone was clipped, but there was nothing antagonistic in his manner. "Warrior down to business" seemingly was his usual approach, even to someone who was his daughter.

"It's Smithy and Finn. We came to find them and got word that they were in the forest. The forest of the Hunters." She tried to keep her words and tone neutral. Relay the facts, she told herself. The worry and problems were for later.

"And why are Smithy and Finn here?"

His words interrupted her thought train. "Oh. Ah, Anu sent Finn to reclaim the sword. To get it back from Colm." She frowned, struck by another thought. "She didn't tell you?"

Daghda's eyes shuttered. "No. Not yet. I was on my way to consult with one of the other warriors about it. I wanted to verify the truth of Colm's words."

"I think Anu felt their truth," Saoirse said. For some reason she needed to smooth things over.

"And Morrigan came with you to find them. You didn't know they were going after the sword?"

"No, yes." She heaved a sigh and began to explain the events that had brought her here with Maura. Everything but the truth about Smithy and even as she relayed the bare facts she felt how weak her story was, the reasoning feeble.

Daghda shook his head. "Let's put aside the explanation for the moment." His horse, as if sensing Daghda's need to be on his way, shifted. "Come, I'll bear you up behind me, and we can ride on."

"What about Maura?"

"She can fend for herself. She'll know where we've gone. From your words, it appears there's no time to be wasted."

Saoirse nodded, accepting the explanation, but his stiff

demeanour and edged tone told her there was something more to it. Ah the secrets, the lost memories, she thought, leave me all at sea. And then she remembered Smithy and his own situation. It could be worse, so.

SAOIRSE SHIFTED UNCOMFORTABLY in her seat behind Daghda on the horse. The journey had been quick, sped on by horses that seemed not to tire and an urgent need that was now taking hold of Saoirse so fiercely she didn't pay attention to the discomfort of her perch, or that it was Daghda's waist she was clutching tightly.

She couldn't think too much about it and her mind might tell her so, but the rest of her refused to listen. The tale it would tell, some ballad all right. A ballad that would be no mournful lament, a ballad that wouldn't have a trace of lilt or jiggity jig. No, it was still all *Clueless Cailín*. Or make that girleen. She would make it all pub song, late nights, joining in. Ridiculous. A woman with no memory, not so bad or strange. Spending time with a father that seemed a stranger, but not. Altogether not so bad, so. But the more of it, the magic, the strange events that brought them together, brought her to the here, the now and even the before of boarding school was even too much for any Irish ballad to sort out, let alone a pub song, now she thought about it. Best leave it, so. Best to leave it in all its shapes and forms to a real balladeer who might infuse the real sense of what it was. A tale to be told, so it was. A tale for the night that was in it, and all the nights after it.

She pushed that thought away and all the thoughts that went with it. Daghda was an enigma and the feeling for this father was no different than the feeling for the one before. Or less, since there was nothing there for him. Wasn't that the real tale?

Ahead, the forest's edge drew close and she realised they were here. As if to confirm her thought, Daghda stiffened and called a halt. Without a word, he helped her down and dismounted. The others prepared to follow but he signalled them to remain mounted.

"We'll go, the two of us."

She nodded, glad that he was allowing her to accompany him. Perhaps some of her very thin explanation indicated that it was important she be present too.

They approached the forest, Daghda leading, his hand resting on his sword, the tendons flexing in his forearms. It was quiet, but it loomed large before them and when they entered, the trees, everything, seemed to close around them. The familiar odours of mouldering leaves and damp loamy earth suggested nothing untoward. Lichen and moss clung to the tree trunks and branches, like every forest she'd been in. But soon the whispers started, soft and rustling at first, eventually becoming a harsh staccato. She tripped a few times, certain that the roots had moved. Present where they weren't before.

Daghda halted and she drew up right behind him. He scanned the area, his head turning only slightly. Saoirse cast her eyes around. A flicker up in the branches caught her attention. Then another and soon the branches of the tree to her right were lined with birds. They weren't crows, at least she didn't think so, but maybe a type of crow? Were they Maura's? She tried to take comfort in that thought.

Behind her, someone spoke, his voice filled with suppressed anger and something else. She didn't understand the words, but turned toward the voice. Daghda moved in front of her, blocking her view for just a moment before she stepped to the side. Three men, all carrying spears, faced her, their dark hair as straggly as their beards, their mouths full lipped and belligerent.

Daghda said a few words, his voice strong and commanding. The man who'd spoken before answered him, gave a nod of acknowledgment and then gestured to the other two. They turned and headed down a forest path. Daghda moved to follow them, but Saoirse placed a restraining hand on his arm.

"What's going on? Who are they?"

"The Hunters. Well, a few of them. They've been expecting us. Or that's what they say. Ogma has been keeping them entertained in the meantime. But, he says, now is the time for payment."

It took Saoirse a moment to realise that Daghda had meant Finn when he'd mentioned Ogma. "Payment? What does he mean by that?"

"I don't know. I imagine we'll find out. But I'm certain I'm not going to like it. Bargains with the Hunters are to be avoided at all costs."

It wasn't long before they arrived at a small clearing where a few round huts were arranged. In the middle was a huge hearth, encircled in stone, and wooden stumps and logs arrayed for seats. There were others present, about four in all, similar in appearance to the three that had escorted them. One was a woman, fierce faced, dark haired, arms crossed and indeterminate in age.

Along one of the logs sat Smithy and Finn, their feet bound and hands tied behind them. Finn was speaking, his words lilting and infused with a reasonableness that seemed to amuse a few of the Hunters and bore others.

It wasn't going to be the last time Saoirse cursed her lack of language in this world, she knew. But still, this particular time it seemed more important than ever. She studied Smithy who was surly and frowning, until he caught sight of Saoirse. His expression changed to shock and concern, only to finally settle on anger.

Without thought, she moved over and sat beside him, giving a nod to Finn, whose words seemed to have petered out at the appearance of herself and Daghda.

"What are you doing here?" Smithy hissed at her.

"I could ask you the same question," Saoirse said. "Whatever made you come to the Otherworld? Are you a complete eejit or just mad?"

He gave a snort and nodded to Finn. "Blame him."

"Oh. Right. So he dragged you here?"

Smithy gave her a dark look. "Ah, just leave it."

Saoirse swallowed her anger. What was the point? He was here, in the middle of some kind of tangle, and the sooner they got out of this tangle and returned to the other side, the better.

She sighed. "So what's the problem with them, the Hunters? What do they want?"

Smithy gave an angry snort. "They say I made a bargain with them when I was here before. And that it's time to pay up."

"Before? When we came for the judgement?"

"No. The time before that. The time..." he let the words trail off, but Saoirse knew what he meant. The time when he was captured by the Fomorians and was killed.

"What's the payment?"

He gave her a hard look. "Do you think I know?"

She stared at him, realising what he was saying. "You don't remember any of it?"

He shook his head.

"Does Finn know this?"

"I think he's come to that conclusion."

"But you haven't told him."

"I haven't told anyone," he said bitterly. "Except you."

For some reason that gave her a brief thrill. That he'd felt he could tell her but not anyone else. Then she chided herself that it was more down to the fact that she'd noticed and pressed him. Pressed him hard.

"So they won't tell you what the payment is? That's hardly going to get them anything."

"Oh, they've told us what they think the payment is, but I don't know if that was the agreement."

Her mouth formed a large "O". "Does it sound unreasonable?"

"Any payment to the Hunters is unreasonable."

"So I've heard. Chancers?"

Smithy grinned wryly. "You could say that. But with some force behind it."

She was just about to ask about the consequences of refusal when Daghda, who'd been talking to the leader, or the person she presumed was the leader, took a seat on her other side.

He began to speak in the old language and, after a glance at her, switched to English. "Goibhniu, just what were you think-ing, making such a bargain with your ones?"

Saoirse smiled inwardly hearing Daghda express himself in such a modern Irish manner, with a slightly foreign intonation that was his accent when speaking English. It came across unpractised, formal.

"I wasn't. Thinking that is," said Smithy. "I was caught and it was the only way out."

Saoirse looked at him curiously and she caught the slight shrug he gave her. Still, Daghda seemed to have accepted it.

"Well one spear is bad enough, but five swords and five spears?"

"No. No," said Smithy. "Never that much."

"How many then?"

He hesitated a moment. "One each."

Daghda nodded and Saoirse tried to assemble her features

into something that didn't shout "what the feck, you don't know that".

"It's what I would have said," Smithy muttered to her.

"Let's hope they accept that," she said.

Smithy grunted. "Oh, you can rest assured they won't."

Daghda rose, pulling himself up to his full height. Finn joined him a moment later. Smithy sighed, and with only a moment's hesitation stood and came along Daghda's other side. Saoirse stared at their backs, tense with contained energy. Oh, feck it, she thought, and made herself get up and stand beside Smithy.

Daghda spoke and Saoirse watched the faces of the Hunters carefully. It didn't take any special intuition or magic to read their reaction or know what Daghda had said. Anger darkened all their faces and most clenched their spears hard. Daghda remained impervious to their reaction as he continued to speak, his voice firm and loud.

A loud flapping interrupted the interaction. Wings everywhere, swooping birds, flying close to everyone's heads. Instinct caused most of them to raise their hands above their heads in a protective gesture. All but Daghda. He spread his legs, crossed his arms and waited.

And then Maura appeared.

SAOIRSE HAD her head in her hands. She couldn't look, not just now. The "never more" wish of the raven going through her mind, and wanting said raven to mind his own and go away. Mind "her" own, she chided. For this raven, now Maura, was making things worse. So much worse. But isn't that what Maura did? Or rather Morrigan. For that's who she was now. Her black hair flailing everywhere, her eyes glittering. Leathers, boots, and all that was Maura had vanished. Black cloth flew around her, like wings, a tunic, yet not, sectioned, shredded and fierce. A terrible beauty, a raging force.

Shouts had sounded from among the Hunters from the moment she appeared, her ravens, crows, rooks and other birds, flying madly among them all. The confusion was there, the fear and the anger. Maura had raised her arms and the birds eventually settled around her and on her.

Daghda spoke angrily to her and she gave him a cold look in return. She faced the Hunters and spoke. Finn started forward, his hand on his sword, biting out words that caused her to turn to look at him. She cocked her head, gave a wicked smile and shook herself like a bird.

"What is it, what's going on?" Saoirse whispered to Smithy.

"I don't know, do I?" Smithy said between clenched teeth.

Spears were raised, all the Hunters turning towards Daghda, Finn, Smithy and Saoirse. One of the Hunters poked Smithy with a spear tip and Smithy jolted back when it hit his skin. He reached for his sword and Finn pushed the Hunter away, frowning at Smithy, who remained where he was, his hand resting on his sword, but nothing more.

Maura spoke again, her voice strident, her eyes taking in everyone. She pointed at the leader of the Hunters and barked out some more words. He frowned at her, crossed his arms and nodded slightly, grunting. Maura turned to Daghda and spoke in the same tone, her eyes hard, her lips pursed. His eyes blazed at her for a moment, but eventually he nodded, his hand clenching the sword hilt as he did so.

Maura gave a nod and spoke a few words. When she finished, she gave dark looks to all of them and vanished.

Saoirse let out a breath she didn't know she'd been holding. Jaysus, Mary and Joseph. She looked at the others, seeing the resigned and vexed look on Daghda's face, the relief Finn displayed and Smithy's misery and frustration. She felt her own frustration, along with fear of the unknown and all the potential it held.

"What's happened?" she said to Daghda.

He turned to look at her, his eyes blinking for a moment as if he'd just remembered her presence.

"Maura has mediated a deal on her own terms."

Saoirse gave him a confused look. "What does that mean?"

"One sword and two spears."

"One sword and two spears? Is that all?"

"That's too much," said Daghda, a trace of anger in his tone. "All of it is too much."

"What exactly is the danger?" she said.

"A magic sword and two magic spears in their hands?" said Finn incredulously. "That shower of crafty feckers? Too much danger."

Smithy groaned. "I'll make it right. I'll find a way. When I fashion them, I'll find a way."

Saoirse looked at him in disbelief. And how was he going to fashion them, she wanted to know.

"And exactly why did the Hunters agree to this compromise, now. What did Maura say?"

Finn glanced at Daghda and spoke. "She said if we didn't all agree she would help the Fomorians come and make us agree."

Saoirse stared at them. "She would do that? But...but why?"

"Because she's Morrigan," said Smithy. "She's war, destruction. That's who she is."

21

LUKE

I awoke with a headache that fought hand and fist with the ache in my arm. I touched my arm tentatively. The heat was there but it didn't appear as angry as the night before. I closed my eyes for a moment and tried to gather my thoughts. The scent of laundry detergent with an undercurrent of some meadow flower wafted from the sheets. Ah Janey. What had I done?

I'd allowed my weakened inebriated state to get the better of me. Dum de dumdum. Yes that old tune and beat, just couldn't get rid of it along with my eejit self. Or maybe I was working on the eejit self because who knows what would happen to my arm in the days to come. Or myself, for that matter after drinking some strange concoction given by a woman who appeared to be warm, nurturing and nothing alarming, but feck, I knew better.

I rose slowly and cast around for my clothes. I saw them folded neatly on a chair against the wall. My shoes, the silly boat shoes I'd worn in Clonakilty were under the chair. I knew I'd nothing to do with the folded neatness but at least I still had my boxers on.

With a groan I got out of bed, steadying myself for a moment while my head remembered where the rest of my body was, and then grabbed my clothes. I made short work of donning them, or at least as short work as was possible considering the state of me.

Once dressed, I made my way down the narrow flight of stairs. Old house, stone made, but warm, inviting. I tried not to sink into it, to allow its warmth, its friendly nature to take me and at a clipped pace made my way through the empty sitting room to the kitchen. A brief thanks and then leave, was the plan.

Only somehow, brief thanks became tangled in "sit down and let me check your wound" no nonsense voice of Kayla's, as she pushed me into a chair, swathed in a kimono dressing gown, her hair unbound and falling down her back.

I sucked in my breath, trying not to notice the curves in just the right places, or the way the light caught the gold in her hair. I opened my mouth to protest her invitation that was more of an order, but was stopped short by her hazel gold eyes studying my own which then spread to the rest of my face. She placed the back of her hand against my cheek and then my forehead. I closed my eyes, immediately uncertain, off balance once again.

As soon as her hand rested on my forehead, my headache eased. I blinked, opened my eyes as her hands began to massage my temples and then cupped my chin, moving my head back and forth. My breath caught, just for a moment. This was Nurse Kayla, not seductress. Nothing seductive about curing a headache and checking for infection. All safe, all calm, no dum de dumdum beat necessary, said my head and the other head agreed all too readily.

Seemingly satisfied with what she'd observed, she turned to my arm and placed a gentle finger on the bandage around my wound, carefully prodding the edges. There was no responding dart of pain. Just the throb that had dulled even since I'd come downstairs.

She clucked softly and then brought the chest over to the table from the worktop where she presumably had placed it in readiness for my appearance. I tried to rise, to utter the thanks and leave before I opened myself to more potential opportunities to ...to what? Work her evil on me? To ensure I was vulnerable and then hand me over to Balor, or someone else? She would have done that last night, while I was sleeping from the herbal concoction she'd given me, if that were the case. That was me reasoning to myself. And surprisingly, myself still argued. But there you are. Who could you trust? Not even this dum de dumdum, or whatever beat and rhythm you wanted the tune to have. It had the same title. Eejit. The Eejit Jig. Played at a mad pace by myself. Followed on by the Eejit reel, polka and slide. A true set, a set with so much craic you'd grin and nod until your face split and dine out on that through Christmas next.

Too busy arguing with myself, I was. Too busy and helpless in the face of Kayla's gentle but persuasive touch who had my bandage unwrapped and my wound bare before the Eejit set was half played.

Her hands were washed and she sat beside me. I looked at her face, all concentration, focused, inward. Her fingers probed gently, pressing the edges, lightly touching all parts around the wound. I could feel it then, a small cascade of pulses, rhythmic sensual, coursing through my muscles, down my arm to the ends of my fingers. I inhaled, surprise and a touch of alarm at the sensation.

She gave a little shush, a soft whispering breath that transformed into a very low hum, a tune that kept time with the pulsing. The tune and the pulsing extended beyond my arm to my chest, swaying, rhythmic like the waves rolling, over and over. I fought to keep my eyes open and not to succumb to the growing sense that I was being enveloped. Enveloped and connected. Connected to the waves, the water and the sky above it. Rising high, towards the warmth and assurance of the sun. Expanding outwards, reaching up and across the expanse of sky with the ocean below.

I opened my eyes, tried to fight the feeling and found her eyes were on me, her expression filled with wonder, bewilderment and something more. She blinked and looked away. The moment was gone and with it the pulsing, the connection broken. She took a deep breath and reached for a pot in the chest. Back to Kayla, local healer.

The door opened after a brief knock and a man walked in, rural friendly with a nod, grin and "how's things." Wellies, faded T-shirt and better days work pants told me all about him, but not enough.

"Ah, Seán Óg," said Kayla, looking across at him, as if glad for the distraction. "Grand day out. Will you have a cup of tea?"

"Ah sure, perfect." He narrowed his eyes, nodded to me. "Tending another injured puppy, is it, Kayla?"

I watched him help himself to a mug and then the teapot, trying to ignore the bristling at the puppy label. He certainly hadn't reached his fortieth birthday and was probably not far past his thirtieth. And he was called Seán Óg. Anyone with the Irish moniker "young" attached to their name like Seán had would deserve the puppy title more than I would

Kayla ignored my stiff body language, if she'd noticed it at all as she began to clean the wound. I hissed as she touched a sensitive spot. Your man leaned against the worktop, surveying it all.

I'll thank her and then leave, I reminded myself. Not long now. Go back to the B&B and...what? Find another place, I dithered. I was still tired, though the ache in my arm had reduced to almost nothing, but the night before was there, not quite a hangover, though definitely hanging over me.

Myself and I dithered away, dither, dither about what to do while Kayla finished up her ministrations and your man chatted to her. I blocked it out, the best I could, like I blocked out his shock of wild blond hair, blond beard and that "I'm salt of the earth" feel of him. *In* the earth would suit me better, but I didn't know why and I didn't want to know.

"Terrible, so, that news about the mines. And now the fish," said Sean Óg.

"The mines?" asked Kayla.

"You've not heard?" said Seán Óg.

She shook her head, her fingers delicately spreading a soothing paste on my wound. It cooled any remaining heat and I closed my eyes, absorbing its effect that spread slowly from my wound to the rest of my arm.

"No," said Kayla. "I haven't seen or read any news since yesterday morning."

"No one mentioned it at the pub?"

She flushed. "Ah, no, I don't think so. I didn't hear anything."

He nodded and pulled a face, a hmmph escaping. "The mines, there down the road. Poisoned. Someone dumped a load of toxic chemicals down them. I was talking to Tadhg and he's said they closed the visitor centre."

Kayla paused in her work, lifted her face to Seán Óg. It was the concern that caught my attention most. This was more than just passing news on for her, I could see that.

"The mines?" she said softly. "Poisoned? It will seep into the land, destroy everything around it...why? Why would someone do that?"

Seán Óg shrugged. "Ah, you know. Probably some bastard looking to get rid of chemicals from their factory or something cheaply."

"What kind of toxic chemicals?" I asked, curious now.

Seán Óg looked at me, clearly surprised I would have anything to say.

"They said on the news, but I can't remember. Thank God my farm is the other side of the village. The last thing I need is for my sheep to eat poisoned grass. But still, it's a fecker for the museum and visitor centre."

"And the land," said Kayla, worrying her lip. "You said something about fish, too? What's happened there?"

"I'm not sure exactly. Tadhg just said that an oil tanker has foundered off the coast from here. Big oil spill. Dead fish have already washed ashore."

"An oil tanker? Near here?" Kayla's tone was incredulous. "That seems impossible."

"I don't know," said Seán Óg. "Maybe it got blown off course from Bantry in the last storm."

Kayla gave him a sceptical look.

"Have any steps been taken to contain it? And to protect the wildlife?" I asked. I could see the alarm in Kayla's face and I felt the need to re-direct the conversation before I ended up doing a little toxic damage to Seán Óg. Feck's sake with the Eeyore outlook. Where's the optimistic "could be worse" sentiment always present.

"Oh, I expect they're pulling out the stops. The fishermen'll be out as well."

"Is everyone from the tanker safe?" asked Kayla. "Did they have to take them off the ship?"

Seán Óg looked at me, and as if reading my mind, decided to amend his approach. "Don't know that either. I'm certain they'll ensure they're safe."

Kayla looked back at my arm and resumed her work. "Yes, I'm sure you're right."

Seán Óg sipped his tea noisily, studying her actions. "I'll find out, will I?"

"Drink your tea first," said Kayla.

I laughed inwardly at the "go away now" inference in the remark. Seán Óg seemed to have picked up on it because he frowned.

"I will, so, Kayla," he said softly. "It'll be grand, no worries. And don't they always get those spills cleaned up in the end?"

She looked over at him, forced a smile. "Of course, you're right. It'll be grand." She squeezed my forearm, her eyes fathomless pools as she looked at me. "You're all set now, Luke. It should improve in a day or so and then you can leave off the bandage for a little each day to help support granulation."

I nodded to her as if I understood her last few words, but sure, that's what Google was for.

"Thanks for everything," I said, standing. "I should get back to my B&B, though. I have to clear out this morning. The room's being rented to someone else."

"Oh," said Kayla. "Where will you go? Do you have a room booked somewhere else?"

I shook my head. "I'll check around, though. I'll find something. If not, I'll go on to Ardgroom or Eyeries or somewhere." I had no idea what I was going to do, but felt I needed to show her I had some kind of plan.

"I expect it will be all full, like it is here," said Seán Óg.

It didn't take any super intuition to know he took pleasure in those words, so I forced a shrug. "No worries. I'll be grand."

Kayla placed a hand lightly on my good arm. "You could stay here. Out in the back. I have a campervan that's available."

Seán Óg opened his mouth and then closed it again. And maybe it was that. The knowledge that he didn't want me staying here, or anywhere in this vicinity. Because a few seconds later the words came out of my mouth, surprising me more than anyone else.

"Grand, so. Thanks a million." No reticence, no half-hearted refusal as the custom demanded, to be met by an even more insistent offer. I didn't take a chance, I just uttered the words. And your man didn't look pleased.

Feck off, you Seán Óg puppy, you.

22

SMITHY

Smithy could see the anger in Daghda's eyes and he knew it was directed at him and it was justified. Morrigan, though she'd ensured the bargain was made and adhered to, had only made matters worse for Smithy, because he knew the wrangling and threats would have further shifted the blame for this mess in Daghda's view away from Smithy to the Hunters.

But the time for "what ifs" was over and he must do his part in fulfilling the bargain. And how to explain that he couldn't? All of the weapons might be fashioned, crafted well, but they would all be missing the vital ingredient that had driven this whole bargaining. The magic. The magic that would make them fierce, unrelenting, in the hands of whoever used it. A spear that would find its target, a blade that would cut true.

He sighed and ran his hand through his hair, glancing around at the audience before him.

"I'll have to return to my forge to create the weapons," he said, finally, using Irish.

The Hunters shook their heads slowly, in unison, like a well-rehearsed boy band. Well, it was worth a try, thought Smithy.

"My materials, the forge I use, they're all vital to creating the weapons you want. Unless you just want a couple of spears and a sword. I'm happy to do that here."

Once again, as if the rhythm and tune were still going, the heads shake.

Daghda stared at him, the WTF look on his face clear as any shouted words. Finn choked on a laugh. Ah, look it, it'd been worth a try, so it had, but the fact was that Smithy had created tenfold the number of weapons in this land than he'd ever done across the water. Smithy glared at Finn, whose eyes were now filled with mirth and an expression that clearly told him that quick thinking and eloquence were definitely not one of Smithy's strengths.

"You don't have a forge here, though," Smithy told the boy band hunters. "I'll need to go back to Tara, use that forge. And the metals, I need the metals."

Would the Hunters dare to leave their forest? It was a thin hope, but the only one he had.

Saoirse tugged on his arm. She'd been standing quietly beside him all the while. He knew she was giving her support in the ways she could and he appreciated it, but, truth be told, he found it annoying, and wished she would just let him be. She'd done her best and it'd all been useless. Now, he fought the urge to shrug off her hand.

"What's going on?" she said. There was a hint of frustration in her tone.

"No worries. Just negotiations."

"I heard Tara mentioned."

"I told them that I would have to do it at Tara because of the forge and the metals I need to fulfil the bargain."

"But..." her words trailed off, unspoken between them. Smithy didn't need to hear them to know what they were, the "but you can't make the weapons anywhere", was clear. He gave her a dark look and turned back to the Hunters.

It was the arms crossed move, again in sync. Were they considering it? Feckityfeck. Well it was better than some of the other possibilities – dismemberment, skinning, death – but then that will happen after all was said and done anyway, once they found out he couldn't keep the bargain. The Hunters would demand it. But at least at Tara he might have a chance with his old friends and fellow warriors there to at least allow him time to escape.

"Tara, then. But two of us will go with you," said the Hunter who'd been their speaker earlier. He pointed at Finn. "And he stays here. As surety."

Smithy started to open his mouth to object. No, he wouldn't sacrifice Finn to this madness that was all Smithy's fault. He began to give his own shake, only rapidly and more forceful than their gestures, but Daghda held up a hand.

"Done," he said. "Let it be so. We'll go ahead and make preparations. We'll let you know when all is ready."

The three boy band members exchanged looks. Again the head shakes. "We go now. All of us. Together."

Fingers dug into Smithy's arm again. He looked down at Saoirse's worried face.

"We're off to Tara," he said. "Along with the three stooges."

"But why did he point to Finn?"

Smithy frowned. "He has to stay here. As surety."

"Surety?" she asked and then realisation showed on her face. "Oh feck."

"Exactly," said Smithy.

SMITHY KNEW from the looks he was getting that people were both glad to see him and annoyed with him at the same time. It hadn't taken long for word to spread about the events with the Hunters, he thought sourly. He was sure that Maura had done her best to help it along. It had her markings all over it. Joy and anger mixed. Good craic. He'd crack her with it the next time he saw her. In fact he was surprised she wasn't here now, in the hall.

They'd arrived yesterday. The journey hadn't been long, sped on by the wind that took the horses and had contained a shred of amusement with the sight of the boy band clutching for dear life the mane of the horse they shared. But he was tired, though he knew half of his tiredness was due to his growing knowledge that he couldn't extricate all of them from this mess.

He saw Saoirse approach where he stood at the back. She'd only now appeared in the hall, after the others had gathered to make the formal statement of the bargain. And then. Well, the "and then" had kept him awake all night. He'd risen finally and gone to the forge, before even the dawn light had topped the horizon of the distant hills. The metals were all there.

Saoirse came alongside him and placed a hand on his arm, her eyes filled with concern. Would she ever give over with the concern? He sighed.

"How are you?" she asked.

He inhaled deeply. "Grand."

She dug her nails into his arms. "Smithy." Her tone was clipped.

He looked at her. "What do you want me to say? That I'm well and truly fecked?"

She shook her head. "No. I want to hear you say that you'll try to do this. That we'll try to do this."

He arched a brow. "We?"

She nodded. "Yes. How else could it happen? Think. We did it before."

He frowned at her. It was almost a scowl. Did this woman not understand? He had nothing. "I have no tunes, no music. Don't you understand that?"

Saoirse shook her head. "No. You're wrong. You have the music. Still. Locked inside of you. And we'll find it, open you up. For all of it. All of it, do you hear me, Smithy? All of it."

Her voice was fierce, and for some reason a note or two of her tone reached him. Touched that shrivelled bit of who he was and stroked it, soothed it. Would she make him believe her? Could he?

He covered her hand with his own and gave her a grateful look. He sighed, because the feeling leaked away, the notes faded and nothing had changed. "I will do my best. Of course. But don't place too much faith in me. It's not worth it, because I know better."

She shook her head. "Just try, that's all I ask."

Before she could say anything more Smithy heard his name. Or his true name. It was time. He was called. He straightened and moved forward. But Saoirse grabbed his hand. He gave her a puzzled look.

"Both of us," she said softly. "Remember? We do this together."

She gripped his hand hard and with half-hearted resignation he allowed it. They walked on, the two of them, Saoirse, holding his hand like a vice, while he struggled to find his "no bother" self that would have to carry him through.

He stopped in front of Daghda and the three boy band imitators, Your Ones Three. *Fadhb ar bith-fibe er bih.* There, say "not a bother" in Irish three times over and all is solved. And an echo of other words came after. Strange words. He tried to grasp on to them, listen out more deeply to the echo in his mind, but it faded.

Then he heard the words Daghda said, their meaning

inferred only by the gestures, the facial expressions and the looks of firm resolve on Your Ones Three. He gave them a curt nod when Daghda finished and opened his mouth for the "no bother" words in Irish, when others slipped out. It startled him so much he nearly lost his balance and would have, if not for Saoirse gripping him tightly.

Daghda nodded and gestured to the hall entrance which he presumed meant "off to the forge".

Daghda held back Saoirse, who'd started forward with Smithy, and gave a shake of his head. "It's safer if you remain here, Bríd."

"I'm going with Smithy. I mean Goibhniu. I'm helping, I'm a smith."

Her voice was firm, strong and it filled him with pride. This woman, will you look at her, echoed through his head. She gripped his hand tighter, if that were possible and he tried to convey his own strength back.

"Bríd," began Daghda, but she gave him a steely look and he stopped. He sighed. "Fine. If you wish. But I'll go with you."

Smithy began to protest, but a slight shake of Saoirse's head cut him off. They all headed toward the entrance, including Your Ones Three.

THE FORGE WAS LIT, the heat perfect. Smithy picked up the tongs. Saoirse, no Bríd, placed her hand over the hand that held the tongs and picked up the metal bar with her other hand. He waited for a moment, waited for that hum, but there was nothing.

With a barely repressed sigh, he took the metal bar with the tongs and held it so that the bar was in the centre of the fire. There was no modern protective equipment, bar heavy leather gloves that encased Saoirse and Smithy's hands. He did his best to shield himself from the metal's brightness as it slowly heated and glowed with the chemical changes taking place. Soon it would be his turn for the alchemy. The "not a bother" loomed more as a bother and he tried to distract himself to focus on the heat and a tune. A Blacksmith's tune. Sure there was one, there were hundreds. And the songs, well plenty of those as well. One rose up, ah sure. Why wouldn't it? The tune of the hammer against the anvil would provoke any fiddler, flautist, guitarist and what have you, yes more, to offer up something.

Something pulsed in him, something that told him yes, the time is here. He removed the tongs from the fire, the small metal bar glowing red and near blue with its heat. He reached for the hammer, but Saoirse was there first, taking it up in her hand. He closed his hand around hers, knowing she couldn't possibly have the strength to beat it out to the shape it would take. A spearhead. An arrow shape. A shape that would pierce a breast-plate, skin, a heart. And by the will of all the gods, not his.

He pressed Saoirse's hand to begin the hammering. The first blow rang out loudly, but it was strong and true. He pressed again and after a moment or two of ringing blows, they established their rhythm, a courtly dance at first but still the one two, one two that held promises of a reel, or at least a slide.

He sank into the rhythm and a few moments later he heard her, a soft tune, nothing more than hum, and it was a hum, though it came from her lips, her voice, rather than inside him. He heard it though, and it took hold of him, a small dazzle at the beauty of it as it hovered and swung to and fro, the hammer becoming the bodhran, the driving guitar, the idly, didly mouth music that made him smile.

Maybe it was the smile, maybe it was the feel of his arm moving with hers but he entered that tune that had jaunty written all over it, sure the joy of it was pure fun. Nearly pure drop. Craic all over and he grinned, who wouldn't?

The spear point joined in too, taking on its own grin, its sideways curve that was only a hop and a skip towards the curvy point and the bevel in the middle which rose up to clap the hand as that point slid through to the top to say woohoo.

He felt it all, seeping through his bones and then a tidal rush. Her hum vibrating, a soft whisper at first, and then more insistent. It began to rouse a hum from him, tiny, but still there. It rose to meet the other hum to form a harmony of hums and it all seemed right. Until it didn't and he collapsed.

23

LUKE

I sat at the table and rested my arm there, just as I had every morning for the past three days while Kayla dressed my wound. She studied it closely now, her fingers light on the outer skin, now slightly puckered under the pull of the scab forming. It was red in places, but it no longer ached and or even itched a little. Her hair fell forward, loosed from its long plait and surrounding her like a curtain. I wanted to reach out and stroke it, run my fingers through it.

Her scent filled the air I breathed, unique and complex as I'd come to view her. I could talk to her all day and still learn nothing and everything and still want more.

A small jolt of pain in my arm pulled me out of my reverie. I hissed.

"Sorry, sorry," she said. "There's a bit of pus here, just under the scab. I need to see beneath it and make sure all is as it should be."

"Ah, you're grand. It just took me by surprise, that's all."

She looked up and grinned at me, her hazel gold eyes full of humour.

"So you feel no pain if you'd known ahead of time?"

I returned her grin. "I'm an invincible god, didn't you know?" The words danced out all glee and the best craic, the irony private, but still fun to throw around.

Kayla didn't lose a beat. "Of course I know. But pain is pain, my gentle warrior."

The glee and craic were all hilarity and jumping about at her wit, but I took the words in and felt their warmth.

"And you, the goddess of the sea, with your wavy hair all loose and wild." The poet had taken over, Keats crossed with Yeats and a bit of Seamus Heaney thrown in, a "belle dame avec merci". At least I hoped so.

"More prodding," she said, her head bent again, my comment unremarked.

Prodding. She prodded with her fingers while I wanted to prod her mind and other parts of her body. Luscious, curvy. I seemed to have gone into overload in the past few days. But I knew it was more than that. I'd spent a lot of time in her company since my arrival. Nights were the only time I inhabited the campervan. The house was warm, inviting, its spirit laced with joy. Joy from her daughter, but most of all her.

Her daughter Bláthín, walked in, as if summoned, her normally rosy cheeks pale, her eyes slightly glazed. She wore her school uniform slightly askew, the trousers partially twisted, the jumper not entirely pulled down. Her fair hair was still knotted, not yet tamed into her customary plait that matched her mother's.

"Luke," she said. Her voice was thready, a far cry from the usual cocky, vibrant tone I found endearing. "You will take me to school again, yeah?"

It was half question, with a hint of demand. Unlike the first day, when she just pulled my hand and gave me the "come on you're taking me to school," phrase that allowed no denials.

"I will of course," I said. "But are you sure you're up to it? You don't look like you should be going."

Kayla turned to study her daughter and it only took a moment for a frown to appear on her face.

"Sit there," she said, pointing to a spare chair. "You're not to go anywhere until I fetch the thermometer. I'll just finish up here a minute."

She began to wrap the newly tended wound with a firm pad and bandage. It stung like feck, but as a warrior, I would show none of that, gentle or no. I could give a serious argument to the gentle part. And the warrior too. Those days were too long past to figure in any label describing me.

Once the wound was fully dressed, she rose, closed her box and washed her hands. When she'd left the room to fetch the thermometer, I looked over at Bláthín. The shadows underneath her eyes were like bruises and her blue eyes still glazed with pain. Her pale skin looked a sickly green in this light. Suddenly, she rose and dashed from the room to the small downstairs toilet just off the little entryway at the back door. From my chair, I could hear the retching.

I rose, uncertain if I should go to her, ensure she was okay, but Kayla walked in at that moment. She didn't need to ask where Bláthín was, the retching was audible still. Kayla placed the thermometer on the table and went to tend to her daughter.

I could hear the reassuring words, filled with warmth and compassion and Bláthín's tearful reply. Normally a sturdy, self-sufficient ten-year-old, her tone was higher pitched and vulnerable. Though I knew Kayla was who Bláthín wanted and she was more than capable of giving Bláthín all the comfort needed, I found myself wanting to add my own words. To find something to cheer her up, to make her feel better.

On impulse I went upstairs, determined to fetch Bláthín's raggedy, stuffed rabbit which she insisted was a hare (who was I to argue with a fierce ten-year-old?). His hind legs were long and floppy, but that was more likely down to its decrepit state and homemade nature than the original intent.

As I passed along the short corridor to Bláthín's room I was careful not to disturb Kayla's mother who hadn't stirred, which was unusual. Pausing at her door, I heard a soft moan.

"Nana?" I didn't know what else to call her. Kayla had introduced her in a very informal manner, but now, from my lips it did seem incongruous.

I heard another moan, this time louder. I opened the door slowly, just enough to see inside. Nana lay on the bed, dressed but for her shoes, her eyes closed, clutching her stomach. Her face and skin were ashen.

I walked over to her, concerned. Her eyes fluttered open, hearing me and I gave her a reassuring smile.

"Is there anything I can do to help? Fetch some tea? A bowl?"

She gestured to me to come closer and I approached the bed. I could see the beads of sweat gathered at her brow and across her upper lip. A bad bout of whatever this was.

She reached out for my wrist and clutched it. "Fetch Kayla. Tell her it's important." Her voice was a raw whisper.

"I will of course," I said. "She's with Bláthín at the moment. She's sick, too. I'd say you two may have the same thing."

Alarm filled her eyes. "Bláthín?" She groaned. "Kayla? Is she all right?"

I nodded. "Not to worry. She's fine."

Nana sighed, relief evident in her eyes. "That's something, then. There's a bit of time."

I patted her hand. "Sure, you both will be grand. Up and around the house before you know it."

She gave me a cryptic look and patted my hand. "Just tell Kayla to come to me when she can. Then bring me a bowl. I'll stay here in my room today."

I nodded and moved towards the door. "Don't worry, Nana. It will all be grand, you'll see."

She just grunted.

I STOOD at the foot of Bláthín's bed, my face filled with concern. I'd tried to convince Kayla to call the doctor, but she put on a smile, and said that she really didn't think it warranted that step. Her mother was no better, either. Neither one had improved in the two days since they'd first fallen sick and I felt it was too serious for home remedies. All the chicken soup and herbal tea in the world wasn't going to cure whatever virus they had.

"Will you tell me a story, Luke?" Bláthín said, weakly.

Her head peered over the covers, her golden curls tousled and knotted. The feverish glaze in her eyes was gone but the paleness of her skin and dark bruises under her eyes seemed to have increased.

"I will, of course," I said.

I'd taken to coming to her room in the afternoon, after I'd helped Kayla around the farm. Being late summer, the cows and sheep were still in the fields. The sheep were shorn, the cows weren't yet ready for market, the calves were fine, the lambs long gone, or so I presumed. The silage had been cut that final time. Soon, she would begin winter preparations, but now it was a matter of checking up on things.

I didn't know if it was the routine, or the small details repeated and comfortingly ordinary that had allowed me to settle, to find some peace in the past few days, despite Bláthín and Nana's illness. And through all this routine, this ordinariness was Kayla, so much a part of the farm, the land and all that was so good about my time here. Kayla and her daughter, who now gave me a wan grin at my response.

She patted a place on the bed beside her. "Sit here."

There was a pleading in her words and I was happy to comply. I made myself comfortable and took up a wise pose, the seanchie, ready to regale his audience with tales wild and wonderful. But what wild and wonderful tale? I searched for something and from somewhere in my distant memory the tale began to come out of my mouth.

"It's the tale of a young man, a stranger—"

"The hero?" said Bláthín.

"Maybe."

Her eyes sparkled a little. I was encouraged. "Well—"

"What does he look like? Does he look like you?"

I opened my mouth "Ah, no. I'm no hero."

"Ah, you are, or you could be if you wanted."

I was surprised to find how much her words touched me. I cleared my throat. "You're a grand girl, you are. Right, so. This stranger, this young man, arrived at a large hall in a fort where many warriors gathered to help protect the king and his people."

"You mean like a castle? With knights and ladies?"

"Of course. Just like that. So, this stranger...this knight, when he arrived was met by the...steward of the castle who asked who he was and what he wanted. The knight told him who he was and that he wanted him to take him to the king—"

"Who was he? What was his name? All heroes need names."

I faltered. "Uh...."

"Luke?" she asked, her tone hopeful.

I smiled feebly. "If you like." I cleared my throat. "Right, so. The steward asked...Luke what service he could provide for the king, because that was the only way he could be admitted to the hall."

Bláthín frowned, considered the statement, and then shrugged. I resumed my tale.

"Luke said he was a good carpenter, but the steward said

they already had a carpenter. Then he told the steward he was also a smith and a harper too. The steward shook his head and said they had those as well. Luke added that he was a healer, a poet and a historian. He then said that he was also a sorcerer and a champion warrior."

"Wow, he sounds amazing," said Bláthín. "Can you do all those things?"

I felt myself flushing. "I..."

"It's an old tale," said Kayla.

I turned and saw her standing at the door, a bemused expression on her face. How long had she been standing there?

"Do you know this story, Mammy?" asked Bláthín.

Kayla looked at me, her eyes unreadable. "It's very old, dote. Ancient. But yes, I do know it."

I stared at her, holding her gaze. There was so much and nothing in her eyes, as they searched mine. She moved towards us and placed a hand on my shoulder.

"Go on with the tale, Luke."

I tried to gather my thoughts, to bring a different thread to this tale I thought I was throwing into the vast size of the seanchie bag of amusement on a winter's night. But the audience had changed and something else had shifted too.

"Maybe you should tell it," I said. "I may not remember it all."

"No, I think you should tell it your way." Kayla said, her voice honey, a warm blanket, a whiskey on a winter's night.

What did I want to say?

"Did they let him in?" asked Bláthín.

I looked at her, paused and nodded. "He told the steward that if there was anyone in the hall...uh, castle, who had all those skills then he would go away."

"But no one did."

I shook my head. "No one did. But the king tested him, to see if he was telling the truth. He won at chess and the king sat him a place of honour. Then, the king's champion challenged him to a contest of strength."

"What was his name?" asked Bláthín.

"Ogma," I said before I could think to change it. Did it matter?

Bláthín nodded, appearing satisfied.

"Ogma heaved up one of the huge flagstones in the hall and pushed it right through the castle wall outside."

"Oh, that's huge. What did Luke do?"

I grinned. "Picked up the flagstone and threw it back inside and mended the castle wall."

Bláthín smiled, delighted. "So he became a knight. The king couldn't refuse after all that."

I nodded. "He did, all right. Not only that, but the king put him in charge of the defence of all of Ireland."

"Of course. He was the best," said Bláthín.

Her words and confident tone caused me to take a deep breath, to will away the emotion that suddenly rose up. Kayla, her hand still on my shoulder, gave it a slight squeeze. It seemed impossible that she should know.

"So," said Bláthín, "did Luke defend Ireland against an enemy?"

I studied her a moment and then nodded. "Yes." I took another deep breath. "But it was a long time after that. The old king had to step down for a time and the new king wasn't a good man. He allowed one group to treat the others very badly, and though this king agreed to give back the throne to the other king, he didn't. And so the old king's warriors began fighting the new king and his band of favourites."

"Did Luke beat them all?"

I paused, wondering how to say the words. The words that

I'd rarely spoken and certainly never told to anyone who hadn't been there.

I gripped my hand into a fist. Sure, it was only a story. Nothing more.

"They saved him for the last battle. The one against the toughest and most powerful man of all."

"What was he called?"

I hesitated.

"Everyone has a name," said Kayla quietly behind me. She sat down. I could feel her presence, even without the hand. It had moved to my arm, resting there, warm, reassuring. A reassurance that carried something more, like an underlying hum that connected me to her, to Bláthín and the room, along with everything in it.

"Bal...." I couldn't finish the name. But Bláthín nodded and the person in this tale became Bal.

"And did they fight?" asked Bláthín.

"They did of course. The two strongest and most skilled warriors. But Bal had something more. He could poison people. All it took was one look. Everyone feared him, especially in battle."

"But not Luke," said Bláthín.

"Oh, Luke feared him. He was right to fear that kind of power and skill. Bal had skill, too."

"But Luke had more skill. And he was smarter." Bláthín's tone refused all argument.

Luke's breath caught at the confidence of her words, the utter certainty that this hero was without flaw.

"Luke knew he had to be careful, that he needed to use cunning and skill to defeat Bal and his men."

Bláthín only nodded. This was obvious.

"So he took his special slingshot, aimed as true as he could and let fly the perfect sized round stone. The stone hit Bal's eye with so much force it knocked it clean through his head. And all that poison was directed at all of his men, so they all died."

"Bal too?"

I nodded my head, for that was the story. That's the way it should be told, if all were right with the world.

"And Luke saved Ireland," said Bláthín. "Did the king reward him? Give him the fairest lady in the land?"

I shook my head. "Ah, no. Luke was glad that he'd saved the king and that the rest of the army against the king fled after Bal died, but Luke was sad, too. Because...because...."

"Because why?" Bláthín sat up, her eyes wide and filled with concern.

Kayla squeezed my arm and the hum of the connection increased, strengthened.

"Because, because he had killed a bad man, but that bad man was his grandfather, something he couldn't forget."

"Oh, that is sad," said Bláthín. "Even though Bal was a bad man."

"He was a very bad man," said Kayla quietly. "And some-times the right things are the hardest things to do."

The words were obvious, but not. This woman whose hand rested on my arm, whose quiet strength had helped me through the telling of a tale that had begun as a light-hearted invention I was going to weave in a completely different direction, had led me, along with her daughter, to unburden my heart, if only for a short while.

Her other hand stroked the back of my head and I felt a soft kiss planted at my neck a moment later.

"But I'm sure the king, once the battle was finished and everyone was celebrating, gave Luke the fairest lady in the land," said Bláthín.

"I'm sure he did," said Kayla, a touch of humour in her voice.

24

SAOIRSE

Fresh herbs scented the air, along with something acrid, metallic. Shelves lined one wall as well as a tall bench filled with pots and a work surface. The low bench that now held Smithy had been moved away from the stone wall, but still Saoirse could only hope that the draught that seemed to emanate from the stones wasn't chilling him. The small fire in the hearth at the centre of the room did little to warm the room.

Smithy had managed to rouse himself only briefly after they'd brought him here yesterday when he'd collapsed. Daghda had ordered Finn and a few other men on hand to carry him the short distance from the forge to Diancecht's workroom. The Hunters had objected, not understanding why he couldn't have been treated immediately in the forge and then have Smithy get on with the task, with Saoirse of course. Saoirse was thankful that they hadn't asked her to continue alone. She was too concerned about Smithy to even contemplate attempting something like that.

Daghda had seemed pleased with the turn of events overall. Initially he'd thought that Smithy might have been faking the incident as a strategy to avoid creating the sword and the other spear, and clearly so had the Hunters, but not now. Not with Smithy's pallor and lack of consciousness. This was no avoidance tactic like before. This was something altogether different.

Diancecht entered, his craggy face fixed in a scowl. His robes hung loose on his spare frame as they swept the floor behind him. He began muttering to himself. It was all unintelligible to Saoirse.

He cast a disdainful glance at her. "Any change?"

Saoirse shook her head. "Nothing."

Diancecht crossed his arms and looked at the patient lying on the bench. He shook his head, his expression disgusted. "It's past time for him to rouse himself."

Saoirse gave him a quizzical look but said nothing. Diancecht snorted.

"Time for some drastic measures, so."

Saoirse gave him a nervous look and watched while he grabbed an earthenware cup from his work bench and went over to the small fire burning in the hearth, where a pot was suspended from a metal frame. He took the ladle from the pot and poured its contents into the cup. When it was filled to his satisfaction, he moved over to the bench where Smithy lay.

"I need you to hold him up," Diancecht told Saoirse.

Saoirse hesitated and then complied. It took a bit of effort to get Smithy into position, but she managed in the end. Diancecht bent over and held the cup to Smithy's lips. With a little force he managed to get Smithy to swallow a few gulps. Smithy coughed a few times and his eyes fluttered. Diancecht mumbled something and tried to get Smithy to drink more. He'd managed only a few sips before Smithy coughed forcibly, spluttering and his eyes flew open. He sat up, leaving Saoirse to step back.

"What the feck are you trying to do to me, old man? What is that shite you're forcing down my throat?"

Diancecht stood up, a smug look on his face. "I knew that would do the trick."

"What did you give him?" asked Saoirse. "You haven't harmed him, have you?"

Diancecht frowned at her. "You're questioning me? Didn't I do enough for you already? Brought that useless moaner back from the dead against my better judgement?"

Saoirse flushed. "Sorry, sorry. You're right. I apologise. I trust you."

Smithy narrowed his eyes. "I'm not sure I do. What did you just give me?"

Diancecht shrugged. "Nothing of any import. It was more to make you gag and send heat into your body than anything else."

Smithy shook his head and ran his hand through his hair. Saoirse rested a hand on his shoulder in an attempt to reassure him. He looked over at her and gave a wan smile. But the eyes were distant and her heart sank.

"My head feels like an elephant stomped on it."

"You may have hit your head when you collapsed," said Saoirse.

He stared at Saoirse for a moment. "I collapsed. Oh, right." He examined his hands. "I was making the spear." He looked at Saoirse again. "With you."

Saoirse nodded. "Yes, and I think it was working." She didn't want to say more. Not with Diancecht in the room. At least not until Smithy decided to mention it.

"The spear. We made the first spearhead. Nothing more."

She nodded, but didn't know where to go from there.

He frowned.

"How do you feel now?" she asked.

He paused and shrugged. "Fine, I suppose. Except for the headache." He looked up at Diancecht. "Can I go now?"

Diancecht narrowed his eyes and gave him cryptic look.

"There's nothing wrong with you, Goibhniu. Nothing at all. Except what you perceive in your heart and your soul. And I can do nothing about that."

Smithy's expression darkened. "What's that supposed to mean?"

"What I said, Goibhniu, what I said." He pronounced Smithy's name with particular emphasis and Saoirse knew it meant something. But Smithy was giving nothing away, if he understood what was behind it. At least Diancecht had said that there was nothing wrong with Smithy. At least physically. But did that cover magic?

She sighed. Oh feck it all. She was tired of dealing with all of this. The feeling that she was having to work a task blind, with no instructions.

Smithy, as if sensing her mood, took her hand and plastered a smile on his face. "I'm grand, Saoirse, so I am."

She just nodded. What else could she do?

THE "WHAT ELSE COULD SHE DO" sentiment seemed to echo in her mind as she walked with Smithy back to the hall and to find Daghda. He was there in the hall, off to the side, having a conversation with one of his men. A small group of mostly men were clustered on the other side, laughing and talking. Smithy and Saoirse's steps echoed as they crossed the flagstones and the two men turned.

With the hall emptied for the most part, Saoirse noted the brightly woven tapestries and ornately wrought long shields that decorated the walls. There was a grandeur about the place that finally penetrated Saoirse's mind. This was a seat of power, there was no doubting that. The "what else could she do" sentiment seemed a bit feeble in the face of all this indisputable reality. Was going along with Smithy's deception in the hopes she was protecting him really the wisest move?

Daghda greeted them, interrupting her thoughts.

"How are you feeling?" asked Daghda.

Smithy shrugged. "Fine. Sorry for the alarm."

"He has a headache," Saoirse said. She felt compelled to add something cautionary about Smithy's health.

"What did Diancecht say?" asked Daghda.

"He says I'm fine. There's nothing wrong with me."

"Physically," Saoirse said in a low voice. Smithy gave her a dark look for her effort.

"I'm fine," Smithy stated firmly.

Daghda gave him a sceptical look. "You collapse twice and you say you're fine?"

"Diancecht says there's nothing to worry about."

"Those weren't his exact words," said Saoirse, frowning.

Smithy glanced over at her, a flash of anger crossing his face. "There's no problem, really. Just a fluke. Perhaps a temporary blood pressure thing."

"Blood pressure?" said Daghda, frowning.

Saoirse and Smithy exchanged brief looks. "Nothing really," said Smithy. "It can happen to someone if they're under a lot of pressure. But it's grand, really."

"Pressure?" said Daghda.

Smithy shot a meaningful look in Saoirse's direction. "There's been a lot for me to take in lately."

Daghda nodded slowly. "I see."

Saoirse pressed her lips together, fighting the growing anger inside. How dare he blame her, the fecker. She started to open her mouth to challenge him, but Smithy spoke first.

"What about the Hunters?" he said.

"Still here," said Daghda. "Waiting for you to continue."

"Are you going after the sword, still? What about Finn, I mean Ogma?"

"I was just discussing it with my men. Apparently Ogma has escaped. He's on his way now."

"Escaped? How?" Saoirse asked. She couldn't imagine the Hunters allowing that.

"Morrigan," said Daghda.

He added nothing more, as if that explained it all. But it just added questions to the questions that had lined up in her mind like a queue for a U2 concert.

"I'm just on my way to meet him," added Daghda.

"Good. I'll come with you," said Smithy. "If I can slip out with you now, I won't have to forge the rest of the weapons." He looked at Daghda. "I'll go with Ogma to recover the sword."

Daghda gave a thoughtful smile. "It's a plan. It could work. At least for now. We can't defer them forever, but maybe long enough that we can come up with an alternative that won't place two magic spears and a sword in their hands. Or at least get something big in return."

Saoirse had listened to this exchange, giving Smithy furious glances. But he avoided her looks, keeping his eyes fixed on Daghda.

Right, so. That's the story is it, she thought. "I'm coming with you both."

Both looked at her in astonishment.

"It's a nice thought," said Daghda at the same time as Smithy said a flat, "no".

"But really," Daghda added in a kind tone. "It wouldn't be safe for you."

"Why?" she stated in a loud tone that had a belligerent edge to it.

"Well," said Daghda, suddenly patient. Was this a new approach? A "soften her up to bend to my will" approach? "You don't have the language, you aren't skilled at weapons and you don't know the, uh, area."

"I have some skill with weapons," she said, firmly. "I've been practising with Smithy, uh, Goibhniu. And Maura, er um, Morrigan, gave me some training. I don't need the language or knowledge of the area if I'm with Ogma and Goibhniu. And besides, if I go with them the Hunters can't ask me to create the weapons."

"I don't think they'd ask you," said Smithy.

She gave him a dark look. "You're certain about that are you? You know them and their habits so well you can tell me they wouldn't do anything to get their hands on the rest of the weapons?"

She knew she was baiting him, but she was also telling him that his lack of memory was a big liability. And his body. A body that could give out at any moment. Regardless of what Diancecht said. Or maybe because of it. That because there was nothing wrong with him physically, it would be impossible to predict what could trigger another collapse. Or any other sort of weakness.

Smithy frowned and looked at Daghda.

Daghda sighed, folded his arms and spoke. "It might be best. Given all the options."

He looked at Saoirse and she found herself colouring under his scrutiny. What did he see there? A daughter? A stranger? Someone he loved? She just couldn't begin to understand her relationship with him or what it was before, when she really was Bríd.

Who was she now? It was a question that lurked at the back of her mind. She no longer felt like Saoirse, or at least not the ex-barista and Trinity graduate. But she still felt nothing like Bríd, the goddess. She was somewhere in between. The "In Between Girl".

LUKE

I watched the sink fill with water and the soapy suds form from the washing up liquid, musing yet again. Bláthín's words at the end of my tale had hung over me the past few days since I'd told it. My tale. Did Kayla understand how much it was my tale? My story? A brief part of it, but key in making me who I was now. The tale without Bláthín's romantic ending, though, regardless of the certainty she'd had when she added it. No, my tale, the real tale, was dark, ending included. It was an Irish tale, ancient, riddled with power, violence and flawed gods. Spin Rapunzel darker, Sleeping Beauty enmeshed in brambles that can never be penetrated, Cinderella's slipper lost forever – those were the kind of tales that made up my story.

Only music kept me from sliding further into the darkest part of my story, with a bit of wave riding. And I'd done neither of them since arriving at Kayla's. I would have drowned if not for Kayla. But she wouldn't always be here to save me. Her presence, warmth, her something.

I'd go to the next session, sort myself out. And maybe cheer up Kayla in the process. She'd tried hard to keep up a sunny outlook lately, but I could tell she was worried about her daughter and Nana, who were no better. And feckin' Sean Óg popping in every morning full of doom and gloom news about the mines and the oil spill didn't help.

Kayla walked into the kitchen singing softly under her breath. I looked over at her as she came alongside of me and squeezed my arm.

"Thanks a million, Luke. That's very kind of you."

"No bother at all. It's the least I can do."

"It's not the least you have done, *a chara*, and I'm grateful for it all."

A chara. She'd called me friend. I was glad of it, but I found a small part of me was disappointed that I wasn't somehow more. More what? More of a Keats poem, or Yeats' Aengus, wandering through the hazel wood spying that glimmering girl with apple blossoms in her hair.

"What were you singing?" I said. Anything to cut redirect my thoughts from the path they'd wandered into.

"What?" she asked, surprised.

"Just now, when you came into the kitchen you were singing something under your breath."

She paused, alarm flashing across her face so quickly I could almost have persuaded myself that I imagined it. She smiled. "Oh, it was nothing."

"Did it have a title? It sounded vaguely familiar."

"Probably. I'm sure you've heard it before. *Máirín de Barra.*"

"*Máirín de Barra._* That's what you were singing?" I raised my brow.

"Yes. Why? Do you know it?"

I nodded. "Yeah. I know it." I knew it well enough to know that she hadn't been singing that air. Why would she lie? But did it matter? Maybe she knew a different version of the one I'd known.

"I have to go out, Luke. Do you mind keeping an eye on my mother and Bláthín?"

"No, of course. But did you want me to go with you?"

"No, no, you're grand. I should be back by the afternoon."

She brushed my cheek with the back of her hand. "You're a grand man, Luke."

I stared at her, puzzled. There was a hint of sadness in her eyes, but before I could say anything she pecked me on the cheek and with a brief thanks, walked out the door.

A "belle dame", she was without a doubt, but I couldn't help hoping that there was more than thanks involved.

I stared at the shut door, rubbing my arm. It was grand now. More than grand. Except for the itch of the scab that was tight across the skin. It had healed with amazing efficiency and speed, even for me. Her touch, something. Her touch was something, it sang across my skin and through it, a pure form of music and light, wound and blended in one. She'd been my music in these past few days, I suddenly realised, a tune that was elusive as it was powerful. Earth music, sky and air music, sea music, a triad that was difficult to explain or replicate. I itched for my uilleann pipes, my fiddle, mandolin. Something.

I went into the small sitting room and retrieved the mandolin from its case. I'd put my instruments in the house rather than the uncertain temperatures of the campervan. I spent most of my time here, really, and it seemed only natural that my instruments would too. And now, in these few moments, I wanted to play this tune, I needed to play this tune, to find that triad and explain it in the only way I could.

I settled into the mandolin, tuning, twisting pegs, listening for the feel of it. I tuned it the old way, the not quite half tone off, the vibrations slightly different, a tuning of ancient ways and old paths. The only avenue to this tune, this elusive triad going through my head.

I plucked the strings, slow at first, searching, listening. The "ah sure" still elusive, just out of reach. I retreated inside myself, listening for it, trying to feel it, touch it but it danced away, skittery and teasing. Or was it teasing? Was it just so deeply buried, embedded in the core of me, all the elements that made me and everything else what they were.

I plucked out a "getting to know you" riff, something that just came. A "myself", "who the feck are you" and all that shite that really had me snorting with derision any time I'd heard it. The "ah get over yourself" outlook had served me so well, but it didn't get me this triad. No, feck it. That triad, that sea, air, earth, was found in the root of me. I understood that now.

I plucked on, the tune taking a different shape, beyond the light banter that just showed the fun and joy of the initial acquaintance of the chancer, lover and session player, blended in the all player. The shape became brutal, dangerous, and coated in blood. The core of me signalling, "stay away I cause damage". A "put a hashtag on that and wrap it around me", kind of tune.

I explored that tune, trying to find the triad, even though I knew it wasn't there, never there, but its power and darkness latched on to me, my fingers and what they plucked on the strings. It wrapped around me, tighter and tighter and I gave into it, sure, what harm for a moment only, and it pulled tighter and I drove into it, knowing it was already mine, this tune, of course it was, this gobshite tune, for that that was me, how could it not be?

My arm began to itch, a slight distraction, like an annoying fly, but the itch grew, becoming strong and powerful, a power that overwhelmed what was going on with the strings, and my fingers on those strings. I broke the tune and raised a hand to scratch that itch. I pulled up the sleeve of my T-shirt and put a finger to scratch at the edge, it responded with a tickle, and the tickling vibrated through the rest of the scab. I rubbed it gingerly with my finger, all around the edge and then moved into the centre of the scab. Tingles, vibrations radiated out along my arm, to my fingers and back up into my chest.

I sat there, unmoving, my full attention centred on this experience. The tune was there now, back again, but stronger this time. No more skittery, "slide away from me" action now, this tune was there. I picked up the mandolin once again and began to pluck, finding my way in again, only this time it was different. This time the tune was ready and waiting. I worked my way towards it, its subtle, sensual melody, a thread that slowly unwound to form a whoosh of wave, a vibration of earth, a breath of wind.

I kept it going, more certainty added to the sound as I plucked it out, feeling it, now, so strongly that it made my chest ache. Would I try it on the fiddle, I thought after a while? The uilleann pipes might be too loud with Bláthín and Nana upstairs, most likely sleeping. It's what they did most days now, waking only to eat a little soup, or whatever Kayla could persuade them to get down.

I stopped, put the mandolin to the side and was just after getting up from my seat on the sofa when I heard a voice from upstairs call out. Nana. Ah feck it. Did I wake her up? I went to the bottom of the stairs and listened.

"Luke?" Her voice was weak enough, but I could still hear a hint of steel in it.

"Yes?"

I climbed the stairs and headed to her door. When I arrived she was struggling to sit up, her face gaunt and pale, her skin paper thin. Her hair was loose, grey and tumbling down her back. I rushed over to help her, cushioning the pillows to support her.

She gave me a grateful smile and took my hand, holding it

tight. I looked at her and her gaze was intense, her eyes filled with things I couldn't understand. Stories ancient and older than me. I blinked.

"You have it. It's there, within you. Keep it, now."

"Have what?" I said. I was confused, but then again, somehow I knew what she meant.

"You have the tune, you have her."

I gave her a puzzled look, but she only squeezed my hand. "She's been waiting for you. So come, play for me, now. She'll need you when she returns."

"Kayla?" It was all confused ramblings from an old woman who was ill. Sure, that was it, wasn't it? Smile and indulge her, that was the best thing to do. So I smiled. I nodded, did the indulging. I played the tune after I fetched the mandolin, while I fought the feeling that there was nothing rambling or confused about her words.

I WAS STILL PLAYING the mandolin, only now downstairs again, when Kayla came through the door. I'd left Nana asleep, the tune I'd played soothing her and her words lingering around us as she drifted off. She'd asked me to play the tune for Bláthín, but when I'd peeked in her room, Bláthín was asleep too, though there was a bit more colour in her cheeks.

The tune still rolling around in my head, I'd gone downstairs and settled once more on the sofa, couched the mandolin on my lap and resumed playing. This time I added a few flourishes, elaborations that supported the melody and gave it wings went it needed, gravitas at other times and pure wishes for it all. It was in my head, my body and all of me, in a way that I'd never felt the music before. Sure, I wasn't flying it, it was flying me, soaring high, swooping, diving, and all that was in between.

And then she came through the door. The kitchen door first, moving through it to the threshold of the living room. Haloed by the light, pure luminescence in the late morning sun, her eyes large and filled with grief.

"Oh, Luke," she said.

The words pierced me, wrenched my gut open. The words? The tone? The beauty of her as she stood there, full and ripe, burgeoning with all that was her? Warmth, understanding, comfort and that lush earthiness, that hummed and hovered around her. The tune, the melody, that still echoed around me, even though I'd stopped playing, was her. It was all about her. Sure, wasn't it obvious? The thought was there only for a moment and it was gone, but I felt the remnants linger.

"Something wrong?" I asked, knowing it was all about distraction. Distraction was best, so it was. And there was something. I could see it in her eyes, and her tone told something more than its usual. Grief?

Kayla nodded. She looked away, but not before I could see tears glittering in her eyes. She sank down in the chair opposite me. "It's getting worse."

"What is?"

She licked her lips. Oh, feck me. I looked away. Distraction, lad. Distraction.

"The mines. I went to check on them. The poison is spreading. It's as if they poured more down there. It's penetrating deeper into the earth and wider."

Her words drew my attention. "Is there no one treating it? The government? Office of Public Works? Surely it's a heritage site?"

She nodded. "They've been trying all right. But it's as if each attempt is being thwarted. Either more toxic waste is being dumped or something else prevents the clean-up." She shook her head. "I just don't understand it."

"And they don't know who's behind it?"

Kayla frowned. "No. They don't."

I put the mandolin aside, rose and went over to her. There was something about the way she said those words, the emphasis on "they" made me wonder if she knew. "Who do you think is behind it?"

She looked away a moment, but there was something in her eyes. "I don't have any proof," she said eventually.

"Who are they? And more to the point, can we stop them?"

She smiles sadly. "I'm trying to get help."

"Can I do anything?"

She gave me a sad smile and took my hand. She gave it a squeeze and was about to pull away, but I held on to it, using my hold to pull her up to face me.

"What aren't you telling me, Kayla?" I studied her face, her eyes, looking for the answer.

She forced a smile on her face. "It's nothing, really. I'm just worried. The oil spill isn't cleaning up easily. The wrecked tanker is still leaking."

I frowned at her. "The oil tanker is still leaking?"

She nodded.

For the first time I considered the possibility of an oil tanker wrecking off the coast here. I suppose it was possible an oil tanker would be in waters that close to the tail end of the Beara Peninsula. Whiddy Island, where they had refinery tanks that held some of the country's oil reserves, wasn't all that far away. But this didn't seem enough.

"Who owns the oil tankers?"

She paused, pursed her lips. "I'm not sure."

I snorted. "You know. I just don't understand why you won't say."

I placed my hands on her shoulders rubbing them gently. She looked at me and I could see the tears lurking at the back of them. I stilled my hands, the urge to comfort, to reassure, to make that connection with her, suddenly halted and I knew.

I blinked. How was it possible? How did she know, because what other answer could make sense?

"Balor Energies," I said flatly. I dropped my hands. "I'm right, aren't I?"

She sucked in her breath. That action only confirmed that it was so.

I turned away, my emotions raging, tangled, fighting each other. What the feck? What was I supposed to do with that?

I felt a hand on my cheek. She pulled my face towards her. "I'm sorry, Luke. I know it's difficult for you. But he's not a good man. And he has nothing but bad intentions towards this land. Towards everything. He's an angry, bitter person who wants to wreak havoc."

I looked at her. "Who are you?" I whispered bleakly. "What do you want with me?"

"I want nothing from you, Luke. I want only for you to find peace. To be your real and true self."

I stepped back from her. "Who are you?" I repeated.

"I'm Kayla," she said. "I'm as you see. And I mean you no harm."

I shook my head. "You know who I am, though. Don't you? No, no, don't bother. I know you do. I just want to know how."

"I know you for the man you are," she said. "I don't deny that. I know the true man. Not the wanderer, the fun-loving womaniser, the trad musician, though that's in you, there's no doubt about that." She gave a wry smile. "But foremost, you are a brave, talented, strong man who knows what has to be done. A hero."

I narrowed my eyes a moment and then forced a laugh. "Oh, right, so. Come here to me, let me tell you my hero tales. My horse, the surfboard. My enemies, the waves. And my reward, oh, the fair lady. I always get the fair lady. If not then, all I have to do is play my whistle." I gave a dirty laugh and raise my brow. "That's the sum total of my hero tales."

She sighed, squeezed my arm and turned away. "The time is near, Lugh," she said softly in Irish. I flinched and was about to object again, but she interrupted me. "I need to check on Bláthín and Nana. Have they stirred at all while I was gone?"

I stared at her until her question penetrated my thoughts. "Uh...not Bláthín, though she was looking better when I checked on her. But Nana, yes. We talked a little. She'd heard me playing this tune and asked me to come up and play it for her." It seemed ages ago, now and hardly worth the importance I'd given it earlier.

"Tune? What tune was that?"

I looked over at the mandolin and shrugged. "Oh, just some old thing that I was messing around with."

She looked at the mandolin for a moment. "Play it for me."

I frowned. Well why the feck not? It would save me thinking what I didn't want to. Save me from taking the steps to leave that were stirring around me. The "put on the walking shoes and get on the road", mode. The mode that seemed to be my norm, now.

I picked up the mandolin, sat down and held it for a moment to get myself settled, oriented. I searched for the tune in the air, inviting it back, a visitation whose welcome was half fearful at this point. Was it fire I was playing with? Mixing earth, air and water in such a way, to such a woman? This Kayla who was more than she was? My mind, my body were unsettled, skittery as the tune when I'd first met it. What would it do to me now? What would she do to me when I played it?

Amidst this tangle, tumble I began to pluck the notes, the string vibrated with sounds. The sounds became loud, fierce and uncompromising. The notes grew, multiplied and expanded into more than what it was. The tune swirled and raged around me, a driving force, a weeping sea, a gale of such force I could hear no thoughts but this tune. Felt nothing but this tune. I was the girl with those dancing shoes, unable to stop, only it was my fingers plucking the strings.

Kayla, came over to me, rested her hand on my arm. I looked up, my fingers halted. The room fell silent. She leaned down, touching my head with hers. "It's calling you, Luke. They're calling you."

"What do you mean?" I whispered. My heart was racing, the music was still there hanging, waiting for me to connect to it again. Her touch, her voice, it was all there, in the music. I reached up to touch her face, to pull her in so I could connect her lips with mine. She pulled away, shaking her head.

"It's the song of the land, Luke. It's calling you." She muttered something else, so low that I only caught a few words. It took me a second to realise that the words were *the time has come* and that they'd been spoken in my original language. The language from across the waters. The Otherworld.

26

SMITHY

S mithy's sword dug into his side, reminding him of so many things that were wrong about his current situation. And adding to it all was the heavy mizzle that had seen fit to find the bare spot on his neck and made the mound of earth damper than even the boggy stretch of land between him and the tumbling tower that was ahead.

The three of them, Finn, Saoirse and himself, had been hoping to confirm that Colm was hiding here and if so, how many men he had with him. So far they'd seen no movement, or any other sign that there was anyone here, let alone Colm.

"Ah, feck it, this is a waste of time," muttered Finn.

Smithy gave him a curious look. Finn had been off since they'd met him outside of Tara, his usual good humour and easy manner gone, replaced by moodiness and impatience. It was so unlike him that Smithy nearly asked Finn what exactly he'd caught in his gob, but he didn't. His own behaviour hadn't been stellar and Finn seemed so enmeshed in his own troubles that he hadn't pressed Smithy about his past actions.

Saoirse had still been giving him side glances and concerned looks, as well as trying to get him alone so that she could question him closely. So far she'd been unsuccessful, primarily because Smithy had kept close to Finn's side, easy enough as they travelled to this tower.

"Ah, now, give it a bit more time," said Smithy. "Sure, they might be out hunting."

Finn gave him a disbelieving look. "Oh, of course, all the ducks they'd catch."

Smithy shrugged. "I'm sure Daghda's information was reliable."

"Why don't you go back to check on the horses?" said Saoirse. "Get us a bit of food,"

Smithy opened his mouth to object, to offer to do it, but Finn clapped Saoirse on the arm and said, "Thanks. I will, so."

He made his way from the boggy rise crouched low, but in better humour. Smithy sighed inwardly and braced himself.

"What's got Finn in such a mood?" asked Saoirse. "He's not usually like that, is he? At least never when I've been with him."

Relieved at her choice of topic, Smithy relaxed a little. "I've no idea. It's not like him, no. Something Daghda said to him, maybe? Maura? I mean she's always good to wind up Finn, though he usually gives her just as much back."

"Those two do seem to enjoy jabbing at each other."

Smithy snorted. "She's a crow, isn't she? They like to peck at things. Sure, she loves giving everyone the old jab. It's what she does."

"Maybe. But she seems to enjoy it most with Finn."

"It's the king's champion thing. The warrior. She likes to prod him, stir him up. Get the fight up in him."

"She likes that side of him?" asked Saoirse.

Smithy shrugged. "Of course, she would."

Saoirse bit her lip. "Is that why she likes prodding you too? Because you make weapons and she wants that side of you?"

"That side of me?"

Saoirse gave him a direct look. "She was mad for us to get together. Don't say you didn't know that. But her reason for it was so that we'd work together. To make weapons. She wants this war. And to have it, weapons are needed."

Smithy considered her words and nodded slowly. "You're probably right."

Saoirse raised her brow. "I know I'm right."

Smithy just nodded.

"And now she knows there's a problem."

Smithy narrowed his eyes. "What do you mean?"

Saoirse frowned. "You know what I mean. She realises that you have a problem with your memory and you can't make the weapons."

Smithy started to open his mouth, but Saoirse put her hand over it.

"Don't say anything. I know you want to deny that anything is really wrong and yes, Diancecht said you were fine physically. He did add that word, physically."

Smithy shrugged. "So?"

Saoirse sighed. "There's something holding you back, Smithy. Something that is making you forget so much."

He stared at her. He knew she was right. He'd known from the moment Diancecht had said it, and truth be told he'd known before then. The "what" that was going on. He just didn't know the why.

"But I did make a weapon. The spearhead." It was feeble, he knew. She would bat it away like a fly.

"Oh, Smithy," she said, her voice filled with sorrow.

He looked away. No batting, no anger. He could deal with those, put on the big defence. This time, when she "ohsmithyed" him it went right through him.

"Ah, no. You're right. I'm fecked. The spearhead was all you."

Saoirse shoved his shoulder. "No," she said firmly. "It was the both of us. We did it together. But for some reason it became too much for you. It was as though you were overloaded. You couldn't do it any more."

He thought back to the forge and how it felt. "You could sense that?"

"Smithy, when we forge weapons together, we forge ourselves as well, don't you see that?"

She pressed her hand on Smithy's face, gently turning him back to face her. There was so much in her expression, all those emotions, good emotions that showed how much she cared for him. Loved him. It was all there for him. Him. It was too much. Too much of everything.

He brushed his hand along her hair. "Oh, Saoirse, don't be wasting time on me. I'm fecked, like I said. It's too late."

All those emotions in her face folded into one. Anger. Oh and a bit of annoyance thrown in too. Ah, there you are, so much better. He could handle this.

"Smithy, you gobshite, this is not finished. Don't think I'll let you do that."

Words to lay on top of the nice bit of work he'd done came to him. And they were fine and wonderful and would forever solve this problem and sink him to where he should be. Oh it would. Except for the shout, followed by loads of other shouting. There, up in the tower and off toward the small woods where they'd left the horses. Where Finn was now.

He turned to look. Feck. Colm was here, all right. No duck hunting going on. None at all. All the ducks were safe. Shame about himself and Saoirse. And god knows what Finn's safety was looking like now, judging by the men pouring from the woods, battle axes, swords and spears raised and an unholy shouting coming from their mouths.

Smithy had no time to think about the whys and wherefores of these men who suddenly appeared ready for battle. In fact, the battle raged before he could even stand and draw his sword. Men poured out from the tower, all armed and matching your ones behind Smithy for shouting.

It was a clash of two fighting groups, and he and Saoirse were caught in the middle. Smithy just checked Saoirse, who was drawing her own sword and the two of them, side by side, began to do battle. He could see Saoirse out of the corner of his eye match the blows that were aimed her way, but still his breath caught and his gut tightened. He swung his sword in a wider arc, creating a larger defence circle. He had no idea who was the lesser enemy, if there was one, though he'd hardly had the chance to decide. Colm's lot took no deciding, really, he just wasn't certain about their opponents and knew it was best to keep an eye their way as well. But where the feck was Finn? Surely he'd heard the noise.

His thoughts were soon forgotten in the immediate need to fight. Colm's lot were wild, unfocused and just thrashed about. A sly thrust, a quick move and he'd dispatched a few of them quickly. Saoirse got in a few blows and a small swell of pride filled him that expanded when she drew blood and a foul curse from the one.

He spied Colm, off to the side, his hair spikey and his scraggly beard sporting what seemed to be tiny plaits. Smithy nearly snorted at his attempt to look fierce until he realised the man was cutting right and left, and any blow he landed seemed to create deadly results. No opponent was able to get near him. It was as if his sword arm had trained and honed its skill under a completely different place than the rest of him. Colm's footwork was appalling and his stance often ridiculously awful, but the sword arm. No one could argue with the sword arm.

The men behind Smithy appeared to realise it too, because they gradually all turned their focus on Colm, leaving Smithy and Saoirse to fight Colm's remaining men from the tower. He counted five, no, four men left because Saoirse had just cut the arm of one of the men and he dropped his sword. Smithy finished her work and they exchanged a grin, briefly, before fighting on. He could see she was tiring, though, and blood streaked her face from a cut on her head. She was doing far better than he'd would have thought, and he wondered if perhaps some part of her remembered more than she'd learned from himself and Maura.

He caught a blow on his shoulder, a stupid slip on his part because he wasn't giving the fight his full attention. At least his leg had held out and he still remembered how to fight, he thought grimly. There was much he did remember, he realised. It was some of the key things, though, that escaped him. He suffered another blow, this time catching him on the side of the head. He cursed roundly, in Irish and in English. The pain seared through his head and he fought the dizziness. He gripped his sword hard and continued to fight on, giving full focus and increased ferocity. The bastards. He'd have them.

Colm neared him and Smithy saw him out of the corner of his eye. The men fighting him were fewer in number, their comrades fallen, lying still or moaning on the ground behind him. Colm gave a roar, his eyes blazing, a wild expression on his face. The arm kept swinging, each blow landing true.

It was then that Smithy realised the key to Colm's battle prowess. The sword. The fecker had Nemed's magic sword and he was using it on his opponents. No one would be able to defeat Colm, not with the sword in his hand.

The remaining two men of Colm's lot were fighting hard. Smithy tried to take them both on, to give Saoirse a respite and to put them out of action so he could remove her from harm's way before Colm came near enough to fight her. But she was having none of it and the two of them battled the last of Colm's men together. They were fit, skilled and not easily defeated. Saoirse's arm was obviously tiring, the workout too much for muscles unused to it.

Smithy's eyes blurred and it took him a moment to realise that it was blood clouding his vision. The blow he'd sustained earlier had obviously started bleeding. He tried to blink the blood away, but the moment his attention was gone proved to be dangerous and he felt the blow to his arm before he saw it His shield was shoved aside and his opponent's sword found its way into his shoulder. Smithy let out a yowl, but lunged with his sword at the same time. It was a blind thrust, but it found a home and Smithy heard a corresponding howl from the man. The man's sword dropped and he fell to his knees.

Smithy knew his shield arm was fecked. He could fight with his sword, but that was about all. Still, he held on to his sword, turning to help Saoirse with the last man. She was flagging. Blood coated her neck and soaked her pants. She was obviously wounded, too.

Still, Smithy forced himself to raise his sword as Colm came bearing down on them, the remaining warrior near him faltering. As he fell, a bloodcurdling scream cut the air. Smithy and Saoirse both turned and Finn burst out of the woods, brandishing his sword, yelling a war cry that thundered across to them. Mud coated his body and most of his face, so that his eyes appeared large and the whites of his eyes startling.

Smithy turned his attention back to Colm now, who stared at Finn, too stunned by his appearance to do anything.

Before Smithy could make a move, Saoirse lunged across and threw herself at Colm, knocking him down. Taken by surprise, the sword dropped from Colm's hand and Saoirse grabbed it, rolled away from Colm and stood. Smithy, only a few seconds behind her, rushed over in time to place his foot on Colm's chest, his sword at Colm's throat.

"I'd run you through, except that I know Daghda will want to have a chat with you," Smithy said in Irish.

Colm began to reply, but Smithy pressed his sword harder against Colm's throat, so that only a choked sound came out.

Saoirse came alongside of him, breathing hard. Smithy gave her a quick kiss on the cheek. "You're a grand girl, so you are."

She grinned at him, her eyes filled with delight. "I think you mean grand warrior."

He gave a small laugh, loving the comment, the woman beside him coated in blood and grime. Without even a word, Saoirse pulled her belt from her jeans and tied Colm's hands together and gagged him with a strip of linen from his shirt. It was nicely done, tidy and firm. Past experience surfacing again?

Smithy pushed these speculations aside and just focused on the now. These precious moments where all that mattered was the thrill of success that they'd managed between them. And Finn. He turned and saw Finn nearing them, breathing hard, the mud on his body half dried, the wildness in his eyes fading.

"That's a grand look you've got there, Finn," said Smithy.

"Ah, you know, I'm a trend setter," he said.

Saoirse's eyes widened. "Are you naked under that mud?"

Finn looked at her and shrugged. "Served its purpose, didn't it?"

Smithy laughed. "The king's champion, so. Full of dignity."

"Oh, feck off. This isn't the first time it's been done."

"Hmmm. This is the trend you're setting, is it?" said Smithy.

"Whatever works. That's my trend." He nodded to Saoirse. "You got the sword didn't you? I presume that's the sword."

The three of them stared at the weapon in Saoirse's hand. The hilt was elaborately wrought in silver, ancient designs swirling and curving into interlocking patterns. The blade itself shimmered, free of blood, as if it had just been forged. It was unique, unforgettable in design and, from recent experience, powerful.

Saoirse handed it to Smithy. "Daghda will want this as soon as possible."

Smithy grinned at her. "We'll deliver it to him now." He indicated Colm. "And your one. A double bonus."

"Ah, he'll be over the moon," said Finn.

"Especially when he sees you," said Smithy. "What happened to you anyway?"

Finn frowned. "Some feckin' Fomorians. They were waiting in the woods when I got there. Armed and ready for battle. At first they thought I was one of Colm's men. Before I could say anything, they had me bound and gagged and left with the horses. They were in too much of a hurry to start the battle to take much care in the manner in which they tied me, so eventually I was able to work my way out of my bindings and retrieve my sword and go back to help you two."

"Don't forget the part about removing your clothes," said Smithy, sniggering.

"And it worked!" said Saoirse brightly, her gaze directed anywhere but at Finn. "But maybe now you might want to put them back on."

Finn laughed. "If I'm to mount a horse, I think it might be best. A dip in the river though, first."

Smithy grabbed Finn's arm before he headed off. "Did you say they were Fomorians?"

Finn nodded. "I recognised one of them. They're Balor's. At

least he is." He glanced back at the boggy field and grinned. "Was. They're all dead. Every last one, thanks to that sword."

"Well we all know it couldn't have been Colm's skill at fighting," said Smithy. He clapped Finn on the head. "Get yourself to the river, and we'll sort things out here."

Finn nodded and loped off. Sure, things might not be all bad after all, thought Smithy as he watched Finn go.

27

SMITHY

They found Daghda with the king in one of the rooms off the main hall. Smithy smiled wryly to himself. Though he understood Daghda was meant to have given over much of his responsibilities to the younger men, it was more of a notion than a reality, Smithy realised.

Daghda turned when they approached. "Ah. I'd heard you'd been sighted." He glanced at the prisoner clutched between Finn and Smithy. "And you've brought me a treat." His words had been delivered in Irish, but now he glanced at Saoirse and gave a small smile. "You're safe."

It was two words. Or three if you wanted to get technical, but the pleasure that flashed across Saoirse's face gave Smithy a warm feeling.

"She's safe, but not because she hid away from the fight," said Smithy, unable to resist. The pride was clear in his voice.

Daghda raised his brow. "What happened?"

"She was grand," said Finn.

"Fought like a warrior," said Smithy.

"I am a warrior," said Saoirse.

The king rested a hand on Daghda's shoulder. Though he'd

probably not understood the exchange, it was clear they were praising Saoirse. He spoke a few words. Smithy didn't understand this time, but the flush of pride that suffused Daghda's face was evident.

"I want to hear all," said Daghda. "But for now, we must deal with this traitor."

Daghda exchanged a few words with the king and two men came forward. They took Colm from Smithy and Finn's hold and led Colm away.

Daghda snorted. "That, hopefully, will see off any further treason."

Smithy nodded, but they all knew that hope was anything but assured.

Daghda looked to the king. They spoke again and the king nodded. Daghda gave him a grateful glance, before turning to the three of them.

"Come," he said. "We'll go to my quarters so you can tell me the details. That way we'll avoid the Hunters."

Smithy thanked him. The Hunters had been a niggling worry since he'd arrived at Tara. Daghda had assured them that the Hunters were safely occupied in a game of fidchell with some of the more unscrupulous members of the king's household. He didn't know who were the worst chancers and figured the outcome would be deserved by all.

Daghda's quarters were spare enough, furnished with a bed, a table, a couple of chairs to take his ease in. Several chests lined the walls, beautifully worked with ornate carving. He took a chair, which left a spare one. Saoirse headed for the bed, which was large to accommodate Daghda's tall, bulky frame. Finn took the spare chair, grinning at Smithy. Sighing inwardly, Smithy took a seat next to Saoirse on the bed.

Which led him to think of the last time he'd been on a bed with Saoirse. He tried to shove the thought aside, but it was too insistent and too filled with emotion, confusion and so much else that it shoved its way further into Smithy's mind, took centre stage and played havoc with the rest of him. It was a polka, stamped out with such force, it was all he could not to stand up and walk, run towards the door.

Finn was speaking and Smithy tried to focus on his words, but that two four polka beat kept at him, stamping out each idea, each memory, each visual that was cluttered together, arm in arm.

Saoirse slipped her hand in his and he nearly jumped from the bed. The heat that had been warring throughout his body now headed south, where a ceilí took up with determined ferocity. Feckityfeck. My god.

"What do you think, Goibhniu?" asked Daghda.

Smithy blinked. "Ah, sorry?"

Daghda frowned at him. "Are you well? Did you receive a blow to the head during the battle?"

Smithy paused. There'd been no blow, had there? The question was a distraction and he was all over it. Diancecht had tended to their wounds immediately upon their arrival, giving Smithy sour looks and muttered comments he tried to ignore. He was such a moody fecker, that one.

"No, I'm fine," said Smithy. "I just got distracted for a moment. What was the question?"

"Ogma," he said, nodding to Finn, "suggested that you and Saoirse cross the water as soon as possible. The Hunters will know soon enough that you're here. It's best if you're gone, so that they can't make you complete the bargain. Ogma will follow shortly after."

"Do they have the spearhead?" asked Saoirse. She squeezed Smithy's hand, the one he was all too conscious had remained in his since she'd first inserted it.

Daghda gave her a wide grin and his eyes twinkled. The

action lit his face and in that moment Smithy could see the resemblance between the two. She'd been a fierce warrior, and he knew now she had more than a bit of Daghda in her, more than any faint resemblance. The polka danced louder and harder. He barely heard Daghda's reply.

"Not at all. I slipped it away in the confusion of Smithy's collapse. They didn't realise that it was complete. And I may have encouraged that notion."

"Where's the spearhead now?" asked Finn.

"Safe," said Daghda. "But I want Goibhniu and Bríd to take it with them. It will be safest across the water. The Hunters won't be able to get it there."

Saoirse nodded and Smithy stared, his attention caught now. "Are you certain? Someone else might come looking for it."

"Ah, sure, who would find out, or even think to look for it there, even if they were able to travel there?"

Smithy frowned. Daghda might think no one would hear about it and find a way, but he knew better. Word would get out, he was sure. And what would they do with that knowledge, was anyone's guess. Didn't Colm prove that treachery could happen?

"It'll be grand, Smithy," said Finn.

The polka had quietened, slowed its pace and came to an end now, to be replaced by something that was not the _suantraí_ collection of lullabies.

FINN's good humour seemed to have vanished once they'd crossed the water. He had decided to travel back with Smithy and Saoirse and as the boat neared the banks Finn had gone quiet, his face and mood shifting to something more sullen. The misty rain only seemed to emphasise his foul mood.

Smithy really noticed it this time, maybe because Saoirse

had called his attention to it earlier. Now, they exchanged looks at the sharp negative reply he'd just issued in response to Saoirse's question about his departure to his own home.

"Anu will only make me come to her place," added Finn. "I may as well get it over with."

Smithy nodded, deciding not to say anything more. He led the way back up through the woods. He wouldn't bother to stop at his own place, not in the current atmosphere. Besides, it was best not to distract himself with Saoirse's presence in his house. It was difficult at the best of times, but now it seemed to be over-whelming. He'd tried to analyse why this had happened. She hadn't changed. Or had she? He couldn't stop seeing her. Seeing the woman, the whole woman, whose hair, now caught up in its usual plait, flamed around her head like it would set the world on fire. Her leather jacket, which he knew had been Maura's, fitted her so well, though it was stained from battle and travel-ling. She looked...more. More than the pixie boho with her coronet of plaits and funky clothes. Those clothes would return probably, he knew that, once she was back at Anu's, but she'd still be more.

He could feel her behind him, her breathing still even, though the climb was getting steeper. It was all he could do not to turn around to see her, to keep her in his sights. But he forced himself to stay focused ahead. There was too much to sort out in himself, before he even took on anything beyond that. If only the Ceilí going on in his body would stop heading south, setting up a stage in his groin.

He flexed his hands, gripped them hard. Think about your sword skills, you fecker, he chided himself. They had been perfect at the end of the battle. In sync. And why wouldn't they be? Yet he had forgotten his own language. Was it another part of the brain? He'd forgotten things about the past in the world that had his native language. Was that a fluke? He knew it wasn't. Diancecht's mutterings told him it wasn't either. Deep down, he knew all the things he'd experienced since Diancecht had brought him back to life were something to do with the past and his desire to keep it all past. A past that included Saoirse. Bríd.

Saoirse came alongside, startling him. Was their connection so strong that the mere thought of her brought her to him? It was a ridiculous notion, but then again, was it? The connection he'd been trying to deny, to sever, was still there. He didn't have to hold her hand to feel it. He looked down at her, misty droplets clinging to her hair and clothes and wetting her lashes. Strands of music, weblike, spun around inside, tightening, forming knots that were firm against any undoing.

"What's wrong with Finn? Has he said anything to you?" she said to him in a low voice. "He's worse than ever."

It took a moment to switch his thoughts to her words. "No, I've no clue at all."

"Maybe you should ask him."

Smithy weighed her idea for a moment. "Maybe. I'll see what I can do." He doubted he'd get anything out of Finn, but he might try.

"And you, what am I going to do with you?"

"Me?"

She took his hand and squeezed it. "Ah, Smithy, you know what I mean."

He shrugged. "I'm grand."

"No. You're not."

"It's nothing to bother about. I was fine during the battle, wasn't I? No weaknesses, I was able to fight." He grinned down at her. "And you were fearsome."

She returned the grin and shoved against him. "You didn't expect that?"

He shook his head. "I never said you didn't have a natural

skill, but you certainly fought as though you had more than that. It was as if you had the experience of years of training."

She frowned and slowed her steps. "I know. It was strange, Smithy. It all just happened. Came to me without thinking. My arms, my whole body, it just moved for me. A...a kind of muscle memory, I suppose."

"Plenty of muscle, so," he said with a laugh. "Don't question it. It's a good thing."

She smiled slowly. "I guess it is." She paused. "And it's something you should take note of."

"What?" He knew where she was heading, but it wasn't something he counted on or even let himself consider.

"It'll come to you in time, Smithy. The bits you're missing. They'll come back."

He sighed. Even hearing the words gave him hope. But he couldn't afford hope. He couldn't be caught out with hope. Hope was unreliable.

Anu's drawn face was the first thing that Smithy noticed when they arrived. She gave them a smile and her usual warm welcome, followed by tea making and seating themselves around her kitchen table.

"Is Maura back?" asked Saoirse when she'd taken a sip of her tea. Her hair, soaked and nearly dripping, had largely escaped the plait now. Her nose was a little red, too, but Smithy found he liked it. Liked the way her lashes had become spiky from the rain. His eyes drifted to her mouth, which was sipping tea again.

"Maura is back from across the water, but she won't be here. I had to send her to the Beara."

"The Beara?" asked Finn, surprise and something else in his eyes. "Why?"

"I'll tell you in a moment. After you tell me what happened to all of you." She gave Smithy a frown. "And why it was that you went across and not just Finn."

Finn gave her an amused look. "Ah. You might want to ask the other two to explain that."

Anu turned her gaze to Smithy and raised a brow.

"What?" he said. "It was Finn who wanted me along. Pushed me to go with him, telling me what great craic it would be." He gave a little huff of annoyance. "Oh, there was some craic all right."

Finn laughed, his mood a little lighter. "Oh, you know you loved it, you fool."

Anu held up her hand. "Just tell me what happened. Then we can go into why you were there."

Saoirse started to open her mouth, but Smithy interrupted her and began to recount the events that had led to the battle and then the battle's outcome. When Smithy had finished, with Finn adding his embellishments and teasing remarks, Anu looked very pleased. Smithy was glad to see her face lighten, and Finn's improved mood.

Anu nodded. "I can see that all of you more than succeeded in what you set out to do. Saoirse gained insight into her true self, Finn found that there is more than just being a master of words and a king's champion. And you, Smithy. I think understand more about the nature of what is ailing you."

Finn, Smithy and Saoirse stared at Anu.

"What do you mean?" asked Smithy darkly.

"What ails him?" asked Finn, looking questioningly at Smithy. "What do you, mean 'what ails him'?"

Smithy glanced at Saoirse and saw her redden. A cold fury passed through him. "You told her?"

"I had to," said Saoirse softly. There was pleading in her eyes, but also defiance. "You kept putting yourself at risk. And putting others at risk, too, and I didn't know what to do."

"You had no right," said Smithy, his voice hard, icy.

"She had every right," said Anu. "She loves you. You are her other half. When you suffer, she suffers."

Smithy glowered at Anu. "She had no right."

"What is it she had no right to do?" said Finn in a loud voice. "Can someone please tell me what's going on?"

"Smithy has been struggling with missing parts of memory." Anu said. "And possibly some other things, but he's been trying to keep it from everyone."

Finn turned to look at Smithy. "Is this true?" he said in a shocked voice.

Smithy gave him an angry look, but said nothing.

"Yes, it's true," said Saoirse. "He can't remember the language of the Otherworld, for a start. He doesn't recognise people from the past from there either, do you, Smithy?"

Smithy rose from his chair. "I've updated you on what's happened, so I'll be off."

"Sit down," Anu said firmly. "I still have things to tell you."

Smithy frowned and reluctantly resumed his seat, crossing his arms. He was conscious of the angry looks Finn was giving him. He forced himself not to care. So they all knew now. Not a bother. Fine, so. Despite the thought, he instinctively inched his chair away from Saoirse while the word "traitor" echoed in his mind. He tried to squash the juvenile thought, but it kept popping up.

"I had a very disturbing message from *An Cailleach*, recently," said Anu, cutting into his thoughts.

"*An Cailleach*?" said Saoirse, her face puzzled. "What's that?"

Anu gave her a surprised look and then gathered herself. "*An Cailleach* is ancient," she said finally. "She dwells in the Beara Peninsula. She is the Beara, the land."

Smithy hid a smile as he watched Saoirse's struggling to take in the information and make sense of it. To pretend it was all normal to her, nothing strange, no bother at all. He felt a tenderness and squashed it immediately.

"But aren't you that?" Saoirse said finally. "For the whole of Ireland?"

Anu gave her a humorous look. "I am that and more. *An Cailleach* is part of me, she is connected to me and when she suffers, I suffer too."

Saoirse nodded slowly, but Smithy knew she was more confused than ever. Would she even understand that *cailleach* meant "hag", "old woman", but also so much more in this case.

"Like the holy trinity, so," said Finn, his grin back in place. "Only two of them. But she, herself is a trinity, though, I suppose."

Smithy started to laugh at Saoirse's confused expression and quickly turned it into a cough when he caught Anu's sharp glance.

"Oh, right," said Saoirse. "Sorry, now. What was *An Cailleach's* message?"

Anu gave a brief nod. "Something serious has happened. Toxic dumping in the mines and a severe oil spill just off the coast."

"How did that happen?" asked Smithy. Anu had his full attention now. "Two incidents at the same time? Hardly a coincidence."

"No, not a coincidence," said Anu. "Balor."

"You're certain?" asked Finn.

"I am. *An Cailleach* investigated it herself. There's no doubt he's directly responsible. And she fears that's not the end of it. She was certain she caught sight of one of Balor's men at the mine site. He vanished when he saw her."

"One of his company men, or one of his old warriors?" said Finn.

Anu frowned. "One of his warriors."

"But why?" asked Saoirse. "Why would he send a warrior to do something like that and not someone with experience in that kind of thing?"

"Because he trusts them," said Smithy. "And they've done these things before."

"And," said Finn, his voice steely. "They are prepared to take whatever steps are necessary to accomplish their ends."

"So, more poisoning?" said Saoirse.

"More of that, but also possibly to set a trap," said Finn. "To lure us there."

The rest of the words hung in the air. Smithy didn't need Finn to voice them. Balor wanted a battle. He wanted them dead. Especially Smithy.

28

LUKE

I sat on the high rock, looking out to the sea. The faint humming was still there, whooshing in and out inside me, a sound and beat that wasn't a heart, or at least not my heart. I'd come here the past few mornings, staying for an hour or so, when I'd finally get up, and walk back to the farm, to Kayla.

Kayla. The humour of it wasn't humorous, not to me. It pulled me, ripped at me and wouldn't leave me. The name, her, it was in my skin and under it and all over the top of it. There was no "only for nowness" about it. I couldn't shift it, because shifting it meant that I'd be shifting part of myself. A part I wanted, still and always.

Oh, feck me. Mon would have a field day. I finally understood. The wanting, the needing, even though it was the worst thing for me. I could no more leave this place, leave her, than I could leave this planet.

She'd not even forced herself on me, no not at all. I managed it myself, the eejit that I am. There was no seduction, no flirting with instruments. The wound, sure, that was a thing, but purely and simply a desire to help, no siren call intended. And there were no demands now, only an explanation.

Ah, the soft way she told me who she was. The woman of that house, *Bean an Tí* of all that is the Beara. Her sweet ways, sweet words, they punctured me with their very own arrow. A slow weaving, whoosh and I caught the tune from the air, the sea and the very land around me, as I sat in that farmhouse. The disease of the land, a viral tune that only I could catch.

She'd put no pressure on me, none at all. Checked my wound, gave me smiles, fussed over her daughter and her mother (daughter and mother?). A triune of goddesses all in one house. Two of them ill. What did I make of that? She made nothing of it, at least not to me, just continued to fuss and worry like any other mother and daughter. While I watched, said nothing. Drank my tea, ate my food, helped with farm chores and walked the land.

What was I doing, besides wondering if this ever-loving tune would leave me? I didn't know. I just kept on doing the whatevers, and felt the desire to touch her, to do more than touch her. To feel us, together. And each day I walked here, took the steps. Separation of the soul from the body, Yes, Turlough, a new meaning for your harp piece. A blind harper from long ago who knew more than he realised. For every time I took those steps, separated my body from hers, my soul remained behind. With her.

I lifted the sleeve of my T-shirt and looked at the scar forming on my arm. It swirled and curved, a strange design with a Celtic look. In some ways it had more the look of a tattoo than a scar. I marvelled at it, wondering at its creation. Was this Kayla's work? What did it mean? The salve she used, her touch, it had all felt more. More than a nursing touch.

I sighed. Though it made me uncomfortable I didn't feel compelled to dig it out yet again. I didn't feel a dark, underlying current with it. I knew Kayla was bound to the land. She was the land. They were the land. Bláthín, Kayla and Nana. Grandmother, mother, maiden. I sighed again. And how did I fit in there?

The sea looked back at me as I pondered these questions, its whoosh whoosh blending in with the one inside me. After a few moments I rose, the questions still hanging in the air, and began to walk back.

I ENTERED THE KITCHEN, expecting to find it empty, but Kayla was sitting there, her face pale and drawn. I tensed, my body on full alert and a surprising dart of pain and worry shot through me.

I squatted beside her, touched her arm. "What is it? What's happened?"

She turned to look at me, her golden eyes a stormy sea filled with pain. "Oh, Luke, I am trying. Each day, I'm trying, but it's getting worse. I can feel it."

I brushed her cheek with my hand. "What do you mean? How is it getting worse?"

She clutched her stomach, turned away and swallowed. "He must be poisoning other places as well as the mines. I can feel it. Nana is worse and Bláthín is no better. And now...."

She let her words trail off, but she didn't have to complete her thought. I could see it in the large circles under her eyes, the loose fit of her clothing. Had I been too caught up in my own worries to notice before?

"You're ill," I said. "It's affecting you too, now."

She sighed but said nothing. She tried to rise, but I pressed her down in the chair.

"Have you eaten? Shall I make you a cup of tea? Soup?"

Kayla shook her head. "No, I haven't been able to keep anything down."

I cast my mind back to the night before and the laborious manner in which she ate her food. Or had she? Sure, she'd pushed the food around her plate, but how much of it had she really eaten?

"How long have you been feeling this way?"

She shrugged. "Not too long. A few days. It's only this morning that I really felt this poorly, though." She looked at me and forced a smile. "I'll be grand, so."

I frowned. "Has Seán Óg been here this morning and said anything about more toxic waste?"

She smiled weakly. "He was here, the dote. Fixed himself a cuppa and tried to get me to take one as well. He told me he hadn't heard anything more, but he'd find out. Though he was certain the oil spill would be getting worse before it got better. But you know Seán Óg. He loves the drama."

I knew him, all right. Forced aside the rise of anger and something else, and while it was sliding there, the something else sneaked back and gave me a whack in the face. I stood up, the surprise of it, the sheer incredulity putting up their fists against it in defence of it all. But it whacked me in the face again, laughing with its green eyes.

Ah, no call for it. No call at all for that the twat that was the jealousy. I kicked it aside again, but it just laughed and laughed while I was beside myself with weak denial. Myself took it in hand and before I knew what was happening, Kayla was out of her seat and in my arms, my lips kissing her lightly on the forehead.

"Sean Óg can feck off with his tales of woe," I said softly. I could feel her once lush curves now reduced to a slender frame that suggested a frailty that made my heart ache. "We'll get you better, *a stór,* all three of you." I kissed her head, hugging her tightly, willing my strength into hers.

I would find a way, somehow. If this was Balor's fault he would pay. I would make certain of that. But for now I had to try and ensure Kayla, Bláthín and Nana didn't get worse.

"Let's get you to bed, now," I said. "You're not fit to be anywhere else. There's no need to worry about anything. I'll look after you, Bláthín and Nana."

I picked her up in my arms, dismayed to find how little she weighed, and took her upstairs to her bed. I laid her down carefully. The light from the window revealed the grey pallor of her skin. Worry tugged at me. Her eyes were closed now, but the shadows underneath them were like bruises against her skin. I brushed my hand against her cheek. It was soft to touch, warm and inviting. I leaned down and kissed it, felt her breath on my skin. Her lashes fluttered against my cheek and her eyes opened briefly, latching onto mine. I travelled into them, lost myself in their depths, seeing the Mishkish Mountains, Hungry Hill, Bere Island, and the other islands, mountains, the sea, sky and all that she was.

I kissed her lips, tasted the salt of the sea, the sweetness of the honeysuckle and all the rest of the tastes and smelled the scents that were her. They seeped into me and I felt their strength, the power of it all. The life force was there, but I could detect something else. Something malevolent. Poisonous.

I kissed her again. "I'll make this better, Kayla. I promise you."

Her eyes fluttered open again and she gave me a wan smile. "I know you will. I know you will."

I squeezed her hand and rose. "I'll be back soon."

I checked on Bláthín and Nana. Nana didn't stir, her breathing shallow. I stood at the end of her bed and murmured reassurances, something that might have been for my own benefit rather than hers. Bláthín stirred when I entered, her breathing ragged. I put my hand on her forehead and stroked it soothingly. She seemed to settle a little with that gesture, but I knew it was temporary.

I spoke to her, words of the old language coming to me and spilling out. A prayer, a promise, and everything else that I could think of saying to ensure a good outcome.

Eventually, I went downstairs and outdoors, trying to clear my head, form a plan. A hero's plan. But the plan fell well short and came more in the shaped plan of the hipster, cool surfer dude. Dud. A loud "get over yourself" punched the air.

Startled, I looked around, wondering for a moment if it had been a thought that escaped? For it was true. I was a pure gobshite for wallowing in pity. Pity wasn't a friend. Or a friend that would do me any good.

I heard a squawk behind me. I turned around, away from the view of the fields and the hill that rose up behind it and looked at the yard. A large crow stood not a metre in front and began strutting towards me, away from the large shed.

I crossed my arms, immediately understanding that it wasn't a thought that had escaped. No, the words that had condemned me had come from a source that was well and truly used to slinging insults and wild words.

"Maura," I said flatly.

The caw became a cackle, and almost before I could blink she stood there in all her wild black hair, dark eyes flashing.

"Luke," she said, grinning widely. "A lucky day, all right."

"You were looking for me?"

She just started laughing. The belly laugh, leaning over. "Oh, *buachaill*, you are so canny, you don't even know yourself."

"What?" I asked, puzzled. I watched her while gradually, her humour subsided.

She shook her head. "Oh, I have been looking for you. We've

all been looking for you. Up and down the country. Then the coastlines. Looking for the surfer dude. The top shelf musician. Nothing. You slip slided away. Elusive, always just out of reach. And now, when I'm not looking, here you are, so." She began to laugh again.

I looked at her while her words filtered in my mind. "You're not here for me?"

"No, hero boy. I came from *An Cailleach*."

It took me a moment to realise who she meant. "Kayla?"

She looked at me. "Oh, right. Yes. She sent a message."

Again I looked at her, tried to make sense of what she was telling me. Kayla's words about sending for help came back to me. "She asked you for help?" It seemed extreme to ask Morrigan for help. Or maybe not.

"Not me, per se. Anu."

I nodded. "Yes. Of course. And Anu sent you to talk to her. To find out what exactly is going on."

Maura shrugged. "The extent of the damage. And to confirm everything."

I stiffened. "I can confirm it all. Toxic waste dumped in the mines. Offshore oil spills killing marine life. All of it."

"Where's *An Cailleach*?"

"My word isn't good enough?" I said darkly. "She's ill. She doesn't need to be disturbed."

Maura rolled her eyes. "Fine. Right. I was just doing what Anu would want me to do, you gobshite."

I frowned. "I'm sure she would take my word for it."

"Ah, now, would she though?"

I shook my head. "Never mind. It's not important. The point is that we need to act. The fecker has dumped more poison and the situation is getting dire."

Maura raised a brow. "The fecker? Which fecker would this be? There are so many."

I pursed my lips and bit out the words. "The biggest fecker of all. The fecker that was supposed to have died. The fecker who's related to me."

"Oh, that fecker." She nodded sagely. "So he is definitely behind all of this?"

"No question. Kayla looked into it." I recalled the man I'd seen earlier today. "And I've seen one of his minions. One of his personal guard."

Maura's expression darkened. "Ah, now. That does sound serious. Especially if his men are here. Do you think himself is here?"

I thought about this for a moment, then shook my head. "I doubt it. This is all by stealth, a furtive guerrilla type action that doesn't require a fierce show of strength or a heavy battle."

She nodded slowly. "True. Do you know where they're based?"

I shook my head. "Not yet. It won't take me long, though."

A slow smile spread across her face. "Oh, I'm sure it wouldn't. But what I'd like to know is why all of a sudden you're so anxious to help?"

I looked away, unwilling to reveal anything to this woman. This harridan of chaos and blood. "Just accept that I am and let's get on with it."

She snorted. "Oh, we'll get on with it, don't you worry. I just thought it would be nice to have the full picture, so. For Anu."

"I'm sure Anu will be satisfied knowing that I'm here and willing to help."

Maura shrugged. "Fine. But don't think I won't find out." She looked beyond me to the house. "Is *An Ceailleach* inside, then? I'll just have a word."

She began to step around me, but I blocked her path. "I said she's ill and she doesn't need to be disturbed." I bit out the words, enunciating carefully so that there was no question about their meaning.

Maura raised her brow. "I see."

It was two words, but she packed her own meaning into them. I sighed. "Look, just let Anu know that I'll find out as much as I can and then take action."

Maura nodded. "No, worries. I'll tell her. But don't do anything rash. I'll be back with the others to help. You don't know exactly who or what you're dealing with, yet."

"Others?"

"Others. I'm sure you can hazard a guess."

Before I could question her further, she vanished with a flapping of wings.

29

SAOIRSE

Saoirse swung her leg off the back of the motorbike and stood beside it, feeling a little stiff as she unclasped the strap of her helmet. The ride to the Beara had been long enough before it was too long, considering that Smithy had been stiff and tense the whole of the journey. Finn had insisted that they'd go before him, so he could pop back to his own place and retrieve some things. Anu had agreed, seeming to feel that someone needed to be at the Beara as soon as possible, especially when Maura had appeared and updated them on the situation.

The mixed feelings that had possessed Saoirse since the suggestion had been given still continued to trouble her. Smithy had been an enigma since before their return from the Otherworld. Even her blunt words had done little to persuade him to reveal his own state of mind and health or persuade him on some kind of path to healing. Not really. Now, that he'd discovered she'd told Anu about his problems, she could at least understand his anger toward her. At least in that regard. But the battle, the manner in which they fought together, she felt that had bonded them in a way that couldn't be ignored. Apparently, though, Smithy seemed to feel otherwise.

She watched, still unsettled, while Smithy took her helmet, and placed it beside his on the motorcycle seat. He turned and helped remove the straps of the large black zipped bag she'd carried on her back, his eyes focused on the task the whole time. The case was the shape of gun bag, padded and protective of its contents. Smithy hefted it away carefully. It was precious beyond words and they both knew it.

She took in her surroundings, suddenly aware how beautiful it was. Though she couldn't see the sea from her position, she could smell it and hear the cry of the gulls that marked its close proximity. She could also smell the sweet scent of freshly cut hay and the pungent odour of dung. The farmhouse in front of them was old, but solid, its stone frame at home in its environment. The yard beside it stretched back to several sheds and the hills beyond that. Bleating sounded as if on cue, confirming the identity of the grazing animals she saw in the distance.

A dog barked and Saoirse looked beyond Smithy and saw a figure coming down the hills, the dog at his heels. She knew who it was before she could make out his features.

"Luke." She said his name flatly. She hadn't seen him since he'd left her at the railway station in Galway. The fecker.

"That's Luke?" said Smithy coming up behind her.

She said nothing, just stared at the figure as it slowly came towards them, the confusion she felt before heightened. Knowing what she did about him, now, Luke seemed more and less of who she thought he was. What she thought he was. Luke the surfer, Luke the amazing musician, witty and clever in his banter, his manner. Fun to be with. That was the façade. The chancer who invited her to a weekend by the sea, who took her and dumped her at the first sign she wasn't just some easy chick. But he was Lugh, the reluctant hero, running away from those who needed him. Damaged and angry. Fearful enough that he believed she had power that she didn't possess. Or at least that's what she'd concluded.

He came into view, hesitating a moment only when he saw her and Smithy waiting. He opened the field gate, nodded to them and made a big production of shutting it behind him, before walking the short path that led to the gate to the yard. He spoke to the dog, made a small gesture and the animal took off to the shed, its task done.

Luke walked steadily towards them, his eyes on Smithy, his expression neutral. He was wearing jeans, a T-shirt and wellies. Nothing strange or out of place in this rural countryside, but it gave Saoirse a bit of a shock. But not as much as his hair, The dark blond locks no longer flopping, but cropped close to his head. Stubble clung to his cheeks and dark shadows hollowed out his eyes. He looked haunted.

"Goibhniu," he said in a firm voice. There was no question in his voice. He knew who he was. "Saoirse," he added, as if it was an afterthought. "Or do you prefer Bríd?" His tone was flat, devoid of emotion.

Saoirse frowned. "Saoirse's fine." What was the point of explaining the situation to him?

"Call me Smithy," said Smithy. "That's my name...here."

"I see. Very original altogether," he said. "Smithy."

Smithy shrugged. "As you say...Luke."

"I suppose Anu sent you to help me."

"Yes, and Maura should be here soon," said Smithy. His tone was pleasant, giving nothing away. "And Finn."

Luke arched his brow. "Finn?"

Smithy glanced at Saoirse a moment. He cleared his throat. "Ogma. He's called Finn this side."

"Finn. Oh, fine. Well, Anu needn't have sent anyone. I'll be fine on my own. King's champion or no."

"No harm to have us too," said Smithy, keeping his tone reasonable. Saoirse could tell he was becoming annoyed. She wasn't certain the reason, but could maybe guess that he found Luke's attitude annoying. Maybe as much as she found it annoying.

"Why would you object to our help?" Saoirse said, a touch of anger in her voice.

He turned slowly and focused his gaze on her. She made herself return his look, unblinking. She clutched her hands into a tight fist. No backing down this time.

"Your help?" he said. He gave a small laugh. "How could you help, flute girl? Play your music while I fight? Sing them to their deaths? Oh, sorry, sorry, I forgot you inspire poetry as well. Or wait, you'll heal my wounds."

"She can fight," said Smithy. He glared at Luke. "So you can shut your gob."

Saoirse was surprised to hear Smithy's words. That he was defending her. Luke looked at her again, scepticism in his eyes.

"With what? Her tongue? Well, I can say from experience she does have a way with her tongue."

Saoirse flushed. She stiffened, raised her chin and narrowed her eyes. "I can fight with a sword. Would you like a demonstration? I'm happy to fight you."

Luke laughed, and she could hear the tinge of bitterness in it. "No, you're grand. I've no interest in fighting amateurs."

"From what I understand, you'd be lucky to beat an amateur at this point," said Smithy. "How long has it been since you picked up a sword?"

Luke shrugged. "It's not important."

Smithy snorted. "You don't think?"

"The skill is there. There's no need to worry."

"Oh, I'm not worried about you," said Smithy. "Just the poor feckers who will be relying on you."

"And that would be...you?"

A loud caw filled the air along with the swoop of wings. Maura. She appeared, her cheeks flushed, eyes sparkling.

"What did I miss? Did I miss anything?" She looked at each one of them. "Oh, what? Already at odds? And Finn's not even here. Oh, this is great." She laughed.

All them looked at her, their exchange forgotten for the moment. Maura put her hands on her leather clad hips, surveying them still.

"Oh, don't let me stop you," she said.

"You haven't changed," said Luke.

She gave him a puzzled look. "Why would I? I am who I am."

"No doubt about that," said Luke.

"The years haven't dulled her wit either," said a voice behind them.

Finn walked into view, his expression guarded. He wore a quilted leather jacket and leather trousers. His normally wiry auburn hair was slicked back from his face and his blue eyes were dark, serious. He was startling, different to the Finn Saoirse knew. Even the time rescuing Smithy, or the attack at the tower, there had still been something carefree and friendly about him. Now, there was a dark echo simmering underneath the surface. He gave Luke a cold look.

"So, you decided to come out of hiding, finally," said Finn.

"I wasn't hiding. I was...avoiding."

"Avoiding responsibility," said Finn.

"No." Luke's reply was sharp. He took a deep breath. "I made a decision a long time ago and I intended to stick to it."

"A coward's decision," said Finn.

"Well, it should have pleased you," said Luke. "You always wanted to resume your role as king's champion, when I took that privilege from you."

Luke stepped forward, but Smithy put a hand to stop him.

"Oh, this is good," said Maura. "And as much as I'd like to see how it all develops, maybe we could hold it off until we've done what we came for."

Luke looked over at Maura. "You're right. For once. We need to move quickly."

"*An Cailleach*, how is she?" asked Finn, his voice tight.

Luke frowned. "Ill."

Finn nodded, his face expressionless.

"Did you find out anything more?" asked Maura.

Luke nodded. "They're based at Turieann."

"Turieann?" said Saoirse.

"It's an ancient fort west of Castletownbere," Luke said in a clipped tone.

Saoirse nodded, repressing her sigh. She could understand Luke's attitude towards her. But she'd watched the tense exchange Luke had first with Smithy and then Finn anxiously and with some bewilderment. It seemed reasonable that Smithy would harbour some resentment towards Luke for avoiding them, but hadn't Smithy done the same? And Finn's reaction was just as puzzling. Could it just be laid at the feet of an ancient rivalry?

"How many are at the fort?" asked Finn.

"I counted around ten, but there could be more."

The others nodded, taking it in, considering.

After a moment Maura piped up. "Well, what's the plan?" She surveyed the group, her mouth forming a half smile.

"The plan," said Luke stiffly. "Is to take them by surprise."

Finn snorted. "Ah, now. Aren't you the clever one?"

"How?" Maura cut across Finn. He gave her a dark look. She stuck her tongue out.

"Do you have anything specific in mind?" asked Saoirse, keeping her voice calm, reasonable.

Luke looked at her and his expression eased a little. She felt grateful for that.

"The road leading to the fort is narrow, there are a few places we can park and then approach them without being seen. The fort is on a rise, in an open field though, but if we cut through the far field behind it and creep up the back way, we have a chance to take them by surprise."

Smithy, Finn and Maura nodded. "Makes sense," said Maura. She turned to Finn. "You have my gear?"

He gave a curt nod, his eyes on Luke.

"I don't have a weapon," said Luke. His words were a statement, but behind the words, said so evenly, there was a question and a touch of shame.

"We have your weapon," said Saoirse.

She took the bag from Smithy and opened it, withdrawing an oil cloth-wrapped bundle. The weight of it and its meaning was heavy in her hands. Carefully, she presented the bundle to Luke.

Luke stared at it for a few seconds then reached out to touch it tentatively. He looked up at Saoirse, pain and wonder in his eyes.

"Nemed's magic sword?" he whispered.

She nodded. How he knew that without unfolding the cloth, she didn't know, but it confirmed for her that there was no better person to wield this weapon.

"We went to a lot of trouble to get this sword back, so use it well and wisely," said Finn.

Luke looked at him and for the first time there was no animosity. "Of course. Thank you."

"You can thank Saoirse," said Smithy. "She's the one that took it from Colm. After she fought him and his men. And Balor's men."

Luke turned his gaze to her. "I'm sorry," he said. "For

doubting you." He spoke to Smithy. "Balor? He was involved in stealing the sword?"

"Not directly."

He briefly explained the events while Saoirse studied Luke. Was his apology about more than just doubting her skill at fighting? There was nothing in his expression now that would explain it any further. Saoirse just had to hope that he understood that she didn't know who he was when they'd gone to Galway for that weekend. That she'd been in a haze of grief at Smithy's rejection and the betrayal she felt towards Anu. She would find a way to convince him, if he didn't already know or believe it. She could see now that the fecker who'd left her at the railway station was really not the person or fecker she thought he was.

30

LUKE

I pushed the door to the kitchen open slowly, catching myself over the expectation I would see Kayla in the chair, a mug of tea in her hand a smile on her face as she greeted me. The wave of grief I felt surprised me even more. I placed the cloth bundle on the table and ran my hand through my hair. Bracing myself for what I might see, I climbed the stairs. When I pushed open her bedroom door and saw the prone figure on the bed, unmoving, my breath caught in my throat.

"Kayla," I said, moving to her side.

She lay on top of the covers, her clothes dishevelled, her hair tumbling around her. I brushed a strand of hair from her face and leaned over, relieved to hear the faint sound of her breathing. On impulse I brushed my lips lightly against hers. Her eyes fluttered lightly and I kissed her again, my lips pressing hers gently. Her mouth was warm, and I could taste the salt and fresh herbs that seemed to be part of her.

"*A cailleach, mo chroí*, Anu has sent help. We'll make this better, I promise. I'll defeat him." I continued, repeating the endearments, the promises in Irish and in the old language.

She stirred, her eyes opened and she smiled faintly as she

looked at me, joy and something else in her expression. Pride. She spoke in the ancient language. The formal tongue, one I hadn't heard in so long I'd nearly forgotten it. "You have answered the call of the land. You have answered my heart."

I OPENED the cloth bundle carefully, almost fearful of what it would reveal, even though I knew what was inside. The cloth itself was old, yellowed from the oil, the weave still tight and smelling strongly of its purpose, its duty.

When I was finished and the contents were laid open, bare to me, I allowed myself to breathe. I whispered its name, given to me by the sword itself. Retaliator. The beauty I'd remembered was still there, burnished and perfect from the tip of the blade to its magnificent hilt. My hand shook as I took it up carefully, thinking of the last time I'd held it, a time that was just as misty as the clichéd phrase implied.

The last battle, before my grandfather was dead at my hand. Or, fallen, I amended. Daghda had given me the sword on the king's orders, more for its symbolic nature than as a necessity, for he knew that I had the skill to defeat any of my opponents. The odds had been against us, though, the Fomorians force was large and King Bres's treachery had made it worse, taking knowledge as well as key weapons with him. Except the treasures. Daghda had the treasures safely guarded elsewhere. He'd never trusted Bres. Daghda had given me the sword to show that despite the treachery, the most important treasures were still with the Tuatha de Danann, and therefore their power and might couldn't be beaten. Me, the king's champion, the warlord of the Tuatha de Danann, had to show that symbol, use it and let the Fomorians tremble at its might.

I'd wielded it with pride that day. Feeling the honour, the

beauty of its meaning and that finally, finally I was accepted fully as a Tuatha de Danann. Not a half breed whose loyalties could be questioned secretly, or in private. I belonged. I knew who I was and so did they. And the enemy had fallen, hard, quickly. Until Balor's men appeared. A contingent of vicious fighters and no amount of symbolic sword slashing or killing Fomorians seem to stop the onslaught. It was as though they had their own cauldron or well to renew slain fighters. It wasn't until later that I'd realised that's exactly what had happened. The well had been filled with boulders, the cauldron stolen.

With Balor's poisonous eye I knew I wouldn't be able to approach him, though the sword might kill a thousand men while I did it, his eye would seek me out and I'd be doomed. I was fierce in my determination to eliminate him. That's what I said to myself. Eliminate. He must be eliminated. The sword was useless, its magic no match for a man of his skills and power. It was the warrior's heart, the Tuatha de Danann who calculated the next move and with precision executed it. Executed him with my slingshot, confident in my aim, confident that it would succeed in disarming his eye and eliminate him. I would win this battle for my people. Win this war. And I did. My people, the Tuatha de Danann were freed from the Fomorian yoke. The Fomorians were broken. And Balor with his evil, poisonous eye was dead. I was a hero. Lugh the god. The Fomorians were banished. My mother with them. And part of me was banished with her. Though she would have none of me, her father's killer.

Mon had given me her message, his tone sympathetic as he added that it was grief speaking and she would relent eventually, but I knew it was false. And so did he. Fomorians never forgave. I knew that so well, because I possessed that particular Fomorian trait. And the person I couldn't forgive was myself. Despite the self-imposed penance of avoiding conflict and any role in which I might be cast as a hero all this time, it seemed to have found me in the end. And perhaps this was my ultimate punishment. To assume the role I felt the most uncomfortable in.

I swung Retaliator carefully, testing its balance, finding the weight of the hilt and its graceful action all as I remembered.

"Careful, now. I do like my head."

I turned to see Saoirse at the kitchen threshold. I lowered the sword. "Sorry, wasn't expecting anyone to come in. Are the others waiting for me?"

"Ah, no, you're grand. I just thought I would make sure everything is okay and ask if you needed anything more." She gazed at me up and down. "Say, better clothes?"

I looked down at my worn T-shirt, battered jeans, wellies. "I'm not sure I know what you mean," I said keeping my voice flat.

She frowned. "Well, unless your intent is to show where to place their cuts and thrusts, you might want something a little more, uh...."

"Soldierly? Flak jacket and helmet?" I kept my tone the same.

"No, well not really." She narrowed her eyes. "Oh, ha very ha."

I gave a slight grin. I hadn't been able to resist the urge to wind her up. There was a bit of a bite to it, but the edge had dulled considerably right now. Maybe it was because I held the sword in my hand, or that there were bigger things afoot, so that there was only a residual resentment in me at her betrayal.

As if sensing my thoughts she spoke. "It wasn't what you thought, Luke. I didn't know. I promise you."

"What did I think?" I said evenly.

"That I knew you were Lugh, that I had been looking for you, trapped you when I found you and planned to betray you. But I didn't. I didn't even know who I was. None of it."

I stared at her, puzzled. "What?"

"What, what?"

"What, you didn't even know who you were. What could you possibly mean by that?"

"Just as I said." She sighed. "My memory of being Bríd is gone. Lost. Anu said she wiped my mind to protect me." She hunched her shoulders. "Though whether that's true or not, I can't say. But sometimes, or the odd occasion really, it's as though parts of me do remember. I think. Maybe."

"But you were gone, Bríd. Dead."

She nodded. "Another long seanchie tale, so. But yes, I was dead and thanks to the Well of Slane I came back. And please, call me Saoirse. I can't get used to Bríd just yet."

I shook my head at the wonder of it. Though, I should know better than to question anything when it involved across the water. I studied her, trying to find the truth of her words.

"You do look different from the Saoirse I knew in Dublin."

She nodded. "I feel different, in a way."

"Difficult," I said. "Confusing."

She nodded again. "Complicated."

"Overwhelming."

"Overpowering."

"Life altering." I was starting to grin now and so was she.

"Absurd."

"Outrageous."

"Ridiculous."

"Supercalifragilistic."

"And very expialidociously awful."

"Hmmmn. I can imagine."

"Can you really?" she asked.

I paused. "No, I suppose not. Especially since I've been spending ages trying to avoid who I am."

She nodded. "That can be tough, just the same."

"It can," I said.

"And are you ready to be who you are?"

I sighed. "Maybe. I hope so."

"My hero, so," she said, smiling. She cocked her head, considering. "Our hero?"

I winced and frowned. "Don't push it."

"Right, so," she said. "Go prepare."

I looked down at my attire once more. "You don't think I'm equipped for the ball?"

"Not if those balls involve chains or cannons."

"No cannons, I think."

"Just go." She shook her head, grinning.

I smiled at her, feeling something ease in my chest. "Tell the others that I'm just getting my things from the campervan. I'll be there soon."

She saluted me and left the kitchen. My smile slipped away and I rubbed my hand over my face. It was time to join the fight. The war. A war that might lead me in directions I didn't want to go, but for Kayla and all that she meant, I would do it.

31

SMITHY

They were hardly the team of warriors fit for a hero's tale, thought Smithy as they piled out of Finn's car and began the trek towards Tuireann in the growing dusk. Any seanchie would look with disdain at their clothes, their disjointed and very dysfunctional manner with each other. A seanchie would, in fact, have completely re-written everything about them. Except Nemed's magic sword. They would keep the magic sword, but they'd give it a name. Something like "Deathkiller". No, that made no sense. "Deathbringer?" No, cliché, done before. "Slayer", maybe. Ah, but where was the poetry in that? It would come to him, so. He promised himself.

The thoughts kept him going, though, so he played with a few more names, even thought he might ask Herself's opinion. Maura. Or rather Morrigan, because it was that opinion he needed. She would have a name, so she would. His mind kept that little puzzle going, steering away from the "would my body do well, my mind function" question that seemed to lurk at the edge, creep up on him when he wasn't looking, like a child playing "Sly Fox".

The periphery of his thoughts were just under control when

the periphery of his vision acted up and he saw that Herself, now inhabiting the mindset and behaviour of the terrible, awe inspiring war goddess, was seriously annoying Finn, who gave her alternately stony silences and meaningful glares, accompanied by biting barbs.

"You'll not do it," he said.

"I will so," she said.

"No. You won't. It's not right."

"I will do it." A shrug was added.

The "I will" and "you won't" carried on and Smithy still struggled to understand what the "it" was, but the low, deadly tone between the two was such that he knew better than to interfere, or even question what they were talking about. He looked at Saoirse, but she was lost in her own thoughts, with an occasional sidelong look at Luke, and then him. He didn't want that look, no thank you, and he assembled his face into a "not a bother" expression.

Luke on the other hand, wore a thunderous expression, clenched and unclenched his sword hand, swinging the arm, muttering to himself. The actual sword hung by his side, its scabbard attached to a cobbled together piece of leather made to look like a belt. His low slung jeans, torn in a few places screamed more high-end fashion, than battle worthy. At least he was wearing a quilted jacket, though it looked it was fit more for a night out in Dublin. The boots, thankfully, were leather, sturdy and reassuringly scuffed, but maybe not quite Luke's size.

No, not a seanchie's tale.

Maura came to a halt and held up her hand, followed by a finger to her lips. They all fell silent. Well, Finn did, because it had only been him and Maura speaking before. She gestured them to move to the ditch. They closed in, huddling around her.

"I heard something up ahead," Maura said.

Smithy gave her a doubtful look. How could she have heard

anything over the sound of the two of them bickering? He glanced at the others and saw the doubt in their faces. Except Finn. He had his head cocked to the side, eyes narrowed. A moment later Luke's body stiffened, his eyes alert. He held up two fingers. Two of them.

Smithy put his hand to his side, feeling for his sword. Luke moved ahead of them, motioning for the others to remain behind. Finn grabbed his arm and shook his head, pointing to himself. Luke shook his head, his eyes angry. Maura slapped the back of both of their heads and firmly shoved them aside, striding ahead. Seconds later she was gone and a crow was flying upwards.

Not quite a seanchie's tale.

A shout of laughter, a drunken squeal. Up ahead, Smithy could see in the growing dusk two figures swaying as they walked towards him. Words to an old musical began to waft from them in a key unknown to this world. Behind him, Saoirse sniggered.

They arrived at Smithy's group and stopped. Two men, one dark haired with glasses and a beard, the other fair but with the same squared jaw and lanky frame. They squinted at Smithy's group, sloppy grins on their faces.

"Hello, hello," said the one with a beard and glasses. There was an accent. Possibly German, or maybe Scandinavian.

"You are off to a fancy dress party?" said the other, gesturing to Luke's sword.

"Or a battle?" said beard and glasses, laughing.

"Oh, a battle. Definitely a battle," said Luke dryly.

More laughter, this time both of them, long and hard, morphing into guffaws. Eventually they both stopped. Beard and glasses pulled his face into a serious expression and placed a hand on Luke's shoulder. "You are a great warrior. You will be brave. You will be a hero." He tapped Luke's shoulder and raised his hand and tapped the other shoulder. "Rise Sir Knight."

The other one guffawed. "He's already standing, *dum*."

"Oh. Yes," said beard and glasses. He snorted. "Remain standing Sir Knight." He nodded, seemingly satisfied. He looked at the rest of the group. "Fight well, my friends." He saluted. His companion did the same and they ambled off, resuming their garbled version of what Smithy realised was a song from *Les Misérables*.

A twisted Seanchie's tale. Twisted altogether.

Saoirse sniggered again. Finn snorted and it shortly became full blown laughter. Maura appeared, a sardonic look on her face. Saoirse's laughter had joined Finn and even Luke had a slight smile on his face.

"Sir Knight?" said Maura, one brow arched.

He looked at her, frowned and shrugged. "They were foreigners. They wouldn't know."

As cryptic as that remark was, Smithy had to smile. What did anyone know? What did he know? Very little. "Ah, get over yourself" filtered through his mind. Yeah, well.

"What took you so long?" said Finn, looking at Maura.

She gave him a brief glare. "When I saw there was no harm to the two of them, I decided to double check our friends at the fort."

"And?" said Luke, tensely.

"And they're there. Camping behind the mound."

"They're very bold," said Saoirse in her best "mammy" voice.

Luke grinned at her and Smithy found he didn't much care for that.

"Ah, sure they're only lads," said Luke.

Smithy liked that remark even less. He frowned at Luke. "Does Sir Knight have a plan for these very bold boys?"

Luke turned to him, his expression neutral. "Do you have something in mind?"

"A very big spanking?" said Saoirse, laughing.

"I'll give them a spanking, all right," muttered Smithy.

Saoirse put a hand on his shoulder. It was a small gesture and part of him welcomed it and part of him resented it. The part that welcomed it encouraged the warmth that spread through his body because of it. The part that resented it told him he was a fool.

"So," said Finn. "They're camping there, bold as you please and no complaints from the farmer?"

Maura shook her head. "Bold as you please to us. To me. As far as anyone else is concerned there's just a small herd of deer there. Eating grass for all, mating, I don't know."

"Deer," said Finn flatly, his humour vanished once more.

"Yes deer," said Maura, though, rather than the animal term, her emphasis seemed to lean toward the personal use.

"Oh, dear, deer," said Saoirse, with a smothered laugh. Was she giddy, wondered Smithy.

"Dear, dear," said Luke, the grin a flash across his face.

"Oh, feck's sake," said Smithy. He nearly added, "dude" to his comment along with "just shut your gob, surfer boy". Luke's "I'm so cool I'm ice just give me a surfboard, man" attitude that emerged since those drunken twats had appeared was really annoying him.

Everyone had turned to look at Smithy. He glared at them. "Does any of this affect our original plan?"

Maura shook her head. "No, but it might make them less cautious. An advantage for us."

Luke nodded. "They aren't necessarily expecting us. As far as they're concerned, they're here to do a job."

"There's someone guarding the lane and the back entrance, though," said Maura.

"Deer?" asked Finn.

"No, they're posing as walkers."

"Right, so, they can't do that for long." said Smithy. "Walkers will hardly be leaning against gate posts in the dark."

"No, need to pose in the dark," said Finn.

"True," said Smithy. "But they might be less likely to be vigilant when there's little chance of anyone coming along to visit the fort."

They all nodded patiently and Smithy could feel the eye rolling even though every one of the eyes were fixed on him. It was all obvious, all the statements that had rolled right out of his mouth, but he couldn't help it. Anything to stop the stupid little banter between Luke and Saoirse. Why was she so giddy? Was that surfer boy really so funny, so witty and cool she'd been reduced to a fan girl behaviour?

"Right, so," he said, forcing out the words. "Nothing's changed then. It's just a matter of waiting until it's fully dark."

"Yep," said Maura. She pointed to a small gateway down the road. "Will we all pitch up there for the next while?"

"Sounds good to me, these feckin' boots are killing me," said Luke.

"What's wrong with them?" said Saoirse.

"They're not mine. They belong to Kayla's neighbour. He left them at her place a few months ago when they got too wet chasing his sheep in her field. I figured they were better than nothing. But they're stiff as hell and a little small."

No one said a word in reply, though Smithy thought he might have heard a stifled snigger while they headed toward the gateway that Maura had indicated.

The twists had unravelled from the tale, any hope for a seanchie taking it up now vanished.

Smithy could see the men silhouetted in the darkness. Mists had descended with purpose in the last while. There was a chill to it that Smithy knew signalled that, though it was August, the seasons were following the old ways and autumn had well and truly arrived with the onset of Lughnasagh. He appreciated the irony that the fire festival named for the very god squatting beside him was more of a pain in the arse to him at the moment than the weather or season. And tried to ignore the fact that at this moment Luke was whispering quietly to Saoirse. Even in this light he could see Saoirse's fair skin and how she bit her lip as she listened intently to Luke.

"We should put some mud on our faces," Smithy said, his voice louder and harsher than he had intended.

Finn grunted, Maura nodded, but Luke, the gobshite, poked him in the ribs and told him to keep his voice down.

"You're the one who's whispering away like some girly gossip," Smithy said. It was petty, but sure, lookit, the man was an idiot.

Luke opened his mouth to utter a retort but Maura nudged him and said, "Save it. We need to focus."

"That's what I was doing," said Luke between clenched teeth. "Saoirse asked me a question about tactics and I was answering her."

This did nothing to mollify Smithy, and if anything, it made it worse, because the thoughts that now consumed him were riddled with the "why not ask me" theme song "why ask him" being the back-up singers' refrain.

"The time for tactical instruction is past," said Maura, her voice so low Smithy could barely hear her. "Is everyone ready to go?"

After everyone nodded, Luke spoke. "I think it would be better if we split up and break them into smaller groups. Maura and Smithy, you go to the south side of the mound, Finn you go over the top and attack from above – you're the best skilled for that approach – and Saoirse and I will approach from the north side."

Smithy wanted to object, he even began to form the words, but he knew that Luke was right. But only just. As the most skilled he would be able to protect Saoirse, while Smithy fought with Maura. Volatile, uncertain Maura, who might or might not fight against them with all her skill. She'd behaved well so far, because she liked a good fight, but once it was in full swing, she could decide she was bored, and leave. Or she might catch a whiff of a much better conflict somewhere else that she could egg on. In a way, he should be flattered that Luke thought he could handle Maura. He should be, but he was after feckin' hating the idea.

Maura nodded along with the others, except Smithy, until they all looked at him expectantly, and with a sigh, he gave his nod too.

"Right, so," said Luke. "Let's go."

Smithy's first thought was why the feck did Luke get to give the orders? As if sensing his thoughts, Finn gave him a nudge with two fingers. Two very key fingers that told Smithy that Finn agreed with him. Smithy grinned. He returned the favour with the same two fingers. "Good luck," he muttered to Finn.

Finn whispered, "Stay safe, swordmaker and wielder."

Smithy felt a stab to his heart. It was the phrase that had been said to him in the old times. It felt so wrong and so right. He took a deep breath. He must do this.

A kiss to his cheek brought him out of his thoughts. He turned to look at Saoirse. She mouthed something, but he couldn't quite grasp what it was in the light. He bent his head low, his ear to her lips.

"You're a grand man, so you are, *mo chroí*," she said.

The last phrase was so faint that he wasn't certain he heard right. Had she called him "her heart"? Before he could mull on it, Maura jabbed him in the back and they moved off, splitting off into their assigned directions. He led the way, Maura following behind him closely, both crouched to avoid detection. As they neared the Fomorians, Smithy could hear conversation and what sounded like dice landing on a board. Playing games? He grinned. He would play a few games with them, all right. Not a bother. Behind him, he heard Maura give a quiet snort.

He halted for a moment. As quietly as possible Smithy drew his sword, wincing a little at the sound of it sliding along the scabbard. Maura and he had a silent exchange. The moment was now and he moved forward again, nearly tripping over the four men who were lounging against the mound, supporting the board that held the game they were playing. With a few deft kicks he had the board upended and one of the men with it. Above him, Finn gave a bloodcurdling cry as he descended upon the two men playing cards to the left of the four with the board game. The cry was echoed further along by Luke, whose sword was already making contact and creating chaos among the others standing around at the end. A stab of worry over Saoirse was hastily shoved aside when one of the men sprang for him, his sword grabbed from where it had lain beside him.

The swords clashed, and suddenly, as if the gods wanted to get a good view of this battle, the mist halted and a sliver of moon appeared. It was enough to bolster Smithy's confidence and help him swing true as he slipped and slid in the muddy ground. Other clashes sounded around him while his opponent gave as good as he got. Smithy backed up to regain a surer stance and felt a body slam into him. A glance showed it was Maura, involved in her own sword dance, a half smile on her face. She had two opposing her, but the grin held and she dispatched one, with a clever ruse and quick slash.

A second fighter joined Smithy's opponent and it was his

turn to battle two. He gripped his sword harder, though the mist had done its work on the mud, and his hair that was hanging down in wet clumps around his face, his hand remained firmly in place on the hilt.

He fought on, parry, parry, slash, feint and onwards, both of them encroaching on him. A scream behind him caused him to flinch. Thinking at first it was Saoirse, his attention flickered for a second. But that was all that was needed for one of his opponents to get under his guard, and move to slice him open, pushing forward when a sword came slamming down on his shoulder, cutting it to the bone. Finn. The man screamed in agony, dropping his sword, leaving Smithy with only the smallest cut and an opportunity to finish off his other opponent whose own attention had lapsed at the assault to his colleague.

Smithy grinned broadly to Finn, and after a quick scrub to remove the worst of the spatters of blood and mud on his face, the two moved towards Saoirse and Luke who were down to two opponents. Luke finished off his quickly and moved towards Saoirse just as Smithy was doing the same. Luke reached her first and his sword work quickly took the attention of the swordsman and with a long two-handed slash, Luke felled him to the ground.

Smithy's first thought were two words. First one "show". Second one "off". Others followed that were less suitable for public utterance, and might have had many variations of feck among them and with added descriptives like wanker and words of that ilk. That is until Saoirse put her hands on her hips and frowned at Luke.

"I was fine," she said. "There was no need for you to interfere."

Smithy could hardly contain the grin that slapped across his face the instant she'd said those words. That woman, oh, she was all that.

"What?" said Luke, his voice incredulous.

"You heard me. I didn't need help. I can fight. I told you that."

"I never said you couldn't fight. I was just trying to help."

"I didn't ask for your help, thank you."

Luke stared at her a moment and finally just shook his head. Smithy was almost disappointed Luke didn't say anything further to get himself in deeper. No, he was disappointed. Sure, he'd admit it then, gladly.

Maura came up behind Smithy. "Are we done here?"

Finn nodded. "We'll check around, so. Make sure we haven't missed anything or anyone."

"Take care. There's probably some stores of toxic chemicals or things along those lines," said Luke, his tone a little sullen, at least to Smithy's ears. "I'm sure they intended more harm, either in the same places, or elsewhere."

His words provided a sobering effect on the group and they dispersed in various directions. Smithy was tempted to accompany Saoirse, but a remnant of common sense led him in another direction. A direction that found nothing but discarded satchels and a few bedrolls, but gave him a time to reflect on his latest battle, if it could even be called that. But at least he came out unscathed. He didn't let anyone down. He fought hard and well enough. It was good. He should be satisfied with that. He would be satisfied with that. He ran the word through his head, tried it out, like he would lyrics to a song he was composing, tentative, testing their sounds, their meaning with the hope that it would work. It might work as a song, but he wasn't certain about anything else. It certainly wouldn't work in a seanchie's tale. But then this wasn't a tale a seanchie would tell. That had long been established.

32

———

LUKE

I sat in the kitchen, grime and sweat still covering my body from the fight. The others had left, Ogma, no, Finn, driving sullenly away in his car, the high from a successful battle definitely gone. I had no idea what bee had decided to lodge in his nether regions, but I didn't remember him behaving like this at any time before. Morrigan, I caught myself, Maura. Saying the name deliberately was the same, though maybe better. Her fighting skills were undeniably the same fine edged perfection and she had remained unwavering at their side during the fight. Had another bargain been struck with Daghda as there had been in the last battle, long ago? There had definitely been something of that nature, and perhaps more, between the two of them back then.

Maura was gone now, too, vanished into the night sky, wings flapping, queen of the dramatic exit and entrance. Smithy, this time saying the name deliberately, and Saoirse had ridden off on the motorcycle. Smithy, now there was another one with a bee, not just in the nether regions, but in every orifice. Saoirse was a different matter. It was strange to see her again, changed in appearance and manner enough that was at times like meeting someone new and other times, when her humour was light and mine too, an old companion, the familiar banter making her company enjoyable. And while I'd been with that motley group, she was the only person whose company was bearable. I was glad that we'd cleared the air, though all she said was going to take some time to settle in me, to completely dispel the caution I felt with her as well as the rest of them.

I sighed. There would be time enough for that, if only for the next while, because I'd made the promise to go talk to Anu. Though what she had to say, I was certain would make no difference to my decision to return here as soon as possible. Kayla needed me. The three of them needed me and I wouldn't let them down. Now that we'd stopped the feckers from dumping waste and the treatment for mitigating their damage was underway, things would improve. I hoped. The oil spill still bothered me, and I intended to look into that further, but for now, I hoped it was enough to help Kayla, Bláthín and Nana.

I rose and went to the sink. With a few licks and promises to my face and hands, I had tidied up enough to talk to Kayla. I climbed the stairs in my stockinged feet, the tight boots having been kicked off the minute I hit the house threshold.

When I peeked into Kayla's room, she was sitting up in the bed nursing the cup of tea I'd left her a few hours ago, a small bedside lamp providing a halo of light around her.

"Let me get you a fresh one," I said.

"Ah, you're grand," she said, giving me a wan smile. "I'm glad you're back. Safe."

I blinked at her. I hadn't told her anything. She'd been asleep when I left, so I'd just put the mug on the locker beside the bed. The note I'd written and left next to it had only the briefest "just stepped out" message on it.

But I knew better than to question her. This woman, greater than so much, so many. All.

I sat on the bed and rested a hand on her cheek. "You've nothing to worry about. I'm going nowhere."

A light filled her eyes at my words and I leaned down and kissed her softly. She sighed against my lips. The kiss was brief, but its warmth and sensuality were a promise. And I wanted to fill that promise, redeem it for all that it was worth, but first I had to talk to her. I pulled back.

"You know who I am," I said.

She nodded. "Lugh," she said, softly.

I acknowledged the name with my own nod. I took her hand, circled my thumb on the back of her hand. Reassurance, a hint at the promise fulfilment. "And I know who you are," I said.

She licked her lip, her eyes becoming large. "And?" Her words were barely above a whisper.

I squeezed her hand. "And I want you. More than want you. I-I." I took a deep breath. This wasn't banter Luke, surfer dude, chatting up the girls. "I want, no, I would like to be with you." My words stuck in my throat, my whole self, stuck too, in my very feeble explanation of the magnitude of what was going on in my mind. Ah no, strike that. Body. No that wasn't it. All of me? Feck me, I was pathetic even in my own thoughts.

"But I have to go for a short while." I paused, then forced out the words. "To see...Anu. She wants to see me." I shrugged, trying to make it sound unimportant. "But I'll be back, soon. A few days at the most."

"When do you have to go?"

I frowned. "Tonight? She wants to see me as soon as possible."

She nodded, leaned across to me and kissed me tenderly. "Can't it wait until the morning?" she whispered.

I looked at her, read the meaning in her eyes. "Oh, it can," I said, breaking slowly into a grin. Anu would have to be patient a little longer.

She placed a hand on my arm and I leaned down again. This time I took it slowly, brushing my lips against hers, feeling their softness, tasting them. Tasting her. I deepened the kiss, cupped her face with my hands and ran my tongue along her lips. She moaned softly and it resonated through me, a perfect vibration that set me alive. I stood up, whipped my shirt over my head, removed my jeans and socks so that only my boxers remained. She lifted the covers and allowed me to slide inside, next to her.

I was aware she was still ill, but I was content to spend the night with her folded in my arms, just having her touch as much of my skin as possible. To feel her up against my body was enough. I was surprised to find she had on only the barest of T-shirts. She pressed her body up against mine, so that I questioned my original assumption.

"You're with me now," she said in a low voice.

The words were filled with meaning, a meaning that she strengthened when she kissed me again, stroking my face, brushing her fingers along my ears, and down my chin and throat. It was my turn to groan, a low, deep throated sound that I sent across to her. She pulled me closer, slid her arms around by neck and pressed her body against mine. I pulled back a little, just to see her eyes, their golden hazel colour darkened, and the flush of her cheeks. I kissed her lids, tasting the salt of her old tears, kissed her cheeks and each of her ear lobes. Her hair smelled of honey, gorse and wild onion. I kissed her neck and her shoulder, nibbling, biting, wanting all of her. She stirred under me, her own moans echoing mine as we undulated, swayed and found our rhythms. Whoosh and whoosh, like waves we moved. I cupped her breasts one at a time, licking, nibbling, tasting and marking the hills and valleys of her body. Stroking, brushing, moving in rhythm, moving slowly downward, I feasted on her taste, her scent, the feel of her and the sight of every part of her, keeping our rhythm, our whoosh,

whoosh. She stroked and tasted me in return, and we moved in harmony, a heartbeat and song in perfect unison. And when I entered her, when we were fully united, I knew it was more than a coming together, coming as the world shifted and accommodated this new fact. That we were both now complete.

EPILOGUE
LUKE

I was late when I drove up the hill towards Anu's house. I had never been here before and it wasn't the easiest place in the world to find. Back of beyond, but not far, would be the best way to describe it. Cúil Iarharcht indeed. Not that I minded, or cared, really. Anu would have to keep tapping into that reserve of patience that had always seemed endless to me. And I had an explanation. I wouldn't even reduce it to an excuse. No there was nothing about last night that was an excuse. It was the best thing that had ever happened to me and I wouldn't let anyone ruin it.

The night with Kayla was more than a night with any one woman. She was all women, every woman and she laid herself open to me and absorbed me whole into her. Her strength slowly returning as the night wore on, as if she fed from me as much as I fed from her. And when the morning came, though she was still pale, and her strength ebbed a bit again, there was a light in her eyes, the light from earlier that was still there and made me feel that I was the hero, that I could be her hero, her god. And I wanted that more than anything.

I'd still been worried about leaving her, though. Her

returning strength still seemed so tentative, and Bláthín and Nana were no better. But at least they were no worse, I told myself. At her instruction, I agreed to ring Seán Óg and ask him to come and mind the three of them. He'd presented his eager little face not minutes after I rang, bouncing and chipper as I opened the door to him and all full of "take your time, lad, I'll see to them, no worries. Go do your business." I suppressed the "you will not, so" reply to his assurances about seeing to them. He would not. An irrational thought, I knew, but it was there and I couldn't get rid of it. The state of me.

Still, the silly grin was on my face as I approached Anu's house, the cloth bundle under my arm. I knocked on the door. Saoirse opened it and relief washed across her face when she saw it was me.

"Luke, fab, you're here. We've been waiting this age for you."

"Sorry, now. I got held up." That was enough for me to say, I decided on impulse, and it would have to do them.

I followed her through to the old kitchen, where the others were clustered around a fair sized deal table. I had to smile when I saw Anu hovering over the hearth fiddling with the crane like someone from a heritage park. Except for her baggy trousers, slippers and loose shirt, she would have fitted in perfectly. Her long braid was hanging loosely down her back. She turned to greet me and the thought that she hadn't changed much left me. Her face, that had once been both youthful and the same time wise beyond the ages, was sunken along her cheeks and eyes. Her eyes were clouded a little, so that she seemed to be peering at me, struggling to focus. My god. I caught myself with the oft used phrase. But she was, in a manner of speaking, and her appearance had shocked me beyond comprehension.

She shuffled over to the table, gripping one of the chairs with one hand and opening her arm to me with the other.

"Come, Lugh, let me embrace you," she said.

I moved without thinking towards her and clasped her to me, putting the cloth bundle on the table. I could feel her thin frame beneath my hands. I pulled back and studied her. "How are you?"

The question was a normal greeting, but I put more than that in my emphasis and my expression. But she shook it off.

"Grand altogether, Lugh. I'm so glad that you're here. Sit, now. There's tea there on the table for you. Saoirse, sit down."

I turned and took the chair she indicated. I greeted the others. The bees were still there, buzzing about in the two of them. Finn, sour faced, arms crossed, nodded to me without comment. Smithy, stiff despite his attempt at a casual drape of his body across the chair frowned darkly at me. For feck's sake. Maura, who'd been seated the minute before fidgeted and finally rose, walked to the nearest wall and leaned against it. Saoirse was the only one who looked remotely approachable and smiled at me. I gave her a querying look and she rolled her eyes in reply. Fine, so.

"Lookit," said Maura. "I've said all I needed last night. There's nothing changed and Luke was there for it all, so you've no need of me now. I'm off."

"No, Morrigan," said Anu calmly. "It's not only for Luke's part in yesterday and explaining the situation to him that you're needed here. There's more."

"No," said Maura. "I'm off. I told Finn, and now I'll tell the rest of you. I'm off out of it. It's been grand and all watching this show, poking it on, but now I'm done with it."

"Why? What's happened? Where are you going?" said Smithy sharply.

Maura shrugged, her eyes dark, stormy. "I've a few options. I've heard things. Maybe I'll got to the North? Over to Scotland? Or maybe someplace fresh." Her voice held a hard edge to it.

"There's so much potential. America has an appeal. Or maybe Canada. No, I think America."

The others watched, stunned. I studied her, saw the anger, the rage that filled her body and behind it, something else. Was it sorrow? I'd never seen Morrigan like this, not that I'd been in her company in a long time.

"Morrigan," said Anu. "Please sit down. Listen. And then you'll see how much you're needed."

Maura fixed her gaze on Anu, her eyes narrowed. "You don't *need* me. No one *needs* me."

Anu approached her, placed a hand on Maura's shoulder, but Maura shrugged it off. "Get away with you," Maura said. "I told you. I'm off out of it. I'm only here to tell you myself. In person. Out of courtesy. You should thank me for this courtesy, because it's not often anyone gets it."

She pushed past Anu and slammed out of the door. I heard her footsteps echo up to the road, the stomp stomp of her anger clear. Those feckin' bees just kept coming. Soon there'd be a hive, so there would.

"Should I go after her?" asked Saoirse.

"No, leave her," said Anu. "We'll give her time."

"Time for her to go north? Or to America?" said Finn, his tone filled with bitterness.

"Just a little time," said Anu. She looked tired, and I was reminded again how much she'd changed.

"Do you need me to recount the events from yesterday?" I asked, taking a sip of the strong tea in front of me. "I'm sure with the others already giving their accounts you have a full picture."

"No, there's no real need," said Anu. "Only if you have something you want to add."

I shrugged. "No, not really. Only that the oil spill, while dissipating, still has the potential for serious long-term damage and I would like to ensure that the clean-up is as efficient and effective as possible."

"Not only that," said Smithy. "We need to ensure that he isn't able to do it again."

"That goes without saying," I said. I wouldn't be drawn, though Smithy's needling tone seemed to infer that he wanted to do just that.

"Do you know anything about what's been going on?" asked Anu. "I'll tell you all that we know, but if you have anything to contribute, we would all appreciate that very much."

Saoirse nodded and gave Anu a worried look. "I think it's becoming imperative that we stop all of this as soon as possible."

"Of course you do," I said. Still not getting drawn. "What was it you needed to say to me? Only I have to get back to Allihies as soon as possible."

Everyone exchanged looks but Anu. She smiled serenely at me. "It was important to reach you for so many reasons, *Mo Ghíle Mear*." She repeated it in the old language and then English for emphasis. My Shining One. Lugh, the Shining One. She was calling me that. She was calling me. I closed my eyes, wanting to block it out, forget I heard it. I pressed my lips together

"What?" I said calmly. "What do you want from me?"

"I want you to answer the call of the land. My call. I want you to take back your weapons. Your spear. Your slingshot. Your sword. I want you to take them all and defend the land. I'm asking you again. A second time."

I glanced at the cloth bundle on the table, unable to help myself. I'd intended to return the sword to her. To signal that I had been glad to help but I had other obligations now, no less honourable. Now, I clenched the hand that had held my mug and looked up at her. My God. My land, the land that claimed me now. All the land. The land that I was part of, the land that hummed inside of me, loud and true. I could feel it rise up to meet her call. And she had asked me twice, knowing the *geis* upon me. The *geis* that wouldn't allow me to refuse a second request for help. The reason I'd avoided her and the rest of them all this time.

"Who has my slingshot and spear?" I asked hoarsely.

"That would be Balor," said Finn, his voice flat.

Balor. The man I'd defeated. The man who'd come back from the dead. The man who had tried to poison the land of *An Cailleach*, the woman who was part of me, in me as I was in her. This man had done that, and he was taunting me just by his very presence in this land. My grandfather. There was only one answer to that call from the land. And I would give it, because it wasn't just my life or Balor's at stake, it was *An Cailleach*, it was Anu, it was all the land.

I nodded. "I'll help."

I WAS BACK at Kayla's house, in the kitchen making a cup of tea to take up to her, radio on, catching the last of the evening news. Kayla had been restless, some of the colour in her cheeks I'd observed earlier now gone. Earlier, I'd had only a few words from her before she drifted back off to sleep again.

I was still thinking about that small effort at a smile and a nod for a cup of tea that she'd managed to make when I heard a familiar deadly voice come on the radio. Balor's voice talking about the oil spill. He spoke of contrition, reassurance and promises. And the final words he spoke took the breath from me, hollowed me out: *In addition to addressing the oil spill immediately I have volunteered my scientists to address and mitigate the toxic poisoning that the Beara has also suffered. They assure me this exciting new chemical compound they've developed will not only halt the toxic poisoning, but reverse its effects. With the government's permission and approval, the compound was administered late this afternoon on one of the mining sites in a special pilot project. It's hoped that the beneficial effects will be observed as early as next week, possibly the week after.*

I stood there, the words echoing in my head, spreading like the toxic poison that had just been mentioned, while the radio interviewer said his usual banter and chat in that overly earnest, sincere manner they had. A groan, long and loud sounded from the bedroom above me. Nana. The groaning continued. I headed for the stairs, only to be greeted by a sharp piercing cry. Kayla. I took the stairs two at a time and burst into Kayla's room. She was writhing on the bed, clutching her stomach, her face covered in perspiration.

I rushed over to her, swept her up in my arms and rocked her, soothing words pouring from me. Heartfelt, pure, and filled with deadly promise.

"My love, my precious only one," I said in the old language. "I will find him, you have my oath on that, as you have my heart. And when I find him, I will kill him, demolish his soul, his body, so that he will never be able to return."

I made that promise to her, to myself and to all the land.

Look out for the third book in the trilogy coming in spring 2022
    At the Edge of the Otherworld
    In the meantime if you enjoyed this book, a review would be so much appreciated.
    www.https://books2read.com/herogod

A NOTE ON THE MYTHS AND PRONUNCIATION

Some of the names and terms can appear daunting to those not used to Irish. And for those who like to know, I've put a few here in case it increases the enjoyment of the novel.

Bríd – Breed
    Aoife – EE fa
    Anu – An New/An Na (ancient, so it varies)
    Airmid – AIR med
    Ban an tí –ban an tee
    Bláthín – Blaw heen
    Búachaill –bwuock ull
    Cailín – call een
    An Cailleach –an Kall ick
    Cían – KEE an
    Cíara – Keer rah
    Clíodhna – Clee nah
    Daghda – DAHG duh
    Daragh – Da ruh
    Díarmuid – Deer mud
    Diancecht –Dee an kekt

Eilís – Eye leesh
Fadó – fa dough
Gan ainim – gan eye nem
Gearóid – Geh ROAD
Goibhniu – Gub New (another ancient one)
Líam – LEE um
Lughnasagh – Loo nah sah
Mo croí – mo cree
Mo Ghile Mear (@my shining knight) mo geela mar
Saoirse – SEER sha/ SEHR sha (kind of in between)
Seanchie — shan na kee
Siné – shin eh
Sinead – Shin aid
Sláinte –slawn tuh (Munster Irish)
Suantraí – swan tree
Tadhg –Tyg (like tie with a hard 'g' sound on end

The Myths

The myths that are explained and interwoven in this novel are from *The Book of Invasions (Leabhar Gabhala)* part of the collection of Irish myths. I have kept true to the myths, with the exception of a few interpretations and a little embellishment in the case of Bríd and Goibhniu. There is nothing in the myths that say they were together, but they are both smith gods, one female one male, so it seemed natural to link them. Bríd's fate after she married Bres is true, except for the embellishment of her rape. It isn't clear but it seemed a possible interpretation. She did give birth to three sons and died as a result of that birth.

Local myths are also interwoven. On the Kerry/Cork border you will find the Paps of Anu, breast shaped mountains that are always climbed on May 1. At their foot on the Kerry side, it is said by some that the Tuatha de Danann settled there. The site of St. Gobnait's burial and her well is also celebrated. St Gobnait was also known as a smith and there are remains of an ancient smithy there. It is my own view that it might have also been seen as a place where Goibhniu was either venerated or an ancient smith worked and invoked him there, and later became associated with the convent of religious women that was established later, led by a doubtlessly indomitable woman who came to be known as St Gobnait, a name very close to the god's and one that has no English translation in truth. (You can see my idea of her in my novel, *In Praise of the Bees*.) Some see the translation as 'Abby' but that's more than likely just an adaptation because of the 'abbess' aspect of St Gobnait's role.

Lugh's story, even his involvement with the Cailleach, is true to the original myth, except for the part including Clíodhna. He never had a relationship with her, that's my invention. But the rest of her story is as the tales recount, though Mongan's part in Mannanan's wave that washed her away when she fell asleep, isn't true to the myth. There's a site at Glandore called Clíodhna's wave to this day.

Many tales of the Cailleach, or the Hag, are found around Ireland and Scotland and particularly on the Beara Peninsula where there is a large standing stone bearing her name. The largest source of information about the Cailleach of Beara (*Cailleach Bhéarra*) came from the book, *The Book of Cailleach:Stories of the Wise-Woman Healer,* by Gearóid Ó Crualaoich. She is a complex figure with mother goddess and a supernatural female wilderness figure associations that can be linked to Indo European and Norse traditions. A force to be reckoned with.

ACKNOWLEDGMENTS

As usual I owe a great debt of thanks to my alpha team of readers, especially Jean, Jane, Claire and Babs as well as Lizzie and Steph, who gave a great fresh perspective. I also had a fantastic group of beta readers, Saorlaith, Eilín, Síleann, and Eileen who kept my Ireland real and ensured the fadas were all where they should be.

Also I want to thank my fantastic editor, Sandra Mangan, and my wonderful cover designer, Jane Dixon-Smith whose wonderful creative genius have gone a long way to help make my books a success.

And most of all, I want to thank my wonderful readers, whose support down the years has helped to make my writing such a wonderful experience.

AUTHOR'S NOTE

Originally from Philadelphia, Kristin Gleeson lives in Ireland, in the West Cork Gaeltacht, where she teaches art classes, plays harp, sings in a choir and runs two book clubs for the village library. She holds a Masters in Library Science and a Ph.D. in history and for a time was an administrator of a large archives, library and museum in America. She also served as a public librarian in America and in Ireland.

Kristin Gleeson has also published The Celtic Knot Series and The Renaissance Sojourner Series. In addition to her novels, a biography on a First Nations Canadian woman, *Anahareo, A Wilderness Spirit*, is also available.

If you have enjoyed this book please post a review. It helps so much towards getting the book noticed.

If you go to the author website and join the mailing list to receive news of forthcoming releases, special offers and events, you'll receive an e novelette *A Treasure Beyond Worth*, a FREE prequel novelette and its ebook novel *Along the Far Shores* at www.krisgleeson.com

Music is a big part of Kristin's life and many of the books have music connected to them. Listen to the music while you read—go to www.krisgleeson.com/music and download the files. Keep checking back, as more pieces will be added to the library in the course of time.